KING
OF
ITHAKA

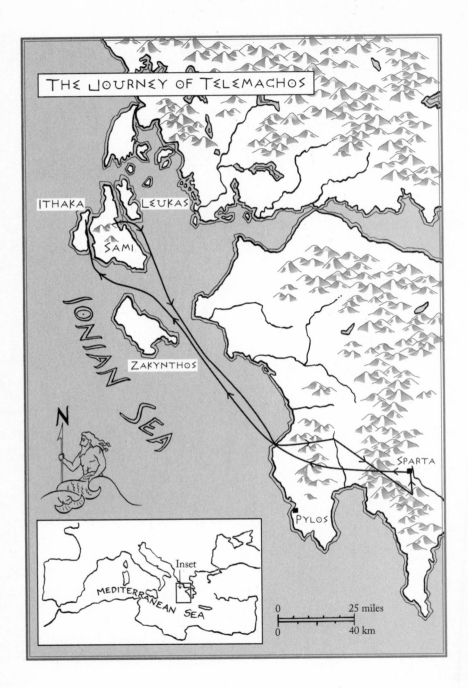

KING
OF
ITHAKA

TRACY BARRETT

Henry Holt and Company ▣ New York

Many thanks to my editor, Reka Simonsen, for her talent and vision; to my agent, Laura Rennert; to Terry Zaroff-Evans, for her meticulous copy editing; to Jennifer Roberts of the City University of New York for her helpful comments; to Greg for his support and for finally learning to leave me alone when I'm writing; to Laura Beth for her close reading and astute suggestions; and most of all to Patrick and Riley for unwittingly supplying the models for Telemachos and Brax.

Henry Holt and Company, LLC
Publishers since 1866
175 Fifth Avenue
New York, New York 10010
www.HenryHoltKids.com

Henry Holt® is a registered trademark of Henry Holt and Company, LLC.
Text copyright © 2010 by Tracy Barrett
All rights reserved.
Distributed in Canada by H. B. Fenn and Company Ltd.

Library of Congress Cataloging-in-Publication Data
Barrett, Tracy.
King of Ithaka / Tracy Barrett. — 1st ed.
p.   cm.
Summary: When sixteen-year-old Telemachos and his two best friends,
one a centaur, leave their life of privilege to undertake a quest to find
Telemachos's father Odysseus, they learn much along the way about what it
means to be a man and a king.
ISBN 978-0-8050-8969-1
[1. Adventure and adventurers—Fiction.   2. Kings, queens, rulers,
etc.—Fiction.   3. Telemachus (Greek mythology)—Fiction.   4. Odysseus
(Greek mythology)—Fiction.   5. Mythology, Greek—Fiction.   6. Ithaca
Island (Greece)—Fiction.]   I. Homer. Odyssey.   II. Title.
PZ7.B275355Kin 2010   [Fic]—dc22   2009050770

First Edition—2010 / Book designed by Véronique Lefèvre Sweet
Printed in the United States of America

1   3   5   7   9   10   8   6   4   2

For my parents, who said "Wonderful!" and not
"How do you expect to make a living at that?"
when I declared a major in classics

It is a wise child that knows his own father.

—*Homer,* Odyssey, *Book I*

HEAR THIS: *I did not hate my father for leaving us. I was, of course, only a baby when he left, but even as I grew up fatherless yet with a living father, I still did not hate him.*

My father and many other men had heeded King Agamemnon's call to leave their farms and their kingdoms and their families to follow him to Ilios and reclaim his brother's kidnapped wife, the lovely Helena. But over the years, as we neared manhood, the other boys' fathers came back. They returned either in person, bearing riches from the treasuries of the fallen city, or only in the words of a messenger reporting that they had died bravely in battle.

I alone did not know what had happened to my father. I questioned my mother, but she, weaving at her loom or preparing meals for the many guests who required the hospitality of the palace even in the king's absence, counseled patience.

No, I did not hate my father for leaving. Going to war is a man's duty. But later, much later, I hated him for returning.

CHAPTER 1

Brax snorted and stamped, his bony knee grazing my ear. I sat back on my heels and pushed the damp hair off my forehead. "Hold still," I said. "How do you expect me to do this if you kick my head in?"

"Sorry," Brax said. I could tell that the thorn in his belly was more annoying than painful, but centaurs are not known for their patience. It must be the horse half of their nature that makes them impatient—and always hungry—and until I removed the thorn, Brax would be irritable and my skull would be at risk.

My nails were bitten down to the skin, and every time I tried to seize the small thorn I only pushed it farther in. I parted Brax's stiff dark-brown hair again and took a deep breath so I wouldn't have to inhale his horse-scent at close range during the operation. I caught the tiny sliver between my teeth and eased it out, then spat it on the ground.

"Hey!" Brax turned, and I dodged just in time. "I wanted to see that!"

"It was only a thorn," I said. "There's not even any blood."

Brax snorted again. "Thanks."

I nodded, the taste of horse sweat still on my lips. Being a centaur has its advantages—speed, strength, and especially the company of girl centaurs—but it must be frustrating not to be able to reach back far enough to pull a thorn out of your belly or scratch your hind end without a branch.

I got to my feet and dusted off my knees. Now we were going to be late. Our friend Damon, who had overheard two girls at the well making plans to meet at the beach for recreation, decided that *we* would certainly find it recreational to watch them. But then Brax had blundered into the thornbush and refused to go on until the annoyance had been removed. He couldn't canter to make up time, since the way to our girl-watching spot was rocky and his hooves slipped on the uneven surface, so I was able to keep up with him.

We took the last bit slowly. I crouched down so I would be less visible through the brush, but of course Brax couldn't do that, so we had to trust to luck that the girls wouldn't look in our direction until we were settled behind the boulders that shielded us. He hunched his broad shoulders and bent his long legs, but it didn't make much difference in his height.

As I flung myself down on my stomach next to Damon, he whispered, "What took you so long?"

"Had to perform surgery on Brax," I whispered back. "Thorn in belly." Damon grimaced sympathetically.

Brax had dropped to his knees and was wriggling forward. He flattened himself as much as he could behind the tallest rock as I settled into the warm sand behind a shorter one. The sun was brilliant and the day even smelled hot. The waves lapping on the rocks of the shore sounded intoxicatingly cool.

"All clear?" Brax asked Damon in a low voice.

He nodded. "They haven't looked up here once."

I raised myself enough to peer over the rock, and there they were. Brax's sister Saba, with her honey-colored back and flanks, was mincing forward into the water. Her hips swayed as only a horse's can. "It's cold!" she squealed to the two other girls (both human), who hesitated on the shore. *Ignore her,* I thought. Fortunately, they did, and Charissa waded in, hoisting her white linen skirt to just below her knees.

"Oh gods," Damon breathed. Glimpses of girl ankles were rare. Charissa walked in farther, her hips shifting as she stepped on the uneven rocks. "Lift it higher," he urged under his breath, and, as though hearing him, she raised the now soggy hem a bit more. She was deeper in the water, though, so we had to be content with the wavy view of her calves through the ripples.

"It's not *that* cold." Charissa had a musical voice. She caught up with Saba, and they linked arms. I've seen vases painted with huge centaurs, their backs as large as horses', but of course this is nonsense. A centaur stands no taller than a human, and the horse half is only the size of a donkey. The two girls stood shoulder to shoulder, their backs to us. Charissa turned and beckoned to the plump and rosy Kyra. She joined them, squealing as the little ripples struck her thighs and waist.

Together the three girls advanced, splashing their own arms and then one another. Damon and I forgot ourselves and half rose to gaze as they laughed and ducked and played. I longed to join them in the cool water, but they would only run and tell someone and we would be severely punished, or at least Damon would. Worse, our hiding place would be exposed.

Brax watched us with a little grin on his sunburned face. He didn't mind that we were ogling his sister. Centaurs don't care about those things, and besides, he always thought it was funny that the sight of girls got us so excited. For centaurs (and satyrs too) it is the scent of female that is interesting, not the sight.

The girls were facing out to sea. They had wrapped their arms loosely around one another's waists and were singing a spring song, their shoulders undulating. Beneath the water their hips must be swaying too, but the bright light winking off the surface made their lower halves invisible, even Saba's. This added to her appeal, at least for me. I've always had friends among the centaurs and satyrs and have never called them hairy-backs or other insulting terms, but I prefer human girls. Not that I'd turn up my nose at a pretty nymph, of course.

"Do you think they know we're here?" Damon asked, settling back on his heels.

"Of course they know," Brax said.

"What?" I was shocked. Girls are supposed to preserve their modesty. Human girls, anyway. Surely Charissa and Kyra would never behave like this if they knew we were there.

"Why did they leave their clothes on, then?" Brax asked. "Don't they usually take them off to go swimming? And why did Charissa lift her robe if it was going to get wet anyway?"

Silence while Damon and I digested this thought. Brax added, "Do you think it's an accident that Damon overheard them at the well?"

The girls had finished their song and were dipping themselves into the water.

Damon squinted up at the sun. "I'd better get back." The regret was plain in his voice. His gentle father wouldn't beat him or even rebuke him if he found the plow lying where Damon had abandoned it, but he would pick it up and finish the field himself, tired as he was from his own work. This would reproach my friend more than a thrashing. He rocked back off his heels to a seated position and stretched. "Telemachos, do you have to go home too?"

I shrugged. "My mother didn't say anything."

Damon grunted and stood, brushing sand off his clothes. He sighed. "Your sister is lucky."

Brax and I looked at him in surprise. "I don't have a sister," I said. Damon knew that as well as I did.

"Just what I mean," he answered. "That's why she's lucky. She's lucky she was never born. Your mother would keep her locked in the house and not let her spend her day at the beach."

This was true. My mother thought that a boy—especially a prince—should do whatever he wanted, at least most of the time, but that girls had to preserve the old traditions. "You're right," I admitted. "Mother says that when her sister Aglaia was a girl she was so wild that their mother kept her chained to her loom all day to force her to do her weaving."

A tale about a girl being chained and imprisoned would normally have drawn Damon's attention like a bee to nectar, but a sudden burst of noise from behind us made me jump and reach for my knife. Damon spun and stood half crouching, at the ready to defend us from whoever—or whatever—was pounding across the rocks.

He lowered his arms as a small figure shoved its way through the brush.

It was his younger sister Polydora, who had been a nuisance to us ever since she could walk. Now she stood, sweating in the heavy weaver's smock she wore over her clothes. One of her black braids had come undone, and she held Bito, Damon's youngest sister—he had three—on her hip. The little girl had a finger in her mouth and looked at me with the same accusatory glare that Poly was fixing on her brother.

"What do you want?" Damon asked. "And what are you doing all the way out here without Father or me?"

"*You're* here," she retorted. Damon sighed. It was no good reminding her that young ladies don't travel by themselves. Poly always did what she wanted, regardless of propriety. I hadn't seen her for a few months, but in that time she apparently hadn't learned to do what was expected of her.

I left them to their family quarrel and glanced without hope over the edge of the rock. Sure enough, the girls must have heard us. They had dried themselves and were rearranging one another's hair. I knew they couldn't have helped hearing Poly's approach—for someone so small, she made a lot of noise—but I had been hopeful that I would catch them still in the process of drying off.

Polydora followed my gaze and then shot me a look of scorn that would have shriveled me if I hadn't been accustomed to it. She turned back to her brother. "You have to come home and finish your work. Father will be back soon, and if he sees the plow—"

But Damon wasn't listening to her. He was staring into the distance, not where the girls had been bathing, but farther out.

"Telemachos." His voice was tense. "Look out there." He pointed straight into the swath of bright sunshine.

"Where?" I squinted. Brax shaded his eyes with one hand and looked out. Poly, still holding Bito, moved closer and leaned over the rock, her black eyes squinting against the sun.

"Move over this way," Damon said. I leaned against him and

lined my gaze up with his. My vision was less sharp than his, and Brax wasn't paying much attention, so it took me a few seconds to make out what he was seeing, but then Polydora gave an exclamation and I too finally saw it.

A sail.

CHAPTER 2

Without a word to my friends or Polydora, I raced home, tripping over a rock and sliding on a patch of gravel before I reached the road. I was out of breath when I finally stumbled to a stop in the dust in front of the women's quarters.

Until only three years ago, I would have passed through that door as freely as through any other in the palace, but when I turned thirteen I was banished to the men's quarters, and I hadn't set foot in the female apartments since. I straightened my clothes, tried to calm my ragged breathing, and knocked.

And knocked again. Nothing.

"Mother!" I bellowed. "Eurykleia!"

Still nothing. I pounded on the door. Would no one come?

Finally, a voice from inside said, "Hush, boy," and the hinges creaked. Their dry squeak was remarkably similar to the voice.

Eurykleia, my old nurse (and my father's before me), didn't look happy to see me. Her face, already deeply lined with age, showed even more creases where her cheek had rested on her pillow, and her wiry gray hair stuck out around her head. Belatedly, I remembered that it was the hour of the women's mid-afternoon nap. No matter; they could rest another time.

"A ship." Before I could go on, my mother stood in the doorway, her clothing loosened for sleep.

"A ship?" Her lips went white.

"Traders. Not a warship."

"But still," she said, knotting a cord around her stout waist, "they might have some word. They might even have seen—" She stopped, but that was enough. *Word of your father,* she meant. *Might even have seen the mighty Odysseus.*

"Eurykleia," Mother said, but she had no need to give orders. Although it had been a year since we had last seen strangers, my old nurse needed no reminding about what to do. She hobbled away, screeching at the slaves to start preparing a meal for guests.

I needed no reminders either. The ship was far enough away that it wouldn't land for at least an hour—if it did land, that is. Sometimes ships went right past our small, rocky island as though it was of no consequence, eager to arrive at the wealthy cities on the mainland. But this one was headed straight toward our main harbor. I hurried to the men's quarters to scrub the dirt and sand from my body and face.

I hadn't bathed properly in a long time, and I had to work the pumice hard to rub off the brownish skin that had built up, especially on my feet. I scraped my heels raw and stopped scrubbing at my toes only when they began to bleed.

I dried myself hastily and found my good tunic. It was too short now, and Mother was weaving cloth for a new one. Still, it was better than my everyday clothing and would have to do. I slid it on over my head. The wool felt light and cool and didn't irritate my skin, still burning from my bath, as the tunic dropped over my hips. My mother's cloth was always fine and soft, even when the garment was brand-new and hadn't yet been broken in by long wearing.

A little oil to try to tame my curls, a good swab of my teeth with a rough linen cloth, and I was ready to go.

Except for one thing. My shoes. I hadn't worn them in weeks. Where had I left them? I couldn't go down to the harbor barefoot like a laborer. These sailors, even if they were only traders, had to be welcomed with all the courtesy a royal family could extend to them.

Cursing the delay, I tossed bedclothes and dirty undergarments around and even lifted up the sleeping pallets to look under them. My shoes clearly weren't in the bedchamber. Where had I pitched them the last time I wore them?

I poked my head into the dark storeroom and sneezed from the dust and the musty smell of the broken furniture and tools that had lain unused since my father's departure and were now jumbled everywhere, along with old farm implements, my mother's broken loom, and various kitchen items in need of repair. I groaned when something moved in a shadowy corner and a dry voice said, "Hey, boy!"

I should have known that my grandfather would be taking a rest far away from where the women would look for him. He was sitting bolt upright, wisps of white hair sticking out in all directions, a wide smile on his face. "Oh no," I muttered under my breath. This was clearly one of what my mother called his "good days," when he was happy and talkative, not curled up refusing to move, even to eat or relieve himself. Normally I wouldn't mind indulging him with chat, but now I itched to get down to the harbor.

"My boy!" Yes, definitely a "good day."

"Yes, Grandfather?"

He looked at me carefully. "Are you my son?"

I shook my head. "No, Grandfather. I'm your grandson." I shifted from one foot to the other, hoping he would get to the point soon, so I could leave. How close had the ship come during the search for my shoes, and now this?

He peered harder at me. "Are you *sure?* I only ask because you look so much like Odysseus." My mother too had said this many times, as had Eurykleia.

"But I'm also different." I tugged at my hair. "See? Brown curls. What is Odysseus' hair like?"

"Straight," he said warily, as though avoiding a trap. "Black."

"And is he this tall?" I straightened to my full height.

The old man shook his head, looking up at me. "No, he's shorter than I am." Maybe that had been true once, but now that my grandfather was bent over in his old age a six-year-old girl could look him in the eye. "And he's bandy-legged. Your legs are straight. And long," he added, as though surprised. He looked me over once more. "No beard."

I felt myself flush. I wasn't happy to be reminded how slow my beard was to come in and hadn't planned to mention that difference between me and my father.

"So am I your son?" At last he would let me go.

The blissful smile returned to my grandfather's face. "Odysseus!" He held out his skinny arms.

Oh gods. I'd have to find some way to convince him, or when I left for the harbor he'd be brokenhearted at a second desertion by his son, and my mother would be angry. But I couldn't stand to wait much longer.

"No, I'm his son," I said.

"You're my son?"

"No, I'm *his* son." I paused. I had to do this right. "I'm your son's son. Odysseus' son, and Penelopeia's. Your grandson."

"I'm your grandson?" Even he had enough wit left to be skeptical.

"No." I sighed. A change of subject might work. "Would you like a cup of wine, Grandfather?"

His eyes lit up, and he licked his lips. He nodded, and as I moved to the door he said, "And don't weaken it too much!"

"Of course not," I reassured him, although I planned to send him only a cup of water with barely enough wine added to color it. At last I could go.

I made my escape. At the kitchen door I nearly collided with my mother. "Mother, have you seen my— Oh." Dangling from her hand were two worn sandals. I bent to put them on, leaning on her shoulder for balance. When I straightened, my toes hung off the fronts, and my heels scraped the ground behind. I pulled them off again. "I'll wear them once I get there. Maybe the traders won't look at me too closely. Mother, tonight can Brax—" I began, but she was shaking her head even before I finished.

"No, dear. No forest people at the table. Not when we have guests. Strangers wouldn't understand how it is here. They're used to bigger cities, I expect, where humans stay with their own kind."

"You don't even know where they're from!" I protested. "Maybe they're not from a big city. Maybe they even have satyrs in their crew!" But she wouldn't change her mind, and secretly I knew that the idea of half-goat, half-human sailors was absurd.

"The donkey is ready," Mother said, her forehead creased by

a worried frown. I repented of my childishness and kissed her cheek.

"I'll make sure they come," I promised. "Don't worry; the fame of your kitchen must have reached to wherever they're from. They'll come, you'll see, and they'll spread word that the palace of Odysseus is as hospitable as it ever was." A rare smile crossed her face, and then fled. As I turned to go, I called back over my shoulder, "Have someone take a cup of wine to Grandfather." She would know how weak to make it.

"Oh, is he having a good day?"

"One of his best," I assured her. I settled onto the donkey's back and kicked her sides.

"Don't go in the boat," she called after me. I didn't answer; she knew that she didn't have to remind me, that the thought of getting in any kind of water vessel turned my stomach. Her warning was a habit more than a real instruction.

The donkey trotted willingly down the road as I drummed my heels into her flanks. I always gave her something for her greedy little stomach as soon as we arrived at the harbor, so now she moved eagerly and didn't try any donkey tricks on me. Her hooves kicked up pale dust, and I hoped that I would remain relatively clean until I'd met our visitors.

We passed farmers in their fields, and at the sound of our passage they looked up to see who was in such a hurry. They must have known where I was headed—word of the ship would surely have gotten to them while I was making myself decent—and although I knew they wished me luck, none of them would dare bring on the malice of the gods by saying this out loud. So, instead of risking divine interference, they sent their voices after me with friendly catcalls and jeers.

"There goes the young prince!" one man called out, straightening from the hoe over which he was bent. "Where's he off to in such a hurry? And look how he's polished himself up!"

"I hope she's human this time!" shouted another. "Nymphs are dangerous for a boy of his age!"

I flushed. The wood-nymph episode had been two years ago, when I was only fourteen, but somehow people had found out about it (I suspected the girl herself of spreading the word, after embellishing it with who knew what imagined details), and I knew they would never let me forget.

"He's going to the harbor," said a man doing something high in a fruit tree. "Maybe he's in search of a mermaid this time."

Raucous laughter came from everyone within earshot. I felt my cheeks grow hot again, and I touched the donkey's flanks with my heels. She laid back her ears as though to say, *I'm going as fast as I can!*

The briny smell of the ocean, never absent on our island, grew stronger as I approached the beach, and mingled with the odor of the bait that the fishermen had loaded into their buckets that morning. When I slid off the donkey's back and rewarded her with a dried fig, the ship was just entering the harbor. It was out of the swath of sunlight now, and I saw it clearly. It was a trading vessel, as I had seen, and was neat and trim. Its red-and-yellow–striped sail had come down and the oars were out. I heard a faint voice that grew louder as the boat neared, guiding the oarsmen to steer left, to steer right, to *pull,* damn it, and finally to ship oars.

While I had been getting myself ready at home, the tide had turned. Now it was coming in, and the waves slapped on the rocks that had been piled up as a breakwater for the fishing boats. I was not the only one waiting. Vendors had set up braziers and were roasting fragrant slices of lamb and goat, threaded onto skewers, over the coals. The savory scent tickled my nostrils, and I bought a stick of meat from one of them. As I chewed, I watched more than one fisherman on the shore mending nets that looked perfectly sound. They were as curious as I about the ship that was approaching ever closer. They avoided my eye, hoping, I knew, that I wouldn't order them to return to their real work.

A group of old men, their age excusing them from the fields and the sea, perched on rocks warmed by the sun. I couldn't make out what they were saying in their murmurings, pitched just high enough to reach one another's ears, but I was sure they were curious about the origin of the ship, what it was carrying, and—like me—if the sailors had any word of Ithaka's king.

Clio and her daughter Sophonisba hadn't yet made an appearance. This was wise. In the noonday light, made doubly bright by the sunshine bouncing off the surface of the sea, the mother would have been shown to be quite old and the daughter quite ugly. No matter; they would come out later. By the gentle moonlight, the sailors would not notice their appearance, and their trade would likely be brisk.

A small group of women and children, seated by the boats that had been pulled up onshore, busily cleaned what the men had caught that morning. Gulls swooped down, screaming at one another to back off, and then flew away, trailing purple and black and pink fish-guts, which they swallowed before diving back for more. The smell of fresh fish innards mingled with the rotting ones that the gulls had missed yesterday. Far away, Mount Aenos, the tallest spot on the island, stood like a sentinel guarding my home.

I sighed and turned my gaze toward the ship again. One lucky fisherman had been the first to row out, to guide the pilot close in and then to ferry passengers ashore. How many were left behind as guards would depend on the value of whatever it was they were carrying. I squinted into the sun as one, then two men lowered themselves into the rowboat, which struck out for shore, while the other boats bobbed around.

"What are you carrying?" one of the fishermen called. The reply from the ship was unintelligible. "Where are you bound?" asked another. This time I faintly heard the answer, "Temesa." I had never heard of it, but then I had never been out of my father's kingdom.

I took my position on the largest rock, which served as a kind of landing stage for the fishing boats, well back from the waves that licked against its base. I shaded my eyes as I watched the rowboat approach. When it bumped against my rock, one of the fishermen waiting with me reached down and helped a man out. As he stretched his legs to climb up, I saw that he was about Damon's father's age, with the powerful arms of a sailor. He was as tall as I and much broader. His dark curls were grizzled and were almost as kinky as his untrimmed beard. The second man was a bit younger, lankier, with a keen eye. He wore his brown hair tied back out of his face, and his beard was copper colored in the bright sun. Both were sun-darkened, and their hands, which I gripped in greeting, were callused.

When they were safely ashore and the older man had tossed a coin to the fisherman, I began my speech. "Welcome to the kingdom of Ithaka," I began, hoping my voice would stay steady, but the younger man interrupted me.

"Ithaka?" He turned not to me but to the older man. "I thought this island was called Sami!"

"It is." The older man nodded. "Ithaka's that piece of rock we saw sticking out of the water off to port a few hours ago."

"Then why's this boy saying—"

Was nobody going to ask *me*? For the third time that day, I felt my face grow hot, but this time it was with anger and not with shame. How dare they ignore me like this? At sixteen, I was hardly a boy.

I raised my voice above theirs. "Welcome to the kingdom of Ithaka," I repeated, and they turned and stared at me as though at a turtle or a seagull that had uttered words. "You are on the island of Sami, one of three islands in the kingdom. The others are Leukas and Ithaka. My father, Odysseus, is the prime landowner of Ithaka through his father, Laertes, and the king by right of conquest of all three islands. He has united them into the king-dom of Ithaka. We welcome you travelers to our home and extend to you the hospitality of the king's palace."

They were still staring at me. What was the matter? Was it my too-short tunic, my too-small sandals? I started to fidget, then forced myself to hold still under their gaze. Finally, the younger man broke into a gap-toothed smile. He clapped me on the shoulder.

"Thank you!" he said. "We'll accept your hospitality. All right with you, Mentes?" The older man didn't smile, but he nodded again. His serious gray eyes followed me as I led them off the rock and onto the beach.

Returning to the palace was awkward. I had one donkey, and we were three men. I couldn't mount and leave guests to walk, and I didn't want to offend one by offering a ride to the other. So all three of us went on foot. Feeling foolish, I led the donkey, her gray head bobbing with each step.

The road rose steeply from the harbor, and we all leaned forward as we climbed to the palace. The donkey's little hooves slipped a few times, but she kept her footing, as did I in my increasingly painful sandals. As soon as the ground leveled out enough to allow us to catch our breath, I learned that the older man, the one called Mentes, was the chief of the people of Taphos and captain of the ship that was bearing bronze to the port of Temesa. His passenger, Sikinnos, son of Thrasidaios, was a dealer in metals.

Dusk was falling when we arrived at the palace gate, and the shadow of the city walls stretched over our path. We paused to catch our breath, and I looked up at the gateway, trying to see it with the eyes of a stranger. It was built of huge pale stones, its opening wide enough for a large cart, although the road had fallen into such disrepair since my father's departure that it had been years since anything with wheels had come through it. Above the opening, the painting of two lions rearing at each other, teeth and claws bared, was faded, but still impressive. The bronze gates themselves had long since been removed and melted down.

My mother stepped out of the shadow. Next to her was my grandfather. She had somehow gotten him cleaned up, and he stood leaning on a staff, wearing a spotless tunic. She must have impressed upon him that this was an important occasion, because the dreamy smile of that morning was replaced by a serious expression, and he gripped his staff with a firmness that I remembered from my childhood. She herself was wearing a spotless white robe and she had made up her face for visitors. Over the white cosmetic she had painted three red suns, one on each cheek and one on her chin. But she couldn't hide the anxiety in her eyes, at least not from me.

The younger man, Sikinnos, approached first, bowing to my mother, who gazed at him as though from a lofty height, even though he towered above her. "We thank you for your hospitality," he said. My mother inclined her head.

"You are welcome to what we can offer." She turned to the other man.

"Thank you, madam," he said gruffly.

All was going well, but then my grandfather raised his head, blinking like someone who had just woken up.

"Are you my son?" he asked Sikinnos in his trembling old voice. He answered himself: "No, too tall." The younger man appeared to be trying to think of something to say, but Grandfather ignored him and turned to Mentes.

"Are *you* my son?" His tone held little hope.

The sailor's reply came after a moment of hesitation.

"No. But I sailed with him."

⟨HAPTƐR ϟ

My mother didn't faint, nor did she forget that she was mistress of a household with guests to welcome. But she gripped the wall for a moment and swayed almost imperceptibly. Then she let go of her support and said to the two sailors, "You must be tired and hungry. Please, come with me to the banquet hall."

She turned and led the way. My grandfather seemed to be leading her, but I knew that she was, in actuality, guiding him. I followed with our guests, handing the donkey's rope to a slave, who took her away to the stable. As we passed the dung heap, which was steaming gently, the old dog resting on it to warm his stiff joints hauled himself to his feet. He trotted after us, wagging his tail, the barnyard odor preceding him. He pushed his nose into the hands of our two guests as they walked, begging for a stroke or a treat.

"Go away, Argos." I nudged him away with my foot. "I apologize, sirs, for the dog. He's no good as a watchdog, as you can see, and not much better as a hunter."

"Why do you keep him, then?" Sikinnos asked.

A good question. "His father was my father's last dog. He trained old Argos before he left." Before they asked any further, I added, "The old one wasn't much good either. But we're keeping his descendants for my father's return."

I had spent the journey up from the harbor hoping that I had left the servants enough time to prepare well for our guests, and I held my breath as a slave pulled the hanging aside so that we could enter the hall. To my relief, it looked splendid. Mutton-fat torches burned against the walls, their heavy smoke escaping through the ceiling hole. It being a warm spring evening, no fire was lit in the pit in the center of the room. The crack that ran along the far wall from top to bottom, caused by an earthquake a year or so before and repaired only recently, was barely visible in this light.

The windows brought in the cooling air together with the fresh scent of the herbs that grew outside the hall. The biggest table had been set up and benches were ranged all around it, leaving barely enough room for a latecomer to squeeze between the diners and the wall. Our usual dinner companions, neighboring landowners and their hangers-on, could be trusted not to miss a meal that would be even better than usual, owing to the presence of guests. They looked up from their plates and wine cups as the strangers came in, their conversations trailing off.

The senior man of the family should have made the introductions, but this was clearly beyond my grandfather's abilities—even on a *good* day like this one. I stepped in.

"Friends," I said. I knew they had stopped talking out of curiosity about the strangers, not out of respect for me. "Please make welcome these travelers: Mentes, chieftain of the seafaring Taphians, at present anchored in our harbor, and his passenger Sikinnos, son of Thrasidaios." I walked with them around the table, saying the names of the most important of the various men who appeared nearly every evening, and especially when there was company. The table was large, and Mentes had to squeeze to fit his broad frame around its corners. Since Sikinnos was nearly as slender as I, he had no trouble.

"Amphinomos, son of Nisos," I said. My neighbor was so tall that, even seated, he looked the sea captain nearly in the eye as he nodded at Mentes and Sikinnos and inquired courteously after their health. The sailors answered as courteously. Amphinomos smiled at me as I passed to the next guest, his eyes crinkling in his weather-beaten face. My heart warmed a little; Amphinomos had always been friendly. When he was not hunting, he was out on the water, and although he was not an old man, his face was lined and sun-darkened.

"Eurymachos, son of Polybos." Only a few years older than I, he was already balding, which gave him a comical look. Eurymachos barely glanced away from the kitchen door to salute my guests.

I continued around the table. The beggar Pylenor put out a leg in an attempt to trip me, but I was expecting this and steered our guests safely past him. "Antinoös, son of Eupeithes," I said reluctantly as we approached the only man still talking to his neighbor. Antinoös looked up, flipped the long black hair off his handsome face, and nodded at my guests without speaking, turning to rejoin the conversation he had left. My face flamed and I choked back the words that tried to force their way out of my throat. His constant discourtesy to me was bad enough, but rudeness to a guest in the palace of Ithaka was inexcusable. As I squeezed past him, Antinoös turned on his bench and passed a hand roughly over my cheek. "Still nothing." He burst into coarse laughter.

I clenched my fists to keep from slapping his hand away. Antinoös never lost an opportunity to mock my lack of beard, and when strangers were present the humiliation was almost more than I could stand. I made myself smile and moved on to take my seat.

Mother had placed Sikinnos on my grandfather's right. On Grandfather's left was the captain, and my mother was next. Once we were seated, a maid came around with a large bronze pitcher to pour water over our hands. As the water splashed on the floor, I glanced at our guests, but they seemed unimpressed that such a valuable object was in such humble use. Perhaps they had not noticed it.

My stomach growled as the servants brought in the supper. We started with one of my favorite dishes, flatbread, still hot from the oven, spread with pickled fish. The pungent scent teased my nose as I lifted it to my mouth.

A servant rounded the table with difficulty and laid a board between every two diners. Three more servants followed, one carrying a heavy pot and the second a ladle with which he spread the pot's contents—thick wheat porridge—onto the board. The last servant bore a platter divided into sections, each containing something savory: roasted garlic, leeks in wine sauce, salted fish eggs, lentils with herbs, and many other dishes. The diners spooned what they liked into holes they made in their porridge, which stiffened as it cooled.

I always had a good appetite and tonight was no exception, even with my eagerness to hear what our visitors might say about Odysseus. I knew that they were too well mannered to talk about anything so serious while we were eating, though, so I controlled my impatience. Fortunately, Mentes concentrated on eating, and

I didn't have to try to chat with him. I would have had no idea what to say to the leader of the seafaring Taphians, a people of whom I had barely heard and whose habits were unknown to me.

Others around me were having no such difficulty. Our neighbors had all known one another since birth, and they laughed and joked and teased. Antinoös, who owned the land adjoining ours to the west, threw a crust of bread toward Pylenor the beggar, and then roared with laughter when a dog seized it instead. Gentle Amphinomos handed the fellow a piece that was still smeared with a little fish roe, and the beggar snatched it, gnawing it without thanks. Phemios the bard sat on his stool in the corner, his hands folded on the lyre that was leaning against his round belly. There was no point in his singing or playing anything now; his reedy voice would never be heard above the unmannerly noise of our guests.

Even through the hubbub, I knew that Sikinnos was having rough going with my grandfather. The old man seemed to think, gods knew for what reason, that this young man was interested in the details of a hunt on the mainland decades earlier in which my grandfather had gotten separated from the rest of the hunters and had spent a week wandering in the forest, until rescued by someone he swore was Pan himself. "Not just a simple satyr—oh no," he said scornfully, as though Sikinnos had doubted his word. "There's a difference. A *big* difference. He never spoke, for one thing, and you know how hard it is to get satyrs to shut up. But this one didn't say a word. Not a word. And his pipes! Why, when he played them . . ." I couldn't think of any way to rescue our guest without showing discourtesy to my neighbor on the other side, with whom I was sharing the board of porridge, so I tried to shut out my grandfather's voice as he droned on.

I glanced at Mentes and found that he was looking at me. He didn't appear abashed at being caught staring, but kept his calm gray eyes fixed on mine. I looked away, and then back. For a flash I thought I saw, not the grizzled Taphian sea captain, disheveled from long days at sea, but a tall and noble woman on whose head flashed a gleaming helmet. I blinked, and I saw only Mentes. Now he was smiling at me.

My dinner companion poked me, and I realized he had asked me a question. I apologized and asked him to repeat it, and went back to our conversation. I sneaked glances at Mentes, but he was no longer looking at me. What was it that I had seen earlier? *A trick of the torchlight*, I thought. *Or maybe this wine isn't as watered as it should be. I must speak to the servants.*

I knew it was difficult for my mother to refrain from asking Mentes about my father, but propriety forbade her bringing up serious topics until after everyone had finished eating. It was only after the boards had been cleared—I noticed that she had hardly touched anything—and all the diners had eaten their fill of figs and apples from our orchards, that she asked, "So you have sailed with my husband?" Her composure was admirable. I think I was the only one present who heard the strain in her voice. She could almost have been asking about a stranger.

The chieftain leaned back and nodded. The other diners fell silent. Some leaned forward, and all were paying attention. They were worried, I knew, that news would come that would force them to stop living off my father's land like crows fattening themselves on grain stolen from a farmer's field.

"Can you tell me about it?" My mother's voice was low. "We haven't heard anything about him since—since—"

Mentes nodded again. He swirled the wine in his cup and

stared into its depths as though seeking words. Then he looked up and met my mother's gaze.

"I last saw him seven or more years ago." He took a gulp of wine. My mother flinched. "Lady, I'm sorry, but I don't know if he's alive or dead. And if he's alive . . ." He didn't finish the thought. He didn't need to. *If he's alive, why doesn't he come home? Has he found another life, one that suits him better? Has he willingly condemned my mother to widowhood with a living husband, me to orphanhood with a living father, the kingdom to anarchy with a living king, while he plays husband, father, king somewhere else?* I squeezed my eyelids shut and tried to force these questions back. I opened my eyes again. My mother was ashen, and I knew that her thoughts were the same as mine.

"Thank you," she said as evenly as though he had been giving her information about some mere acquaintance. I had to admire her Spartan training. Emotion rarely escaped her unless she wanted it to. "And now, some songs, perhaps?" She signaled to Phemios, and he struck a few notes on his lyre.

"Hear this," he sang, and started a bawdy tale about Dionysos, his voice wavering off key. I cringed, knowing that our guests had probably heard accomplished bards tell magnificent tales set to beautiful music. I wondered what they were thinking of Phemios, and of us.

I pretended to listen, laughing when the others laughed, sighing when they sighed, but my mind was elsewhere. The bard finished his song with the usual "And now my tale is told," and then made the rounds of the diners, who each put a morsel of food in his bowl, until it overflowed. They were always generous with my father's storehouse.

As soon as I was able, I slipped out of the hall, managing to hide a half-empty jug of wine in my tunic without my mother's noticing. I took a torch from one of the supports against the wall. But before I had gone many steps, I heard someone following me. I groaned. My mother must have sent a servant after me to re- trieve the wine. I turned, resigned to surrendering it, but then saw that my pursuer was not a servant but Mentes, coming after me with the rolling walk of someone more used to a ship than to solid ground.

I waited, the torch sputtering and smoking above me. It was growing heavy, but I dared not shift it to my other hand, for fear that the man would see the jug of wine and would think I was pilfering drink. Which, I had to admit, I was.

"Listen," he said when he reached me, his tone serious, "I meant what I said. I don't know if your father is alive or dead, but I suspect that he's alive. He's a tricky one, Odysseus, and he knows how to land on his feet. He's very good at looking after his own interests, is your father."

I nodded, my mouth suddenly dry.

"My counsel to you is to go out in search of him. Find out if he's dead, in which case your mother should marry again and you can make your way in the world. Or if you learn he's alive, you can try to bring him home." Hanging in the air between us was the question: *Why wouldn't he come home on his own?* We both ig- nored it, and Mentes went on, "Either way, you're old enough now to take the journey."

"But where should I go?" To my horror, my voice squeaked. I shifted the torch to my other hand to cover my embarrassment, not caring now if he saw the jug.

He appeared to take no notice, either of the jug or of my treacherous voice. "Go to King Nestor, of Pylos." He raised a hand as he saw me beginning to object. "I know—it's a long way. But you can make it in a few days. And Nestor knows everything. He'll treat you well; he holds the laws of hospitality strictly." He paused and looked at me, his gray eyes sharp, even in the torchlight. "You must go. You and this kingdom have been orphaned too long. You're not a child; you need to set things in order here."

He gave my shoulder a squeeze and turned back to the banquet hall, leaving me with my jaw hanging open and the wine jug dangling forgotten from my hand.

CHAPTER 4

I watched Mentes go. It wasn't the distance to the mainland that made me reluctant to journey there, as he had thought, but the fact that to get to Pylos I would have to go in a ship. My memories of sailing still gave me nightmares. You never knew, when you set foot on a boat, if you would ever see your home again, and I wasn't willing to take that risk. My father had loved the sea, had left eagerly to cross its wide expanse, but once his sail had dipped below the horizon, he had disappeared as though swallowed alive by its vastness. No, the sea was treacherous. I wanted no part of it.

A soft whistle followed by a sound between a cough and a whinny coming from the oak grove behind the house broke my thoughts. I knew where to find Brax. He was always confident that I would be able to steal some wine and meet him in the glade. As I approached, he trotted over to me. I stuck the torch into the ground and cleared a spot to sit on.

"Good dinner?" I detected a wistful note in his voice. Condemned to a horse's stomach, he had to be content with foods made of oats and barley, although the smells of our feasts tantalized his human nose. Once, a few years before, I'd dared him to try human food, and he had sampled a sausage and some dried fish. I didn't see him for days afterward, and when he finally reappeared, Saba told me that he had kept them up for two nights with his groaning.

I nodded and poured some wine into a cup before passing him the jug. I knew I had better drink what I wanted now; I wouldn't see the jug again until it was empty. Brax took it with a sigh of contentment and settled down on his knees and then onto his belly. I leaned back against him. The night had turned cool and his broad side was warm.

"What were the guests like?"

I shrugged. I didn't tell him about the trick my eyes had played on me in the torchlight, turning a squat sailor into a tall woman. He would tell Damon, and if Polydora came to hear of it she would tease me unmercifully.

"Any news?" he persisted. I shook my head.

"I saw that one stop you outside the hall. Was he asking where the latrine is?"

I shook my head again.

"Where to find a girl?"

I grunted a negative.

"So what was it?"

I sat up. "He thinks I should take a voyage to find him. To find my father. Or at least to find someone who knows what happened to him."

"Are you going?"

"No." I lay back again, balancing the cup on my belly. I looked at the torchlight flickering across its surface. "What's the point?"

Brax started to say something, but a belch interrupted his words. I chuckled and some wine slopped out.

"Hey, don't waste that!" Brax made a grab for the cup, but I snatched it away.

"There's enough for you in that jug."

"You call that enough? You humans . . ." And he was off on his favorite topic, the inferiority of humans to centaurs, satyrs, even wood nymphs.

My mind wandered as he went on and on, thinking of the wood nymph I had known two years before. Her kisses had been as soft as moss, and she had smelled like the forest after a spring rain. Where was she now? I wondered. Did she ever think of me as I thought of her? I tried to remember everything about her in the hopes of crowding Mentes' words out of my mind.

The torch burned down and went out. Brax snored next to me. Despite the late hour, a full stomach, and several cups of wine, I felt restless. I rolled over onto my belly and spread my arms wide. Was it the wine, or did I feel the island of Sami, the kingdom of Ithaka, breathing beneath me? The trees rustled; was it the wind in the leaves, or were wood nymphs and satyrs moving through the branches? Or were the trees themselves gesturing to me?

Everything here was alive, and suddenly I loved my island with a ferocity that I hadn't known I felt. How could I leave the fields and Mount Aenos and the orchards and the beaches, even to find my father? And how could he stay away from all this for so long? No, surely he must have died. The king of such a place would never be able to keep away.

I propped myself up on my elbows. My head was fuzzy. If it hadn't been so cold, I would have fallen asleep like Brax, but I was starting to shiver. All I could think of now was my bed.

Centaurs don't really feel wine or the cold, and, unlike me, Brax would have a clear head when he woke, so I left him and the spent torch. At the door to the men's quarters, I paused. A good host would never let his guests be chilly; I would put some blankets in the guest room before I turned in, no matter how much I longed for my own bed. I went back to the storeroom and rummaged in a chest until I found two woolen covers that my mother had made years ago but that were still free of moth holes. They smelled sweet from the cedar of the chest and I buried my face in their softness as I made my way to where Mentes and Sikinnos were being housed.

I still heard sounds of the banquet, with Antinoös and his cousin Pisander shouting the words of a drinking song along with Phemios, but I didn't hear our seafaring guests. They must have left the hall early, being accustomed to a sailor's hours and needing their sleep. Sure enough, as I approached I heard them talking.

"You've got to feel sorry for the boy." It was Sikinnos. I froze. What boy—me? Why should they feel sorry for me? "He's never been anywhere and he thinks that this tumbledown farmhouse is a palace."

"Come, now." Mentes sounded drowsy. "It's not that bad."

"When he met us at the shore, I thought it was a joke," Sikinnos continued as though not hearing him. "That tunic barely covering his privates, those sandals with his bleeding toes sticking over the edge! And, when I heard him speak, I thought the dignity was a farce. But he means it, doesn't he?"

A grunt.

"Not a bad-looking boy, though," Sikinnos said as if to himself. I felt a fiery blush climb up my neck and inflame my face.

"Did you see I was talking to the old man? He was actually interesting. And the food was first-rate." His sentence was interrupted by a yawn that made my own jaws ache. "Spartan women know how to run a household, even out here. I haven't seen makeup like that in a long time, though. Not since my grandmother died, I think."

A pause, then another grunt from Mentes. The pause after it was longer, and I was about to tiptoe away before they detected me there eavesdropping, when Sikinnos spoke again.

"Do you think there's a chance his father—what's his name, Odysseus?—do you think he's alive?"

I couldn't tell if the sound that came from Mentes' side of the room was a snore or a snort of derision.

CHAPTER 5

I should have stayed awake all night, thinking about Mentes' advice, wondering about my father, but as soon as I wrapped up in my blankets I fell asleep. I've always been a sound sleeper, and besides, I had been wondering about my father all my life. I had received many words of advice about how to deal with his absence—and had ignored them all—so, although the sailor's intensity was new, the thought of making a voyage to find Odysseus was not. Others had suggested it but I had long determined that I wouldn't go. Even if I had loved the sea as he had, the world is so vast—where would I look first? No, going to sea was not for me.

Then why was I even thinking about it? What was it about Mentes that made his words enter my heart and squirm there, not giving me any peace?

I woke with a headache and a stiff neck. As I dressed, I wondered if Brax was still asleep in the glade. With his centaur's head for wine, though, he was probably up and about already.

As I should be. I remembered belatedly that my mother had set aside today as justice day, when the people of Ithaka would bring their complaints to her. Roads could fall into disrepair, the harbor could silt in, the palace gate could gape wide open—but two farmers' argument over the placement of a boundary stone a hand's width to one side or the other was too important to wait. So as long as my mother had me or my grandfather by her side to lend an air of manly authority to the proceedings, she could make judgments. We both knew that after a feast like the one of the night before my grandfather wouldn't be of much use, even symbolic, this morning.

I glanced at the sun and saw that it was mid-morning; our guests must have left. It was embarrassing that I hadn't been up to see them off, but there was nothing I could do about that now. At least Mentes wouldn't be around to nag me about going in search of my father.

I swallowed a piece of bread and gulped down some cider. I hastily threw on my old tunic—it was dirty, but at least this one was longer than the one that had raised the scorn of our guest— and ran into the hall. But I was too late. The last petitioners were filing out. I recognized them as two brothers who had been arguing over their father's inheritance ever since the old man had died in the winter, leaving little more than a tiny tract of land with ten olive trees. Their faces were creased from the sun and now from scowls; I saw that my mother had not been successful in making them agree.

"What do you expect with a woman in the seat of judgment?" one grumbled to the other as they passed me.

"Nothing," his brother said. "Nothing at all. Jug of wine?" The first nodded, and they turned their steps toward the village and its tavern.

I spent the rest of the morning shooting arrows into the straw man that Amphinomos had made for me years earlier. As each arrow found its way home, I imagined that the battered figure was one of our dinner guests. "Antinoös," I said between my teeth as an arrow hit the painted face, picturing that sneer disappearing as he fell. "Eurymachos," I said as the next arrow found its way to the target's groin. Ha! That would teach him to ignore me.

But the noonday sun had wilted my enthusiasm even for archery, and now Brax and I were spending the heat of the day in the shade of a large fig tree. I told him what Mentes had said.

"So what are you going to do?"

"What do you mean, what am I going to do?" I rolled onto my back and crossed my arms under my head. Despite having slept late, I felt groggy in the heat and wouldn't have minded a quick nap. But Brax seemed restless. His skin twitched to get rid of the flies, which merely circled briefly before settling back down on his hide. Twitch, circle; twitch, circle. The rhythm was putting me to sleep.

"Are you going to Pylos, as that sailor said?"

I sat up. "Why would I do that?"

"Well, you keep saying you want to get married—although I can't imagine why—and it doesn't look like your mother will ever let you. She can get married again too if Odysseus is dead. So you should either hold a funeral feast for your father and take over the kingdom and tell your mother to tend to her spindle like a good woman and marry one of your neighbors, or find out where he is and let him run things. Then you could fix the roads and the defense walls and raise an army. And get married, if that's what you want."

I waited. There had to be something more than civic pride and concern for my future going on here.

"And you could open the storerooms." Aha! That was it. "We could eat and drink whatever we wanted." He smacked his lips. "Remember those honey cakes Eurykleia made last summer?"

I did. But something he had said made me uneasy.

"Brax," I said, "the defense walls aren't really falling down, are they?" He twitched his tail at a fly and the end of it flicked my face. "Hey!" I ducked.

"Sorry." Brax shifted his hindquarters farther away. "See for yourself." He nodded at a squirrel that had jumped down from a tree and was now scampering along the top of the wall near us. It dislodged pebbles onto us as it made a mighty leap to cross a gap where stones had fallen in an earthquake. I sat up, feeling as though a blindfold had been removed from my eyes.

The change in the defensive walls had been so gradual, I realized, that I hadn't really paid attention to it. Were they this bad all around the island?

"If those traders yesterday had been pirates . . ." Brax let his voice trail off, and I felt a thrill of fear run through me. I silently cursed my stupidity, or my blindness, or my refusal to see what must be obvious.

What was I thinking?

"If those traders had been pirates," I finished for him, "we would have been overrun." Our storehouses would have been looted, and the men of Ithaka would have been killed. A neighbor in my mother's bed would have seemed kindly compared with what a marauding pirate would do to her.

And even if pirates never came, one of our neighbors might decide to wed my mother against her will. I could do nothing about it. I had no army, no guards, nothing. The only reason we had a full storehouse was my mother's care and prudence. But that would end instantly if raiders came from the cold and hostile sea. I shuddered.

If my father was alive, he should have come home long before now. It was only a matter of time before someone decided to take his place in the kingdom, in the palace, in my mother's chamber. Now that I thought of it, I was surprised that no one had attempted it. Perhaps fear of my mother's Spartan relatives had stayed their hands. But that couldn't last forever. Sparta was far, far away.

But Pylos was far, far away too. I had never been farther than my father's ancestral island of Ithaka—and that only once, at my coming of age three years earlier. Little Ithaka was so close that you could see it from a high point on Sami, like Mount Aenos. The thought of sailing in the open sea, out of the sight of land, made my palms leak cold sweat, even here in the hot and dry field under the fig tree.

"I don't know," I said. "How could I ever find him? The ocean is so . . . so *huge,* Brax. I don't even know how huge. What if King Nestor isn't any help? Where would I look next?" And my unvoiced question was: *How would I even recognize my father?* I hadn't seen him since I was a few days old.

Brax looked at me thoughtfully, a straw dangling from his lips.

"You know what you need to do."

I looked a question at him.

"You need to ask Daisy," he said. I shuddered.

⟨HΛPT⟨R 6

Her name wasn't really Daisy, of course. But nobody—human, centaur, nymph, satyr, probably not even a mermaid—could pronounce her name. The last part of it was said to sound something like "Daisy," so that's what we called her. We didn't call her anything to her faces. Not that many of us had seen her faces. One old woman who had consulted her decades earlier still turned greenish when asked about their meeting and refused to talk, and people said the reason old Kleandros the idiot alternately slobbered and wept in front of the temple of Poseidon was that he had gone down into her cave on a dare as a young man and had lost his wits in the process.

"Daisy?" I asked Brax. "You want me to talk to *Daisy*? You're out of your mind, my friend."

"Well, if you're afraid . . ." He didn't need to finish his sentence.

"I don't notice you offering to go talk to her in aid of the kingdom," I pointed out.

"Not my kingdom. Anyway, I wouldn't fit." He was right. The opening would be a tight squeeze for me, and there was no way a mostly grown centaur could manage it.

"I don't see why *I* should go, even. What can she tell me?"

"Nothing. You're right. Don't go."

Now I found myself arguing the other side. "Maybe I should. She knows everything and can advise me if Mentes is right about going to Pylos." I glanced at Brax. He was chewing on a long straw, working it between his teeth to clean them. He didn't appear to be paying much attention to the conversation. "Maybe I need to do something special, some god I need to sacrifice to, and she could tell me that." Brax nodded as though uninterested. "But I still think Damon or someone can ask her for me."

Brax stretched. "No. You're the prince. You should do it."

"Well, I'm not going."

"I don't blame you." Brax shook his head, and his long hair whipped in the air almost as ferociously as his tail. Luckily, I was out of range.

"But I thought you said I should go."

"Of course you *should*. You need someone to counsel you about whether to go in search of Odysseus. Why should you take the advice of that sea captain—what was his name?"

"Mentes."

"But it would be stupid. You know what they say about her."

They said a lot of things about Daisy. "What exactly do you mean?" I asked.

"That she eats men." He picked up an acorn and tossed it from hand to hand. He threw it into the woods. "That she wears their bones like a necklace. Better to live without a father and a king than to die and be eaten in Daisy's cave."

"I never said—"

"That's all right," he said. "I understand. I won't tell anyone. Likely they haven't even thought about consulting Daisy, so nobody's wondering why you haven't. Nobody would think you were a coward."

"I'm not!"

"Oh, I know that. *I* know you're not. It's just . . ."

"It's just what?"

"It's just that people talk. You know. They say that you like it better the way it is, that life is easy for you. 'No need for the boy to test his strength with his father's bow,' they say. 'He could never bend it anyway, so why strain himself trying?' and 'It doesn't matter that the boy is so much taller than Odysseus—he'll never put on his father's armor in any case,' and 'That donkey is a good enough mount for a prince who'll never go to war.'"

"What?" I sprang to my feet, my groggy head clearing.

Brax shrugged. "Hey, brother, I'm just telling you what they all say."

"Who?" I demanded.

"I don't know. Everybody. You want to see if the girls are down at the beach again? Damon should be through with his plowing soon."

I wouldn't let him change the subject. "So everybody thinks I'm a coward?"

"No, no," Brax said, in what he obviously meant to be a soothing voice. "Not *everyone.* Most people think you just don't care. Let's go down to the beach."

Don't care? But I didn't have the heart to argue, so I followed him to the water. The girls weren't there, but we waded and splashed, cooling off, and after a while Damon joined us. He brought a bunch of grapes, which we shared while drying off in the sun. I allowed myself to be distracted, and as we walked slowly up the hill, the sun setting, I pushed all thought of what Mentes and Brax had said out of my mind. Damon left us at the turnoff to his father's farm, and Brax and I continued to the palace.

As long as there was no off-island company, Brax was always welcome at our table, despite his appetite and his poor manners. My mother was careful to see to it that any wine at our end was well watered and scant in quantity. Brax knew why she limited him—I've never met a centaur who could stop drinking once he started—and he accepted it with his usual good humor. He knew that I would always find a way to sneak a flask out to him after supper.

Of course, the meal was much simpler than it had been the evening before, when we'd had guests, but as always, it was good. Each place was set with rounds of warm bread topped with slices of tangy goat cheese, and bowls of apples were placed all around the table. We helped ourselves. I ate Brax's cheese and he ate most of my bread and apples.

Brax had backed away from the table (narrowly missing stepping on some feet as he did so), and I was standing to leave when Pisander stood up too and said, "Stay a minute, young man. I have something to say that concerns you." Brax looked at me inquiringly, but I had no idea what Pisander wanted either. I felt a sudden suspicion that Antinoös was behind whatever Pisander wanted to talk about. "You can go, hairy-back," Pisander said, but Brax settled down on his haunches like a big dog and crossed his arms over his chest, a little smile on his face. While I grew hot at the insult to my friend, Brax didn't even seem to hear it.

Everyone had fallen silent, and I realized from the way they were looking at one another that they knew what was coming.

A queasy feeling rose in my stomach. I half stood, then sat back down on my bench to wait, my hands and jaw clenched.

My mother had been giving instructions to a servant, but at the sudden quiet she looked up inquiringly. She dismissed the man, who, I saw, lingered outside the door.

Pisander seemed to have trouble getting started with what he had to say, and as my mother gazed at him with her usual composure, he began to fidget.

"Penelopeia," he finally said, "as your neighbors and as subjects of the king of Ithaka, we're concerned."

She said nothing.

"A delegation of farmers came to some of us this afternoon. They expressed dissatisfaction at your judgments of the morning."

"With which judgments in particular?"

"Well, not with the judgments themselves. With the judge. With you. With the queen deciding—"

"In the absence of the king, it is customary for the queen to hear the cases." Her voice was even, but I detected a note of tension.

"Of course," broke in Eurymachos. "But that's when the king is gone a short time. Sixteen years, Penelopeia! For sixteen years he's been gone! If he were alive, wouldn't he have returned by now?"

"We don't know that." My mother had to raise her voice over a murmur that was coming from the other guests.

"Yes, we do," Pisander said. "He's either dead or in captivity or . . ." He flushed and glanced at one of his fellows as though looking for help.

"Or what?" my mother challenged him.

"Or he doesn't want to come back," Antinoös finished for him. Pisander looked uncomfortable at this insult to the queen, but Antinoös merely took a gulp of wine.

The murmur ceased. My mother's face was stony. The silence lengthened. Finally Eurymachos stood up.

"What Pisander is trying to say," he said, "is that it's time Ithaka had a king. Not an old man, not a woman, not an idle boy—" I stiffened, and Brax's hand came down lightly on my shoulder. He left it there while voices rose around us.

"A king," another one of our guests took up.

"We need a king!" said yet another, and before I knew it, the entire room was ringing with the shouts: "A king! Ithaka needs a king!"

My mother listened. Then she stood up, and the voices ceased abruptly.

"You're right," she said.

CHAPTER 7

"I can't believe it," I said to Brax. "I just can't believe it." The night air blew cool through the window of my bedchamber, but I burned with anger. Would she really remarry? What would become of me, then? Who would be my stepfather?

He said nothing.

"All these years she's refused to believe that my father was dead, and now she says she'll marry one of them as soon as she finishes weaving a shroud for Grandfather?"

Brax was still silent.

I scowled and flopped over. My bed felt hot and lumpy. Brax had lain down on his straw, but I knew he was awake.

"My aunt Ktimene should be the one to make his shroud, anyway. It's a daughter's duty, not a daughter-in-law's."

"Maybe your mother wants to make sure he has a good one," Brax said. "Maybe your aunt Ktimene isn't as good a weaver as Penelopeia."

"Nobody is."

"Well, there you go, then," Brax said.

If things continued in this way, soon there would be a wedding. One of our neighbors would preside over the hall of Odysseus, making judgments, telling me what to do, maybe sending me away to sea—and then what would happen when my father returned? For surely he would return soon. What would he do when he found his place occupied by a former neighbor, someone he used to command?

"No," I said. "It can't happen." Brax changed the subject. But for once I had trouble sleeping. I finally dozed off at daybreak.

When I awoke it was full daylight, and Brax was gone. His going had not disturbed my rest, but then, hardly anything did. My mother said that I could sleep through an invasion of maenads— although I thought that a troop of wild women parading through my house might be enough to wake me.

I lay in bed and considered. If I *were* to go in search of Odysseus—not that I had made up my mind, but if I were—should I take the advice of a stranger about where to go? But if not Mentes' advice, whose? Reluctantly I considered Brax's words.

Daisy, I thought. *Daisy! Surely no one would expect me to be foolish enough to go into her cave and lose my life, or at least my mind. Daisy! No, my friend,* I mentally addressed Brax. *Not going to do it. Not for a father I don't remember, who went willingly into battle before I even knew him and didn't care enough for me or my mother to come home when the war was over.*

I lay there until my stomach told me it was time to get up, and then I pulled on enough clothes to be decent and wandered into the hall to see if the servants had left something for my breakfast. They hadn't, of course. My mother's household was run much too well for that. They had cleared the food, giving broken bits to the dogs and the beggars, and had even removed the large table and set my mother's loom in the corner.

My mother looked up at me with a quick smile before turning back to her work. The shuttle was flying back and forth as rows of threads opened, and then shut, and then opened, and then shut. I stared at it, still half awake, soothed by the familiar rhythm of the clacking of the wooden supports. My mother once told me that she had kept my cradle next to the loom for company after my father left, and its sound was still a comfort to me.

I sat on the floor and leaned my head against her leg. She didn't speak, as was her custom when working, but she briefly ran her hand over my hair. The muscles in her thigh tensed and relaxed as she leaned forward and back, moving the shuttle. I watched the cloth grow, so subtly that I saw a difference in its length only when I looked away and then back after some minutes. She must have been coming to the end of it, though, because she reached for the small spool of blue yarn, wove two rows with it, then a few more of the undyed cream-colored wool, then three of the blue. She always ended that way.

"Is that for my new tunic?" I asked as she tied the final knots.

"No, I finished that. It's over there." She pointed with her elbow to the chest in the corner. "One of the women will sew it up for you in a day or two."

"Then what's this for?" I asked idly, not really caring. Something was always needed. I expected it was a blanket for someone's baby, or a shawl for an old man's stiff joints. A sudden thought made me sit up straighter. "Is it Grandfather's shroud?"

"I'm in no haste to get that done. He doesn't look ready to die anytime soon. No, this is to be a table cover. I was ashamed, when our guests were here, to see how stained and torn our old one was." She put down the shuttle and rubbed her wrists. Lately her hands grew numb if she wove for too long.

"Why was Helena worth all that fighting and all those men's lives?" I asked, before I was aware that I was even thinking of the Spartan queen and the war at Ilios.

My mother looked surprised, but she answered readily enough. "Menelaos couldn't let someone come in and take her without going after her. Everyone would think he was weak." She didn't need to explain: A weak king would not remain king for long. Or even alive.

"But they say that Paris offered a bride-price for her. If Menelaos took that and told people that it was all his idea for Helena to go with him, that he was tired of her . . ." But my mother was shaking her head.

"That's not how it's done in Sparta." Her voice became warm, as it always did when she spoke of her homeland. "Menelaos is of the royal house. As you know, he's a distant cousin of mine—of ours. Still, he would not be king but for Helena. In Sparta the daughter of the queen is the next queen, and whoever weds her is the king." She picked up her shuttle again but did not resume her work. "Even if Helena had not been the daughter of Queen Leda, she would have been someone a king wouldn't like to lose. Remember that Helena's father was Zeus. And she was beautiful, and as witty as my sister Aglaia. No," she said, shaking her head and resuming her work, "no king would allow a stranger to whisk her away for *any* bride-price."

What an odd way to choose a king, I thought but did not say. It seemed much more sensible how we did it in Ithaka, and everywhere else I had heard of before today. The strongest man either kills his rivals or convinces them that he is capable of doing so, and they all agree to let him be the king. My father had done the former here on Sami, slitting the throat of the earlier king, as my grandfather had endlessly told me. And then the new king holds his subjects' loyalty by means of gifts. My father had been unmatched in gift-giving, or at least so said my grandfather and Phemios the bard.

"What if my father is alive but unable to return?" I asked suddenly. My mother shook her head. "Or"—I hesitated, but then plunged on—"or what if he doesn't want to return?"

"He does," she said firmly. "I know he does. He did not want to go to war, and he tried every trick he could think of to stay here."

This was new to me. I had thought that he had been eager to join the forces leagued against Ilios.

"He did?" She nodded. "What did he do?"

"He pretended to be insane. He raved and removed his clothes, and he tore his skin with his nails until he bled. He spoke nonsense."

I felt chilled. I had to rethink my idea of my father. "Why didn't that work?"

"Because of you," she said simply.

"Me?" I sat upright. "What did I do?"

"Agamemnon's man Palamedes, who had come to summon Odysseus, suspected that your father's madness was feigned. When your father yoked together a horse and an ox and pretended to try to plow a field with the unmatched pair, Palamedes snatched you from my arms and laid you in his path. One of his men held me back as I screamed at your father to stop, and just before the hooves of the horse reached you, he did. He couldn't bring himself to crush his heir." That was understandable; a man who died without a son to inherit his property might as well never have lived. "Your father was forced to drop the pretense, and a few days later he sailed. I have not seen him since."

I sat silent at her knee, trying to comprehend this new thought.

"He wanted to stay?" She nodded. "For your sake, and for mine?" She picked up her shuttle without answering.

"How do you know it wasn't fear?"

She resumed passing the shuttle back and forth, back and forth, until I thought she hadn't heard me. My eyes were starting to close when she finally spoke.

"Odysseus never felt a moment of fear in his life," she said, as though to herself. "Or hate. Or bitterness." I thought she had finished, but then she added, "And never, as far as I know, love."

CHAPTER 8

"**D**aisy's old, hundreds and hundreds of years old," said Kleandros' son. We were in the marketplace, where I had bought a new pair of sandals and given my old ones to a beggar boy. I didn't know if the man was worth listening to. His father's mind had been destroyed by his visit to Daisy—what could he tell me that I would trust? "So bring her food that's new."

"Like new figs?" I asked. We passed a stall where the iron-monger Oribasios had displayed a few wares. I looked at them with interest. It seemed that bronze was no longer good enough; everyone had to have ax heads and plow points made of this harder metal. Everyone with something valuable to trade, that is. It was frightfully expensive. Oribasios kept his eye on me as I handled a ring, chased with fine lines forming a pattern of swirls and ripples. Even I was not above suspicion of theft when handling such precious stuff.

"Oh no." Kleandros' son picked up an iron knife. He tested it against his thumb, gave a low whistle, and put it back down as

Oribasios watched him. "Meat. The younger and the more tender, the better. But she eats hardly anything, because she never moves. Only a mouthful or two. And my father said not to carry any weapons—she can smell metal—and always to go the hardest way." A small group of idle men had gathered around us.

"What does that mean, always go the hardest way?"

"I don't know." He spat on the ground. "You know how his mind is. But when I told him that you planned to consult Daisy, at first he cried and said to tie you up or put you in a box, and when he finally accepted that you were going, he told me to tell you that. Leave your weapons behind, bring her the youngest meat you can find, and always go the hardest way."

"Don't turn your back on her," said another man, who was in the small group of listeners. "She won't hurt you if she can see your eyes."

"Address her respectfully," offered someone else. "But don't stammer and act timid. She likes bravery."

"If you can't understand something she says, tell her that your hearing is poor," said yet another well-wisher. "Don't imply that she isn't clear. It's her accent. It's hard to understand, but she doesn't like being reminded of that."

"What kind of accent is it?" I asked. I had heard speech from all over and had little difficulty with any of it.

"I don't know," my adviser admitted. "It's old, though. I think it's the language of the Titans."

Three days later, I stood by the entrance to the cave at the base of Mount Aenos, clutching a basket filled with eggs on the point of hatching and a nest of tiny pink baby rats, which I had found in the granary.

It was early morning and cold. Everyone, it seemed, knew of my plan to consult Daisy. They all even knew that it was my mother's promise to marry once she had finished my grandfather's shroud that had finally pushed me into action. Some applauded my resolution, others told me I was crazy, and others acted as mournful as if I had already been devoured in Daisy's dark cave.

I hadn't told anyone except Brax and Damon exactly when I would be going, and now they stood with me as the morning fog swirled around our feet. The torch in Damon's hand looked pale even in the misty daylight, and its smoke hung around our heads.

"Well, good luck, brother," Damon said. I swallowed hard and nodded.

"Come back soon," Brax said. I nodded again, and turned to the cave opening. It was dark and narrow, and as I leaned in I smelled rot in the dank air.

"You don't have to," Brax said. I looked at him. "Really, you don't have to go. We'll tell everybody you went in and asked Daisy but she didn't say anything. Then we can go to the beach. The sun's sure to come out later."

It was tempting. We could hang around here for a while and then go to the marketplace and say that I had met Daisy but she had spouted gibberish. They would believe me, or they would pretend to, and everything would be the way it always had been.

Except it wouldn't. There would soon be a new king in my father's place, and nothing would ever be the same.

I shook my head. "No," I said huskily, and cleared my throat. "I'll go. It's sure to be nothing. I'll tell you all about it when I get back." And before I could change my mind, I ducked my head, squeezed my shoulders tight into my body, and stepped in.

The darkness was almost absolute. I reached back without

turning, and felt Damon place the torch in my hand. Its shaft was still warm where he had held it.

"Thanks!" I called. My voice sounded thin and weak. I looked around by the yellow light of the torch. There was little to see: a narrow passageway straight in front of me, and nothing else. At least there was no chance of getting lost. I took a few steps forward, and the path immediately turned sharply to the right, then to the left. The small sounds from outside, of Brax's hooves shifting restlessly, of the wind rustling the leaves near the cave entrance, abruptly ceased. There were deep shadows where the light from my torch didn't reach, and those shadows were blacker than the blackest night.

I was walking on sand that was quite smooth, as though wind or water had packed it down. The walls were cold, and the thick air was cooler than it had been outside. In the dark sand of the floor, I thought I could make out an occasional footprint. The rank smell I had detected at the cave opening grew stronger with each step I took.

I looked up. The ceiling was marked with occasional streaks of soot, as though someone else with a torch had passed this way before. It was barely above my head, and the knowledge that the entire hill was above me made me feel like it was about to come crashing down on me. I pictured myself as an ant crawling through one of the tunnels in its hill, ceaselessly moving, walking, hurrying—where?

I glanced back, and instantly regretted it. My shadow behind me danced and wiggled along the irregular walls like a malicious imp. I hurriedly turned my gaze forward and kept moving.

The silence was so deep that my footsteps sounded like the tramp of a herd of centaurs. Through the ringing in my ears I heard my own heartbeat.

Then I came to a crossroads. I stood and considered, my breath tight in my chest. Two paths led slightly uphill to my left, and one rose at an angle to the right. When I lowered my torch, I saw that the passageway to the right had the same sandy surface that I had been walking on, and the one farthest to my left had a relatively smooth floor. The last one, in the center, was barely a passageway at all. It was more a narrow opening, with jagged chunks of rock littering the floor as though they had crashed from the roof. If I chose this one, I wouldn't be able to carry the torch, and I'd barely be able to manage the basket as I scrambled over the boulders.

The sweet, heavy smell of decay was coming most strongly from this middle passage.

I lowered my torch and looked at the prints in the dust. There weren't many, and they might have lain undisturbed for dozens of years. There appeared to be more going down the two easier-looking passages. I bent closer and inspected them. A sick feeling hit me in the stomach. Yes, there were more prints on the two side passages—but they all went one way. In.

I examined the central path, the one with the floor filled with lumpy boulders and sharp rocks. I saw a few footprints in the patches of sand between them, but overlaid above the ones going in were footprints coming out. Did that mean that some travelers had given up and come back? Or did it mean that they had made a visit to Daisy and then returned?

At least the ones on this center path returned. So if I went down one of the side paths I wouldn't come out, unless they led to the outer world. The center path was the roughest, and old Kleandros had said to go the most difficult way. But I couldn't trust him—everyone knew that his mind was gone.

Wasn't it?

I chewed my lip. I could go a short distance down one passageway, and if it led nowhere I'd come back and try another. But what if death lay down the other passageways? Or what if it didn't, and I returned, and then I tried another, and that wasn't the right one either? How long would my torch last?

I plunged the torch into the sand deep enough to keep it standing, and, clutching the basket in my left hand, I started crawling over the rocks in the middle passageway.

At first it was merely difficult. Soon it was nearly impossible. By some miracle I managed to keep the basket stable in my left hand, and as far as I could tell I didn't lose any of its contents. But my knees and right hand were bleeding as I climbed over boulders, and I scraped my side against a sharp rock that sliced through my tunic and the skin under my arm. My breath came raggedly, and sweat poured down my face and stung my eyes. In a short time the light of my torch disappeared behind me as the passageway twisted and turned.

The stench grew ever more sickening. It reminded me of the time Damon and I had found a long-dead dolphin on the beach, only many times stronger. And there was another smell, like that of a latrine that had been used for generations and never filled in. How far should I go before giving up? I paused to catch my breath and tried to stanch the bleeding on my ribs. The blood was trickling down my side, irritating me.

Then my ear hairs tingled as a low noise reached them. It sounded like a chuckle.

I felt vomit rise in my throat and forced it back down. The laugh, if laugh it had been, had come from straight in front of me— and not very far. I gave up on binding my side and took a firmer grip on my basket. I closed my eyes and said a brief prayer—not addressed to any god in particular, just to any who happened to be looking this way—and went on.

I blinked. At first I thought I had imagined it, but no, it was there—a lighter patch in the blackness. Maybe the tunnel led to the outer air, where soon I would be standing in some farmer's meadow, having tried and failed. Then I realized that if it were indeed the outer world that was lending its light to my cavern, the air coming down the tunnel would be fresh and sweet. Instead, its rankness was overpowering, making me gag, and I pulled the neck opening of my tunic over my mouth and nose. But that hampered my breathing too much in the thick air, so I let it drop.

As I moved forward, the light grew stronger, and now I heard a low murmuring, like a chant or a song. I looked behind me. Could I escape that way? The blackness was complete. I could turn around and find my way out, I thought. I hesitated, then put out a tentative hand.

I heard a low voice that froze me in place. "I smell a man. No, a boy. A boy who is coming with something for me. What do you bring, boy?"

The voice was female and thick with an accent I didn't recognize. I tried to answer, but my throat closed.

"Answer me, boy." The voice was still mild and even, but the threat in it was unmistakable.

"I bring—" I squeaked, and the chuckle came again.

"Why don't you show me?" I said another quick prayer and moved forward, reaching out a hand and then a knee and then the other knee and then the hand with the basket, when suddenly that hand fell on the empty air, causing me to sprawl backward in a panic and clutch the basket to my chest. The passageway had ended, and before me was a pit.

I paused to allow the world to stop spinning and then leaned forward and strained my eyes. I could see into the pit, because small glowing insects crawled over its walls and tiny bright fish darted in the pond at the back of the hole, illuminating it faintly. I realized later that if I had come upon this cavern from the outside, even on a gray and gloomy day such as today, I would have found it dim. But after the total blackness of the passage, its greenish-blue light seemed bright. The chamber was not large, and the tunnel opening was at about a man's height above its floor.

The murmuring started again, but I couldn't see where it came from. I looked around and saw piles of rocks, some white, some brown, some gray; a big heap of dirt near the end of the room; and that black pond behind it.

"Well?" The voice was coming from the dirt pile, and as I looked, a knob sticking out in the front of the dirt pile moved.

I had to stifle the scream that rose in my mouth, for there, on a heap of what I was to learn was her own excrement, sat Daisy.

CHAPTER 9

I stood before her, my basket in my hands. I felt its edge crush in my grip. The stench was so foul that my eyes watered, making the shape in front of me shift and shimmer in the dim light.

I had no recollection of how I'd gotten down from the opening in the wall and approached her. Still, somehow I was on the cold, rock-strewn floor. The soles of my feet smarted, so I must have jumped. I might have climbed, though. I just didn't know.

Daisy was smaller than I had expected. From the shoulders down to her haunches she was about the size and shape of a large dog, and her broad paws ended in claws, each as long as my thumb. Her body, covered with reddish scales, curled around to a long, thick tail like a lizard's. But what kept my attention were her heads.

She had three of them, all identical. They were female, and the long hair behind them was matted into what looked like a large rug covering her back. The faces were young and fresh; they might have belonged to the daughter of any farmer in my neighborhood. Her eyes—all six of them—were large and brown. Her pale faces weren't pretty, but neither were they hideous. At least not until my eye traveled downward and saw how her three long necks knotted and twisted together into one where they joined her scaly shoulders, her withered breasts hanging down over her grimy chest.

She was still humming or chanting, the faces leaning in as though speaking one to another, but all six eyes were fixed on me. They held the cold light of the eyes of a snake before it strikes. Around her necks she wore white necklaces of what looked like ivory and her tail wore a garland of the same material. I knew what it was, of course, without needing to look closely. It was bones. Human ones. The necklaces appeared to be intertwined finger- and wrist-bones, and several spines were twisted around her tail. Ribs dangled off her back and tail and rattled at her slightest movement. She rested one of her hind feet on a child's skull, and a pelvic bone tilted over the eye of her right-side face.

"Well?" She seemed amused by my scrutiny. Of all the foul smells mingling in the cave, what came from her mouths was the foulest. It smelled of rot and death and terror. I held out the basket, willing my arms not to tremble.

"I know it's not much. I couldn't find—"

The three necks craned, the faces peered forward, and she reached out a paw and wrapped it around the basket. I let go, trying not to flinch at the sight of her claws, encrusted with dirt or blood. She pulled the basket to herself and looked in.

"Ah!" she said.

"I would have brought you a piglet," I said, "but I couldn't find any young enough."

She ignored me. She poked a claw into one of the eggs and

lifted it to her central mouth. The crackling of the shell was audible even through her little moans of pleasure. The other two faces licked their lips, eagerness clear in their eyes as they watched the egg disappear.

"The reason I'm here—" I said.

She shook her heads at me, the mouth of the central face still chewing, and speared another egg. Once again the heads on both sides leaned in eagerly to look at it. I turned my single head so I wouldn't have to see which one of her three took the egg. It was then that I saw that what she was perched on was unmistakably her own dung. How long had she been sitting there without moving?

A swallowing sound. Then another.

"I know why you're here," she said in an accent that blurred her words. All three mouths moved at once, although there was only one voice.

"You do?" I asked. "How?"

The bones on her tail rattled. "Don't you believe me?" Her eyes gleamed.

"I believe you." I tried to sound brave and not to back away. "I believe you, of course I do."

"You are here because there is no king in Ithaka. I know this because I know everything that happens here. I was here before humans were. Before the gods were. My mother was a Titan, and my father is the rock of Sami. My father tells me everything." She speared another egg and chewed it with her right-side mouth. A little string of drool dripped out of the mouth on the left.

"Ithaka has no king, and you want the king. Am I right?" I nodded, my throat too dry for speech. She either saw me or assumed my assent, for she continued, "And what is a king?" She hooked one of the little pink baby rats on a claw and held it up in front of her left-side face as though inspecting it. It squirmed and made an almost inaudible squeak, and she smiled and then popped it into her center mouth. Her teeth, I saw, were very white and pointed.

"A king," I said, feeling foolish, "is, you know, the *king*. The ruler."

"Ah yes?"

I tried again. "Well, he's the one who makes other people do what he wants."

"And how does he do that? Does he kill them if they disobey?"

"Well, sometimes."

"I think he might run out of subjects very quickly, then, if they were independent-minded."

"Well, he doesn't have to kill them very often." I was guessing at this, never in my memory having seen a king. "Mostly they do what he says."

"They do?" She hooked another ratling, and this time fed it to the left-most mouth, while the other two faces looked on in yearning. "Why do they? And don't say 'well.'"

"W—" I began, and swallowed. "They obey him because he's the strongest one. And the bravest. And he rewards them generously for their obedience, so they keep obeying him to get more rewards."

She held up a paw, or hand, or whatever it was, with its four fingers, or toes, held upright, and counted off: "So you say the king is the strongest, the bravest, and the most generous. Correct?"

I nodded. One finger, the one that would be the index finger on a person's hand, remained up. I looked at it. She looked at it. She looked at me. I tried to meet her gaze but couldn't fix on any one face, with her six eyes staring at me gravely.

"I think there's something else," she said. "Something else that a king is. Isn't there?"

I looked at the remaining finger and thought. The strongest, the bravest, the most generous. What was left?

"I don't think so," I said. "I think that's all."

"Perhaps you're right." She lowered the last finger to join its fellows. "Perhaps you're right. Are there any more of those ratlings?"

I peered into the basket and found two more. I offered them to her on my open hand. She speared them, her claw tip tickling my palm, then swallowed them both with the left-most mouth.

"Um. Very good rats. Very fresh. Very new. Very tasty. You have pleased me." Something about the way she said it, and the way her heads, inclining at different angles, looked at me with their wide-open eyes, suddenly made me too feel very fresh and very new and perhaps very tasty. Cold sweat tickled my forehead.

"And why have you come now?"

Was she trying to humiliate me? "Well, because there's no king in Ithaka."

She bared her teeth. They looked sharp but were not overlong. Somehow this was more frightening than if they had been fangs.

"There has been no king for full sixteen years." The last word lingered in a hiss. "Why do you come now? Why not last year? Why not last month? Why not two years ago?" Her heads tilted and her six eyes narrowed.

"My mother . . ." I faltered.

A gleam of what looked like sympathy came into her eyes. "Your mother. I know mothers." She nodded, all three heads bobbing in unison.

Emboldened, I continued, "They—our neighbors—they've worn her down. She says she'll marry one of them, and soon." I swallowed around the lump in my throat that was threatening to make my voice squeak. "And if she does that, then when my father comes home he'll kill whoever it is she married, and maybe he'll kill her too, for dishonoring him. So you see, I *have* to go now. I have to keep her from marrying one of them."

She didn't answer.

"So, what about it?" I asked.

She gave a little start, as though I had awakened her. "What about what?"

"What about helping me bring the king back to Ithaka?"

"Oh, the king." Her voice sounded drowsy. "Let me think. There must be a way." I sat and waited as first one, then two, then three, then four, then five eyes closed. Small though her meal had been, it must have been enough to make her sleepy. Wasn't she going to give me the advice I had come for? Had I scraped my side and bloodied my feet and knees and terrified myself for nothing?

Before her last eye shut, I said, "Hey!" and all the lids sprang open.

She looked confused for a moment, and then said, "Oh, the king? It's easy. This is what you have to do. Not much. Not much at all. Pay attention."

I leaned forward. *At last. And please let it not be like the Labors of Herakles, or the tasks of Theseus. Let it be something possible.*

"Go in search of him, and then return to the place that is not, on the day that is not, bearing the thing that is not. On that day the king will return." Her eyes began to close once more.

"But—" I said, and three of her eyes opened again.

"You still here?"

"Yes," I said. "I don't understand."

"You don't understand what?"

"What you told me to do—going to the place that never was, and all that."

"I don't remember what I said." The drowsiness in her voice was unmistakable. "So maybe it doesn't matter. Maybe it wouldn't work anyway. Now go."

"But—" I said again, and this time when her eyes opened the anger in them made me draw back. Not fast enough, though. As quick as thought, her right-hand paw shot out and raked me on the side of the face. The burning of the claws was quickly followed by the tickle of streams of blood that sprang from the tracks they had made. I clapped my hand to my cheek.

"I told you to go," she said. "Or would you rather I kept you here forever?" She shook her tail, rattling the human spine and ribs dangling from it.

"No, my lady. I'm going. Thank you, my lady. I appreciate it, I really do. Thank you." Still babbling, I backed out until I reached the wall. Somehow I managed to climb up it and find my passageway, and as best as I could, I fled.

CHAPTER 10

I didn't care if I tore all the skin off my hands, my knees, my feet. I had to get out. Every instant, I expected to feel Daisy's long claws seize me from behind, thrusting me into one of her mouths with the pointed teeth, decorating herself with my bones. My face ached where she had gashed it, and I felt blood running down my cheek and neck, but still I crawled across the jagged rocks.

The image that I couldn't shake from my mind's eye was the small round skull under her hind foot. Gods, how had a *child* gotten down there? Had Daisy climbed out and grabbed him? Or had he—or she—ignored all the terrible stories told by his parents and descended into the cave during a game, only to meet his fate in that ghastly cave?

I scrambled and hauled myself through the darkness, over the rough stones, and after what seemed an eternity I found myself at my underground crossroads. My faithful torch was still burning brightly, although it had consumed nearly all the fat-soaked cloth at its top. The small area was now filled with smoke. Even the smell of burnt mutton-grease was fresh and clean compared with the reeking cavern filled with skeletons and Daisy dung.

I grasped the torch and nearly sobbing, I staggered and stumbled over what seemed like a fine road after the rocky path I had just left, and burst out into the open air, gulping it down like sweet wine.

The sunlight dazzled my eyes. I felt myself falling, and then hands—human hands—grabbed me. Someone eased the torch out of my fist and stuck it into the ground. Whoever was holding me lowered me until I was sitting next to it.

"Brother, you *stink*," said a voice.

"What in the gods' names is that smell?" said another. I shook my head, trying to clear the stench from my nostrils.

"Never mind," said the first voice, which I now recognized as Damon's. "Let's get him home. His face is bleeding."

"And his side," said Brax. "And his hands and his knees." Damon helped me onto Brax's back. Brax grunted. "Good thing he's thin. I won't be able to move fast, you know."

"Just as long as you get him home," Damon said.

The next thing I remember is Eurykleia shrieking at the sight of me—I later learned that she thought I was dead—and then ordering Damon and Brax to lay me on a pallet in the hall, near the fire. She stripped me and bathed me, and put bandages covered with something brown and pungent on my side and my face. They stung, but it was a good sting, as I felt the dirt and foulness of Daisy's cave being drawn out of my wounds.

I lay in my bed for three days. Mother and Eurykleia brought me soup and later bread and cheese, and changed the bandage on my face, sponging off the poison that oozed out of my skin.

Three of the wounds healed quickly, but the deepest, the one under my eye, seeped blood and foulness and refused to close.

I dreamed without cease. A transparent baby naiad chortled and squealed silently in the river, her fellow water nymphs tickling her and pinching her chubby bottom. Mentes reappeared and again turned into a tall woman, but the words coming from her mouth were in the man's voice: *Find out if he's dead, in which case your mother should marry again and you can make your way in the world. Or if you learn he's alive, you can try to bring him home. Either way, you're old enough now to take the journey.* A huge paw reached for my face, its claws ripping and tearing my flesh, leaving four wounds that festered and rotted my cheek away, so that when I put up my hand to feel it my fingers met jawbone and teeth. Men's voices, raised in anger, shouted against fraud and accused someone of deception. That someone defended herself in even tones that were nevertheless tense.

The voices grew louder until suddenly I was awake, realizing that this, at least, was no dream. Shouts were coming from the hall, and the voice raised in self-defense was my mother's.

I shot to my feet, and a wave of dizziness and nausea nearly knocked me down again. I bent over, head down, until my vision cleared, and then lurched toward the hall. I cursed, and one of the scabs on my face cracked open. Blood trickled down my cheek.

Leaning against the wall was a staff, left there by some beggar or a shepherd. I grabbed it and used it to help myself move toward the hall, where the loud voices continued. I burst through the door, expecting every eye to look to me, but they all had their backs to me and nobody turned around.

"Of course I undid some of my work," my mother was saying. She was standing next to her loom, gripping one of its uprights with her right hand. "It was flawed. When my father-in-law dies, how will I be able to offer his body to the gods in a shroud that's less than perfect?"

My grandfather, seated near the cold fireplace, wore his usual anxious smile. He looked from one face to another, clearly not understanding what was being discussed.

"Come, now," Antinoös said. A lock of his long black hair tumbled over his face, and he shook it back impatiently. "When did you ever weave anything imperfect?" A murmur of assent rose from the group of five or six men standing around the loom.

"Sometimes I do," my mother said. "And then I make it over again."

A snort of laughter came from one of the men; I couldn't tell which.

"It's true," she said, but her protest sounded false, even to me.

"We know better than that," Amphinomos put in. "Come now, Penelopeia. We know why you undid your work. It was to keep from finishing the shroud and having to marry one of us."

"I wouldn't be surprised if that's what she does with the boy," said Antinoös. "Plucks the hairs from his chin as soon as they sprout, before we can see them." I gripped the staff. What did the hairs on my chin—or their lack—have to do with anything?

"No, it—" my mother started, but Antinoös grabbed her upper arm and gave her a shake. The sight of his hand on her arm cleared my head.

"Stop!" I shouted, and every head in the room snapped around to me. For a moment they were silent, mouths agape, eyes wide, and then a roar of laughter burst from each throat. Even Eurymachos, who had been like a big brother to me when I was a boy, was doubled over, clutching his stomach. My grandfather leaned back on his stool, his toothless mouth agape with uncomprehending merriment.

"See the hero!" Antinoös cried. "See him with his mighty weapon, and his pizzle waving in the wind." I looked down. It was true; I had not stopped to put on a tunic and was as naked as a satyr. The staff I clutched seemed like a child's toy now, but for a moment I pictured myself swinging it wildly, cracking heads and bloodying noses. What satisfaction it would give me to see them lying still on the floor, especially the arrogant Antinoös, but even Eurymachos and Amphinomos, who had always behaved more decently than the rest of our neighbors. They were my enemies too.

The laughter died down. I leaned heavily on the staff, hoping that no one would notice how weak I was. Eurykleia silently appeared at my side and wrapped a blanket around my waist. I clutched it, holding it closed over my hip.

"What's going on?" I tried to sound like a stern judge, not a querulous little boy.

Antinoös dropped my mother's arm and took a step toward me. I clutched my staff and raised it defensively but he merely gestured at the loom.

"Since you ask, boy," he said, "your mother is a fraud. She's been undoing her weaving at night. She has no intention of finishing Laertes' shroud. That way she'll never have to marry anyone. But I caught her at it, and we've given orders for a wedding feast. Animals are already being slaughtered. Tomorrow she'll choose one of us—or, if she doesn't, we'll do it ourselves. And then Ithaka will have a king, and you, boy"—his eyes narrowed—"you'll have a father."

At the thought of Antinoös sitting on my father's throne and sleeping in my mother's bed, the world turned red and I raised my staff higher.

"Telemachos." My mother's voice was low, but it stopped me, and my vision cleared. I looked at her. Her eyes were dark wells in her pale face.

What was it Daisy had said? *Return to the place that is not, on the day that is not, bearing the thing that is not. On that day the king will return.*

I still didn't know what she meant. I was still smarting from the way Mentes and Sikinnos had called our palace a tumbledown farm and me a good-looking boy, and the way my neighbors thought I was an indolent coward. And I knew that Ithaka was falling into ruin and was vulnerable to attack, both from within and from without.

I could live with all these things, spending my days at the beach with Brax and Damon, entertaining myself with nymphs and girls and maybe even mermaids, while the kingdom assumed a new ruler. But what I couldn't live with was the sight of that man's hand on my mother's arm and the despair in her eyes.

I glared at Antinoös. There was only one thing that would wipe that smirk off his handsome face. I took a deep breath, knowing that what I said next could never be taken back.

"You may proceed with preparations for the feast." My mother winced and looked down. Antinoös grinned and started to turn away. "But it won't be for a wedding," I added. "It will be a farewell banquet."

Antinoös snorted. "I'm not going anywhere."

"But I am," I said. "I'm going to find Odysseus." I looked around at the men, most of them smirking, some smiling outright, some turning back to their wine cups. "And when I return, I'm going to take care of all of *you.*"

Their laughter followed me out the door.

CHAPTER 11

An army was marching, the feet of hundreds of soldiers pounding the ground. *Blam-blam-blam-blam* went their tread, and the sun glinted off their polished helmets and shields, shooting pain into my eyes and out the top of my head like a flaming arrow. A war trumpet shrilled, and its notes said my name in Brax's voice.

"Te-le-ma-chos," it sounded. And again, louder, "Telemachos!"

I threw up an arm to cover my eyes and realized that I was in the men's quarters at home. The pounding wasn't the feet of soldiers; it was the blood in my head, and light was coming in through the door.

I groaned and stood, the world whirling around me. Finding a blessed jug of water and a chamber pot on the floor, I emptied one and filled the other, and then fell back on my pallet and pulled a corner of my sour-smelling tunic over my face, waiting for the agony in my head to ease.

"Brother," Brax said from across the room, "if I couldn't hold my wine any better than that, I wouldn't drink."

"Yes, you would." I sat up carefully. "You'd drink if it killed you." I squinted at the glaring light. "Is it midday? The sun's so bright!"

Brax laughed, and the sound made me wince. "It's long past midday. And it's cloudy. It rained all morning. Don't you remember when the rain started and we all ran for cover in the forest?"

I didn't remember much of the night before. My mother had ordered a sacrificial banquet before my departure so that the gods would smile on the voyage. I remembered the goat and the pig tied to the steps of the temple of Poseidon, and then my stomach churned as I recalled the smell and taste of their roasted flesh. The centaur I thought of as Brax's father (like most forest people, Brax wasn't sure who his father was) had come with skins filled with pine-scented centaur wine, and as the dark fell, the torches set all around had given the market square a strange brightness that only served to make the shadows deeper.

An image flickered through my mind: a long dance that led into the glade behind the palace, with Brax and the little wood nymph and dozens of others, even some of the satyrs, whom we rarely saw. I licked my lips, remembering how salty and sticky my mouth had tasted from the sweat that had run down my face and stung my eyes.

I opened those eyes again, and shut them, then cracked one to look at Brax.

"Where's that nymph?" I asked.

He laughed the high whinny that meant he was truly amused. "Left in a hurry."

"Why?"

"I think she was angry."

"Angry at what?" I asked.

"You, you idiot," Brax said.

"Me? Why?"

"You fell sound asleep. She left with some satyr. Two of your servants had to carry you here. You didn't twitch an eyelid."

I hastened to change the subject. "What are you doing here?"

"Wondering about Damon."

"What about him?"

"Did you see him last night?"

Come to think of it, I had somehow missed him in the crowd. Surely he had been there, though. The banquet had been for him as well, since he was to accompany me. I pushed the thought of the journey out of my mind, as I had done ever since I had proclaimed that I was going to look for my father.

"No," I said. "He probably left early with some girl."

Brax shook his head. "He wasn't there during the sacrifice. And Kyra was looking for him."

This *was* strange. He'd been mooning after Kyra for weeks. If she was there, he should have been too.

I stood again and waited for the world to settle. A few grains of barley, caught in my hair, fell to the floor. The pounding in my head had calmed enough for me to realize that my stomach was churning. I laid a hand on Brax's horse-back for support, and together we went out. We passed through the palace gate and soon entered the town. As we neared the temple, the smell of roasted flesh and toasted barley made my stomach roll again. Brax gave his whinny-like laugh. "Easy," he said. I kept my teeth clenched and didn't answer.

The way to Damon's farm was not long. We turned off the road into a fallow field to shorten the distance even more. The grass was wet from the rain of the night before, and small pools stood where the hard ground had not yet absorbed it. As the farm came into view at the top of a little rise, the sun emerged from behind a cloud, and something glinted on the ground a little distance off. I nudged Brax and pointed.

"What is it?" He peered ahead.

"It looks like a bubble," I answered. "An enormous bubble. Could some foam have blown all the way up here from the sea?"

He shook his head. "No wind," he pointed out. "And even in a gale I've never seen sea foam this far from the shore." I hadn't either, but I didn't know what else it might be.

As we approached, I saw that the bubble had the shape of a woman, although it was flatter. There was something horrible about it, about the way its eyes, as gray and lifeless as snail shells, rolled sightlessly in its head, about the way the grass, visible beneath it, was barely pressed down by the thing's light weight. The smell of stagnant pond rose from where it lay.

"What in the gods' names . . ." I was barely able to speak.

Brax had thrust his two fists out in front of him, thumb stuck through the fingers and waggling, in the gesture that averts evil. "It's a water nymph. And she's dead. Or dying. I've heard of them doing this. Sometimes they get confused when the ground is wet, and they climb out of their streams and go on the land. They usually realize their mistake and get back in the water before it's too late. But sometimes . . ." His voice trailed off.

"Can't we help her?" I asked, my headache forgotten. "Can't we take her back to the river?"

Brax shook his head. "Too late, brother. Let's get out of here. This isn't a good place."

But I refused to believe him. Kneeling, I slid a hand under what must have been the nymph's shoulder. Her thin skin shredded in my grasp, and I cried out, pulling my hand back. In trying to help her, all I had done was make her bleed—or leak—even more quickly. As the last of her life fluid poured from her, her eyes rolled in her head, pointing toward me. I don't know if she was looking at me or if it was just the way she was flattening out that made it happen. I thought I saw a flicker in her eyes, but that might have been a trick of the light. I couldn't make out her expression, in any case. Was she thanking me for trying to help? Or cursing me for coming too late?

In the time it takes to draw two breaths, it was over, and the thin membrane shriveled like a jellyfish stranded on the beach. I stood up, again fighting the urge to vomit. Why would a being of the water leave her natural place and cross the land? What urge had led her to take such a dangerous journey?

"Come on," Brax said. "Nothing to do here. Let's go to Damon's." But I knelt again and gathered the filmy shreds in my hands and walked to the stream that ran near the field. I dropped the shiny, slippery things in the sparkling water and watched as they moved back and forth before settling to the bottom and flowing gently downstream.

Brax was where I had left him, scratching his man-back with a twig. When I approached, he tossed the stick aside and said, "Feel better now?" I didn't know what to say, so I fell into step next to him without answering.

The farmhouse came into view. I was almost as familiar with it as I was with the palace; Damon's mother had always welcomed me there as a second son. I missed her; not as much as Damon did, I know, but I missed her stories and her soft voice. My mother was a frequent visitor there and had taught the two older of Damon's three sisters to spin and weave, and frequently provided a lap and a story for little Bito. She had even made them weavers' smocks, with pockets for their scissors and needles and whatever else it is that women use. Still, that was not the same as having their own mother.

I put two fingers in my mouth and whistled the greeting that Damon and I had used ever since we were small. I strained my ears but heard no answering shrill. The place was oddly quiet. I hung back a bit, but Brax strode on ahead, not seeming to feel anything out of the ordinary. When we were almost at the cabin, the door burst open and out flew Bito, whose birth had caused their mother's death. She ran straight at me, her naked little feet splatting in the mud, her short dark braids bobbing behind her, her arms raised. I caught her up as I always did and swung her in the air before plopping her down on Brax's horse-back.

"Run!" she commanded, and Brax obligingly broke into a trot, one arm slung behind him, holding her against his man-back so she wouldn't slide off. She squealed as he kicked up his hind feet, bouncing her higher and higher. I ran after them.

"Where's Damon?" I asked the little girl, panting. "And your sisters?" Brax slowed, and Bito jerked her head back toward the hut without looking at me.

"Damon's in there with Father. So's Sotera. I don't know where Polydora is. Run!" she ordered Brax again, and he trotted off.

Why weren't the men in the field? A little rain wouldn't keep them from their work. Maybe Damon was sick. This would explain why he hadn't come to the banquet the night before. Brax seemed to have forgotten our errand, so I went alone toward the hut. I liked pretty little Sotera, who was as mild and sweet as milk, especially when compared with her prickly older sister.

But as I approached, Damon ducked out through the door. He held his finger to his lips and motioned me away from the house.

"My father's fallen asleep."

"Oh, is he sick?"

Damon shook his head. "Broke his leg. Mule kicked him."

"Gods!" I said, shocked. "Has a healer—"

"She came by this morning. Says that it might heal cleanly, might not. Can't tell yet. And of course Polydora is nowhere to be found. She should be in there taking care of him. Sotera doesn't have Poly's healing skill, and I don't know what to do with him." He looked at me sideways, as though not wanting to meet my gaze. "There's still the plowing to do. And then all the rest of it." Now he did look at me.

"I'll come with you to look for your father, of course I'll come. But can we wait until harvest is over? With my sisters to feed . . ."

He didn't need to finish his thought. I knew he couldn't leave his family now. But I also knew I couldn't sail to Pylos by myself. I needed at least one companion to take turns on watches, and I had to leave now. Antinoös would never accept a postponement of my journey.

I didn't know what to say. If I commanded it, Damon would have to come with me. And he knew it.

"Sophonisba heard what happened and came by this morning," he said after a moment. "She offered to buy Polydora."

"*Poly?* But she's only a child!"

Damon shook his head. "Not anymore. She's a woman now, Telemachos. And Sophonisba would treat her well. But my mother wouldn't have wanted—" He turned his head away, and I saw he was blinking hard. In a few moments he continued. "But that's not what we want, my father and I, for Polydora to become like Sophonisba. Still, she offered a good price, and with one less mouth to feed and one less dowry to pay, my father might be able to put up with my absence for a few months, if we wait until fall before we leave."

"No," I said. "No, Damon. You can't sell Polydora. You stay here and run the farm. I can go by myself. I can sail to Pylos alone." He looked at me, the doubt clear in his eyes. I knew that wagers were being taken in the village as to whether I would actually even set foot on the boat. Had Damon bet, I wondered, and which side had he taken?

"Truly, Damon," I said. "I can do it alone."

"No, you can't," came a voice from behind us. We turned. There, with his arms crossed over his bare chest, stood Brax. Bito slid off his back and ran into the house, her bare feet noiseless on the damp grass.

"You can't," Brax repeated.

"I have to," I said.

Brax lifted a hind hoof and kicked at a fly on his front ankle. "No, you don't. I'll go with you."

⟨HAPTER 12

At first my mother tried to forbid me to go. "The sea took your father," she told me, as though I needed reminding. "Men were not meant to go on boats. I never saw a boat or even the ocean until I married Odysseus and he brought me here, and I have not seen my mother or my sisters since." Though I knew all this, I let her talk until she had said everything at least twice. My resolve weakened occasionally, but then I would remember Antinoös and the smirk on his face and his hard hand on her arm, and I repeated that she couldn't stop me.

"I'll marry one of them," she said. "Then there will be no need for you to go."

"You won't," I answered. "You can't, not until we know for sure about my father." And after she saw that I was determined, she stopped objecting.

Then, when I told her that Brax, not Damon, was to accompany me, she started again, reminding me of the old saying "as useful as a centaur on a ship"—meaning of no use at all. "He eats so much," she said, "and centaurs make such a mess."

I couldn't deny either charge. But neither could my mother deny that if Damon went with me his family would starve, even if his father grew desperate enough to sell Polydora. My mother had assisted at Damon's birth, and a few weeks later, his mother, nursing him, had been present at mine. The prospect of her friend's daughter in Sophonisba and Clio's house silenced my mother's objections.

So, two days later, I sat huddled on the deck of my boat. It had been my father's, and he enjoyed sailing alone, so it was fitted for a one- or two-man crew, and depended as much on wind power as on oars. This was good, because Brax probably wouldn't be much help in rowing. Most of his strength lay in his legs, not his arms.

I had said my good-byes early that morning. My grandfather wore an anxious smile, as though he knew that something important was happening but couldn't remember what. Eurykleia sobbed, which was hard to bear, and my mother didn't, which was even harder. They remained in the palace and would likely stay there the rest of the day, until I was safely out of sight of land. Nobody had come to see us off, of course; it would be foolish to risk having the gods notice a crowd and decide to interfere with what the mortals were planning, just to prove that they could. Only old Argos trotted out to the gate and looked after me, the tip of his tail moving, appearing unsure whether to accompany me or not.

Before we boarded, though, I did notice more people than usual on the beach. They were trying to look as if they were going about their usual business and weren't there to see the prince and his companion depart on what must seem like a fruitless—and perhaps fatal—journey. Fishermen who should have caught the early tide were once again repairing nets that looked perfectly serviceable, and a crowd of little boys ran across the brown sand, shouting and throwing pebbles at one another.

The presence of these spectators meant that when it came time to climb into the little rowboat that would take me to my father's old boat, I couldn't hesitate. The world turned gray around me as I stepped off the pointed rock and my foot hit the wooden seat. The rowboat rocked, and I clutched wildly at the air for support. The fisherman who had reached up to help me down grabbed my arm and whispered into my ear, "Steady there, sir. I've never capsized yet and I won't now. I wagered my brother a week's catch that you'd make it to your vessel on the first try. Don't make me lose, now!"

His breath stank, but his rough voice was more soothing than Eurykleia's sweetest lullaby, and my heart slowed until I felt it pumping only as far as my teeth, not all the way up to my eyes, as it had when I was on the rock preparing to step down. I even managed to turn and wave to people on the shore before I sat; then, since no one could see below the side of the boat, I clutched the seat with both my hands until I was sure it would splinter. My eyelids clamped down, and nothing I could do would force them open.

Brax was already aboard. I had heard his curses and shouts from the shore as two men pulled him up the slippery plank sloping from the smaller boat and two more pushed him from behind. How, I wondered, would I ever get him off when we arrived at Pylos?

My hands gripped the rail, and I sat with my back pressed against the side of the boat, moaning, but we were far enough away that the people on the shore would see only our sail. I couldn't see even that much, because my eyes were still squeezed shut.

I had not been on the open water for years, not since the last time my grandfather had dragged me, screaming, onto this very boat. He insisted that a child of Odysseus had to know how to handle oars and sail, how to navigate, which rope to pull when, and how to turn, slow down, and do everything else that a sailor had to do. He took me out again and again, despite my protests.

Until that last trip my mother had not interfered; being from landlocked Sparta she did not see the value of knowing how to sail, but she knew it was important to my father and my grandfather, and did not wish to interfere. She said nothing as she watched him peel my fingers off the doorjamb and carry me down the road to the harbor, hanging over his shoulder like a sack of meal. She was on the shore when we returned, my grandfather grim-faced from the ordeal and me weak from puking and weeping. She stood with the water lapping around her ankles, and when I stumbled onto the shore she bent over and took me by the hand, straightened, and said firmly, "Never again." Up till now, she had prevailed, and I had made only the short trip from Sami to Ithaka and back, never out of sight of the land, when I had turned thirteen.

What a fool I was to think I could do this. The sailors had pointed us in the right direction and set Brax to rowing while I had cowered, refusing to look at the gray sea. How far was it to Pylos? And once I got there, I would still have to come back. I moaned again as our boat hit a wave and bounced, rattling my teeth and threatening to bring my breakfast up.

I wondered how long the people on the shore would think of us after we disappeared from their view. I felt hollow as I imagined the fishermen going about their business in an hour or two, worrying about the catch, without giving a thought to us on the sea. I pictured Damon bent over a plow, tending to his father, eating the food prepared by his sisters. Would he think of us at the quiet end of the day? Or would he be so busy, so preoccupied with providing for his family, that he would remember us fleetingly, if at all? Would he continue to go down to the beach and look at the girls all alone? Or would he be too caught up in his responsibilities to indulge in such pastimes?

I was sure of only my mother and Eurykleia. But soon even they would be thinking of other things, overseeing the farming of the land and the tending of the sheep, spinning and weaving, taking care of my grandfather. And meanwhile, Brax and I would be out on the sea, the dark, bottomless, unpredictable sea, the sea that teemed with strange and unfamiliar creatures.

I managed to open my eyes. The air was cool and gray, and I loosened one hand to wrap my cloak around me, holding it tight while I gripped the rail with the other hand. My face was damp from sea spray or the fine mist in the air. At each lurch of the boat, my stomach flew into my throat. Each time the spray hit my face, the salt burned my cheek where that one gash made by Daisy's claws still stubbornly refused to heal.

Brax knelt on the deck, prying the lid off a box of provisions. He must have hoisted the sail, for we were still moving, but I didn't dare raise my eyes to look. The wooden deck was solid, and it lay between me and the dark depths. I would keep my gaze fixed on it. I cautiously rose enough to slide onto the crude bench that ran along part of the side of the boat. My limbs tingled, but it was more comfortable than crouching on the floor.

The wind stirred the dark-brown hair that hung down Brax's man-back as he worked at the nails holding the box shut. Brax would never be worried by such thoughts as a cold death in the water, I knew. Saba and his other brothers and sisters and his mother had probably said their farewells cheerfully and then gone about their usual activities without thinking more about him. They would weep and wail for a few days if they learned of his death, and they would feast and dance upon hearing of his return, but until news of one or the other reached them, they wouldn't think of him often. Nor he of them.

Brax looked up, and I wondered if he noticed how white my knuckles were as we moved, smoothly now, across the water. If he did he didn't say anything, just grunted as he finally worked the lid off the box of provisions.

"Ah!" He pulled out one of Eurykleia's honey cakes. He turned it over with a smile before stuffing it into his mouth and reaching for another.

"Stop it!" I said. I should have taken it from his hand, but I dared not loose my hold. He grinned at me, his cheeks distorted by the cake, and chewed.

"We don't know for sure how long the trip will take," I said. "Those need to last us the whole way." He put the second cake in his mouth, but I noticed that he didn't take a third.

My mother had hired Sebastos, the most experienced sailor on Sami, to plot our course. Sebastos had told Phemios the way to Pylos, and the bard had set the route to music. Then he and I had sung it together over and over again until it was engraved in my mind. I sang it under my breath now, taking comfort in the familiar words.

> Sail to the east, then the south, then the east.
> Steer clear of Zakynthos, which loves us the least.

(As I've said, Phemios was not a great bard.)

> When you come to the land, to the wide sandy shore,
> Proceed down the coast with your sail and your oar.

It went on to advise us to make our way south until we came to the harbor of Pylos. Right now the wind was blowing almost directly from the north, and unless it changed soon, we'd have to take down the sail and row eastward for a bit.

We had plenty of food for ourselves (if Brax didn't eat it all the first day) and more for offering to Poseidon, lord of the sea, when we arrived safely. My mother had also supplied us with bronze pots and other valuables to trade for food and whatever else we needed. These were carefully hidden in the piles of hay and grass that had been set aside for Brax's meals.

Mother had not trusted the servants with hiding the most valuable items, though. These were some knives and cups made of iron. Oribasios the smith had discovered a way to forge iron that made it stronger than anything he had ever produced out of bronze, and the blades kept their edge far longer than any other we had ever seen, including those made of iron by men less skilled than the Ithakan smith.

The few traders to whom Mother had sold pieces of this iron-ware had rewarded her with fine goods in exchange and had begged for more. She always pretended that she had none, seeking to keep word of this new iron from circulating too far and too fast until Oribasios had perfected his technique. So she had told me about a secret storage place my father had had built into the floor of the boat. While it was still onshore being fitted for the journey, I had slid the precious iron into it when no one was looking. These were small pieces—a few rings, a spoon, a tunic clasp—but they were very fine, being smooth and delicately shaped, and decorated with engraved lines and curlicues. She had made me promise to keep my treasure secret from everyone, even Brax, although centaurs have little use for metal and no interest in riches.

I was not to show the precious iron to anyone until I arrived at Pylos, where it was to be a guest-gift for King Nestor.

Now the clouds were speeding across the sky as the wind picked up. The boat bounced a little, like a donkey trying to break into a trot. I grabbed on even more tightly and felt a cold shudder run up my limbs. This was what my life would be until we reached Pylos. When I wasn't scraping my hands raw with rowing, I'd be feeling the terror of being dumped into the dark-green sea.

Spray bounced over the side and smacked me in the face. Brax's high whinny-laugh reached my ears, but I was too miserable to mind. The sky was gray, the wind was cold, and I was heading toward a place I had only heard about but never seen, where no one knew me and I knew no one, where the name of Ithaka was as foreign to everyone as Pylos was to me. I was sitting on a hard wooden shelf that wasn't even wide enough for both my buttocks. All we had were barrels of cold food, and Brax would certainly consume what little wine we'd brought, before we reached land. Meanwhile, back at home, Mother was ordering a warm meal for the men who were hoping that I wouldn't return, and arranging a woolen blanket over my grandfather's bony knees.

I nearly lost my grip as the wind shook the boat. Bile rose in my mouth, and as I leaned over the side to spit it out, I saw that the water was oddly disturbed, like it was boiling.

"Brax—" I started, but before I could speak further, the huge torso of a man, grayish-green, and dripping water and seaweed, erupted from the waves and flung itself at me.

CHAPTER 13

I shot backward, hands and feet scrabbling on the deck, which was slippery with the water streaming from that huge head and chest. The thing clutched the side of the boat, rearing its gigantic self up into the sky above me. But I rapidly slid down to where I had started, since the creature's massive weight tilted the deck to a steep slope. From somewhere behind me came Brax's shrill screams as I slammed into the rail directly under the monster. For an instant I thought I was going over the side, and I clung with all my strength to anything at hand.

The head loomed above me, its shaggy blue curls dripping, its mouth in its blue-gray beard open in a snaggle-toothed gape. "Oshammi shammi!" the beast shouted. Was it going to eat me? I tried to push myself away, but, with the vessel creaking and the sail shaking, I found myself pinned directly beneath it by the steepening angle of the deck.

"Go away!" I cried, hearing how feeble my voice sounded. "Go away!"

The beast moaned but made no move either to chomp my head or to return to his watery home. His greenish fists shook the boat, and I crumpled against the railing. I flung out a hand, trying to find a secure hold, and felt something hard slip into my palm. When I looked wildly around, I saw a knife, its blade glinting and sparkling like a gemstone. I didn't know where Brax had found it, but I silently and fervently thanked him.

Holding on with my free hand, I hauled myself up. Now I was almost face to face with the man-thing, and I was leaning perilously far out over the water.

"Kill it!" screamed Brax. "It's going to swamp us!" His voice sounded far away.

Yet I hesitated. The thing looked at me. His blue-gray eyes were flat like a fish's, yet they held something in them that a fish never felt. What was it? Fear? Sorrow?

Either a motion of the man-fish or a wave knocked me nearly off balance, and I was flung forward again. Before I righted myself, my gaze hit the water, and I saw that at the waist the beast turned into some kind of sea creature, smooth like a squid, not scaly. But there was something else down there, barely below the surface. What was it? Another wave tipped me forward, knocking my gut into the railing, and I saw. It was a common fishnet, like the ones the fishermen at home used, and it was wrapped around the creature's lower limbs.

No wonder the creature was distressed. He couldn't swim tied up like that, and the fish half was dragging the man half under to drown.

On an impulse I leaned forward, wrapping my left arm around a cleat and slashing downward hard and fast with my right hand—but not at the throat or the chest of the man-fish. At the net. He bellowed as I missed and snagged his skin. Dark-red blood oozed out as I hacked at it again and this time felt a satisfying rip as my knife severed a long stretch of the net.

"Ah!" said the man-fish, and he surged upward again. I cowered, expecting to feel his enormous teeth close on my neck. But no, he wasn't attacking; he was pulling his lower body closer. I gripped the knife again and cut, more carefully this time, drawing a little blood again but slicing away enough of the net that with a mighty wriggle of his limbs he flung off its tattered remnants. Then he dived, his long tentacles streaming out behind him. He circled the boat once, flipped his hind limbs in the air so that they crashed down on the surface of the water with a mighty splash, shouted, "Oogoro!" and disappeared.

Silence. The boat had righted itself as soon as he let go, and blessedly, the wind had dropped. The sail flapped, and we were hardly moving.

My legs suddenly lost their strength, and I sank to the deck. I dropped the knife and clamped both hands in my armpits to still their trembling. I was cold, and white sparks danced in circles in my vision.

Then I felt a blanket wrapped around my shoulders, and Brax's warm breath, heavy with honey cake, was on my face.

"Thanks, brother," he said hoarsely as he sank to his knees next to me. "I thought we were dead. I thought it was going to eat us or drown us or something."

"Me too."

We sat in silence while the wind freshened again. I didn't know which way it was blowing now, nor did I care. I heard the distant *eee-eee-eee* of seabirds and watched a troop of pelicans fly by, looking like a phalanx of soldiers advancing on an enemy.

Oddly enough, the sea seemed less frightening than before,

not more. At least now there was no huge green torso rearing out of it. My trembling slowed. I picked up the knife. It had a rough, worn hilt and a bronze blade that had been dulled by being forced through the thick ropes. I didn't recognize it.

"Where did you get this?" I asked.

"What?"

"This knife—where did you find it?"

"Me? I've never seen it."

"Brax, stop it. You gave it to me when that thing came at me."

"That thing was a triton."

"No, it wasn't," I said.

"Yes, it was."

"No," I said. "A triton is a man above, a fish below. This thing was an octopus or a squid or something below. But where did you find the knife?"

"It *was* a triton, and I *didn't* find any knife."

I sighed. I had stopped shaking, but my head hurt, and I was cold and exhausted. "Look. I was holding on to the rail when someone put it in my hand. There's no one here but you and me. So you put it in my hand."

"No," he said. "It probably fell out of some crate and came sliding down the deck and you picked it up."

"Someone put it in my hand," I repeated. "You must have seen something." He was silent. "Brax, did you see something?"

"No, I didn't see anything. My eyes were closed the whole time. I didn't want to watch you get eaten."

I put the knife down again. "So if the person who put it in my hand wasn't you, who was it?"

"A god?" he suggested.

I shook my head. "If a god was going to help us, he would

have hit the triton-thing with lightning or dazzled it with flames. He wouldn't have given me an old knife."

Brax shrugged, clearly bored by the discussion.

"Hey," I said as something else occurred to me, "what were you doing all the way over there, anyway? Why didn't you help me?"

"I went there to weight down that side of the boat," he said with dignity. "The triton was going to tip us over."

"It's not because you were scared?"

Brax snorted and shook his skin as though ridding himself of a fly. "I kept us from tipping over. I wasn't scared. Nothing to be scared of."

"Mm-hmm," I said, my tone telling him that I didn't believe him. But since I didn't say so in words, he didn't have to defend himself, and we let the matter drop.

Waves still bounced the boat, but compared with that huge gray-green face looming over me and the ship tipping way over on its side, the slight rocking and occasional spray over the side seemed almost harmless. Though I still kept one hand on the rail, I no longer felt the need to hold on to it with all my strength.

"What did it want?" Brax asked. I told him about the tangled net. He was silent for a moment. "I would have killed it. You didn't know what it was going to do after you cut the net off. It would have been safer to kill it." I said nothing. I didn't really know why I hadn't gone for the creature's heart. Something in his eyes had made me try to help him instead.

"So—what's in the rest of those cartons?" I finally asked. We spent a little while investigating what Mother and Eurykleia had packed.

We had to take the sail down when the wind changed and a light drizzle started. I stayed close to the mast so I could grab it if the boat did something unexpected, as it seemed to do every few minutes, either tipping in a wave or rising up and then slapping down on the water.

"We're too near to Zakynthos," I said as I moved to the stern and lifted the oars out of their brackets. "The people there aren't fond of Ithakans. Sebastos said they probably wouldn't bother us if we didn't get too close. I'll take first shift." So I rowed while he watched for boats, and then we switched. It was hard for him to get into a good position to pull the oars, but he had a strong back, and once he had tucked his long, bony legs under the bench we made good time.

Dark was falling when we rounded Zakynthos. I kept an anxious eye on the coastline. No sails, no lights, nothing. The only Zakynthians I had ever met were three slaves—two women and a little man—owned by our neighbor Antinoös. They had seemed harmless enough, but, then, they were powerless and friendless in his household.

Brax rowed as I called back directions to guide us around a rock that rose straight out of the water. It reminded me of the sea creature, with a giant head and torso keeping watch over the island. But it was just a rock, with birds nesting in its crannies and seaweed clinging to its rough surface. When we'd rounded it, I still saw no boats, and I breathed a little easier. The fishermen must have returned home by now and were cleaning their catch. In the gathering dark they would surely not see our small vessel.

When the island was no longer visible, I called back to Brax to ship the oars and come up for a meal. I tossed the anchor over the side as he came forward, complaining of sore arms.

Mother or Eurykleia had packed stewed onions, which Brax could eat, and a boiled duck, which he could not. We both ate our fill, and then I took first watch. Brax, of course, fell instantly asleep.

The air cooled yet more as the sun dropped, and I was glad of my woolen blanket. As it grew darker and the cries of the seabirds died out, the other sounds and smells of the ocean grew stronger. The lapping of the waves against the anchored boat took on a rhythm that reminded me of the drums the night of my farewell banquet. The stars were out, but they were the same ones I had seen all my life, and they held no interest for me. Instead, I stared at the sea. Nothing. When I thought my eyes were going to dry up like raisins and fall out, I woke Brax. This was not easy, but I finally convinced him that it was his turn to watch.

I fell asleep quickly, and I woke past dawn. The clouds had cleared overnight. Brax snored. Asleep on watch—I should have known. No harm had been done, though; we had passed the night safely enough. A light breeze was blowing in the right direction, so I set the sail, steering with one hand on the tiller and the other holding on to the edge of the boat. It was smooth enough now, but I didn't trust the sea. It was treacherous, and I had learned that it could change without warning.

As if to prove this, something cold and wet landed on my wrist, even though the ocean was nearly a flat calm. When I lifted my hand to shake it dry, I saw that the wetness wasn't water. It was a small and delicate hand. A green hand.

I froze. What new horror was this, come up from the deep?

As if in answer, the hand took a firmer grip and pulled, but not to bring me down. Instead, someone pulled itself up. Not a gray-green man this time, but a bluish girl. Her eyes were as green as new leaves and her lips were the color of coral. When she smiled, I saw teeth like gleaming mother-of-pearl.

I couldn't move—or I didn't want to; I don't know which. The girl pulled herself up so that her slender waist pressed against the edge of the boat. She leaned forward, and her cold lips brushed mine, leaving a taste of salt that burned and froze at the same time. It woke me from my stupor and I leaned forward, but she let go of the boat, twisted in the air, and dived into the sea, her long, forked tail slipping down in the water behind her.

"Wait!" I cried.

"What?" It was Brax. No use telling him what had happened. He would say I'd been dreaming and would mock me endlessly.

"You were supposed to be keeping watch." I drew my hand shakily across my mouth. The icy heat was disappearing.

"I am," he answered. I didn't bother to point out that he'd been snoring just a moment before.

I ducked into the hold to see what there was to eat. "Brax, I told you to leave those honey cakes alone." I came out with the empty box in my hand.

"I didn't touch them." He got up and tried to maneuver himself so that he could pee over the side. He wasn't completely successful, and I threw a bucket of seawater where he had slopped onto the deck.

"Oh, stop it." I was irritable. I had wanted one of those cakes for breakfast. And I wanted that mermaid. It didn't look as if I was going to get either one of them.

"Really, I didn't. I didn't even know where you hid them."

"Well, somebody ate them, and it wasn't me. And you're lucky that nobody came upon us in the night, when you should have been looking out."

As the words left my lips, I saw a small boat approaching fast from the west, the direction of Zakynthos. I squinted. Two—no, three men, and a glint of something I couldn't see. Weapons? Armor? Or simply fishing gear?

I had no wish to wait for them to come closer so that I could find out. "Take the tiller," I commanded. As Brax hesitated, I said, fear throwing a new urgency and deepness into my voice, *"Now. Take it now, and steer us due east."* He looked bewildered, and I jerked my thumb over my shoulder. "That way. Away from that island." My tone must have convinced him that something serious was happening, for he unlashed the tiller and turned us from our southeasterly course.

I went into the hold, wishing I knew where my mother had had the servants hide the weapons. They were too valuable to stay out in the salt spray, but—

I stopped short. There, laid on the floor in a neat row, were two helmets, a short sword, a long one, a spear, and two sets of thick leather chest-armor. I rubbed my chin. I had been in the storage area twice since we left and hadn't seen this.

"Brax!" I called.

"I'm steering!" he said.

"No, that's not what I mean. I'm asking: When did you get the weapons out?"

"What?"

"When did you—" I stopped. It hadn't been Brax. He would have no interest in a box that didn't smell of honey. He had no reason to remove the weapons, much less to lay them out in a row as though waiting for me to take them.

Someone was on board with us.

I didn't have time to wonder who our stowaway was or what he wanted, because just then I heard voices. They were far off and thin, but from their tone it sounded as though someone was trying to hail us.

I pulled on one of the helmets and strapped on a set of chest armor. The leather was old and cracked with disuse, but at this distance whoever was on the other boat couldn't tell that. Grasping one of the swords in my right hand, I went back out on deck and stood in the bow, facing the rapidly approaching boat. Maybe if they saw that we were a bigger vessel and there were two of us (for they would be able to tell by the way we were being steered that someone was in the stern), they might hesitate to attack, if that was indeed their intention.

But my hopes were dashed as I looked back. In the distance, but closing on us fast, was a light vessel, skimming over the water. Two oarsmen pulled hard as a third man stood in the bow, holding aloft a long sword that he was waving in our direction. He moved with heavy grace, and a dark-brown beard spread over his broad chest. We would never outrun them in this pleasure boat, and we could never outfight three grown men.

What should we do? Die fighting? Surrender and become slaves in Zakynthos mere hours after we left Ithaka? Pray that a sea god would capsize them?

I groaned. Why hadn't I seen the dying naiad for the omen she was? She had left her home, thinking she was going but a short distance to safety, and she had died. The gods had sent her to warn me off my voyage, and I had ignored them. *Stupid, stupid, stupid,* I cursed myself.

"Go away!" I cried, shaking my sword in the air. "We're not traders! We're not fishermen! We're after neither your catch nor your commerce!"

The only answer was an obscenity shouted in a thick accent that I recognized as Zakynthian. The oars kept moving. Then, suddenly, the man in the bow leaned forward, shading his eyes with one hand, as though trying to make something out. What? He turned and spoke to the two men behind him. They stopped rowing and turned to face in our direction, their eyes turned up to the rigging of my ship. For a long moment they sat swaying on the waves, speechless, mouths open. I fought the temptation to turn around myself. I kept my eyes trained on them, trying to project menace.

The man in the bow must have spoken again, and the others nodded, picked up their oars, and started rowing again. But instead of continuing to close the gap between us, they turned and pulled hard back to their island.

I stared foolishly after them before remembering that there was something to look at up the mast. Through the sun-dazzle, I made out a slim figure in the rigging. *That's the intruder,* I thought, and I gripped my sword hilt more tightly. *That's the one who ate the honey cakes and laid out the armor.* The figure wore the helmet and breastplate that I had left in the hold and was sliding down through the lines with skill, despite the short sword in its hand.

I stepped forward, ready to repel this invader. "Brax!" I bellowed. "Come here!"

When it had jumped the final yards and landed lightly on its feet, the figure turned to face me. I felt as though someone had kicked me in the stomach.

"Polydora," I said, and she laughed.

ᚲHAPTᛖR 14

I lowered my sword arm as Brax appeared on deck.

"Poly?" Brax's voice was high with tension or disbelief.

"What are you doing here?" I asked.

"Going with you." She pulled off the helmet, and her blue-black braids tumbled down past her shoulders.

I stood still for a moment, trying to think what to say, when I noticed we were drifting toward Zakynthos. I tossed out the anchor and turned back to Poly, still unable to frame words. Brax approached slowly, hooves knocking on the wood of the deck, and gaped. She unfastened the straps of the chest armor, reaching under her armpit and tugging at the laces. She managed to loosen it enough to pull it off and then tossed it on the deck. All she wore now was a light shift, damp with sweat, that clung to her body. Damon must have been keeping his sister hidden from us, and with good reason.

Poly said, "I need some water. It's *hot* in that hold." I motioned to the goatskin, and she undid the knot, gulped some water, and then let the stream run over her face.

"Don't waste it," I said.

"Oh, don't be such an old woman." She tied up the opening and ran her damp fingers through her hair, loosening a braid. "We'll be on land tonight and can get plenty more."

"What's she doing here, Telemachos?" Brax said as though Poly weren't there.

"How do I know? But it's a good thing she is." I hoped she couldn't hear the admiration I felt for the way she had frightened off the Zakynthians. "What *are* you doing here, Polydora?" I tried to sound stern.

"I'm not going to tell you anything until I've had something to eat." Poly rebraided her hair, her fingers flickering through the black waves. "I haven't eaten since yesterday morning. Well, nothing except a few honey cakes."

I cast an eye back toward Zakynthos. There was no sign of another boat, but when our three sailors reached home they might gather comrades and return to attack us. Besides, if I had to spend another night on the bucking deck, I thought I would go mad. I yearned for the feel of ground under my feet, not this treacherous, slippery surface.

"Put that down," I said to Brax, as he started to open one of the boxes of provisions. He grunted, but I had no time for either his gluttony or his irritation. "We have to make landfall first. I don't want to stay out here in the open ocean where anybody can see us. Polydora, give me a hand with the oars."

She followed me to the stern and settled herself on one oar. I took the other, and we pulled. She was strong, and we rowed in silence while Brax called back directions.

The breeze soon picked up and we stopped rowing. Poly climbed the mast to unfurl the sail, and we made such good time that by late afternoon we were within sight of land. If the directions that Sebastos had given us were accurate, this must be the mainland, somewhere close to Pylos. Even if it wasn't, I ached to walk on a surface that wasn't tipping and rolling, so I had Poly tie up the sail again. I took an oar while she called down directions that guided us into a sheltered cove. The hiding spot made me a bit uneasy; on the one hand, we were out of sight of the open sea, which was comforting. On the other hand, we were also cut off from a quick escape if someone chose to come in the narrow opening to the cove. Also, there were no trees—not even any bushes—to hide us. If anyone sailed in or even walked nearby, our boat, with its gaily striped blue-and-white sails, would be easily visible. Still, there was no reason to fear the people on the mainland. Ithaka had long retained good relations with them.

Unbidden, Polydora jumped off the side of the boat into the sea. The water came up only to her shoulders, so I followed, after passing down a basket of food to her. I heard a splash as Brax hit the water too.

I'd never been so relieved at the feel of solid ground. True, it was foreign soil, and I'd never before set foot anywhere but Sami and that one time on the island of Ithaka, but it was hard earth, with the familiar smell of sun-baked sand and resinous pine trees, and the feel of shells digging into my feet, and the sound of scurrying in the nearby forest as unseen creatures hurried away from the newcomers.

The basket turned out to contain my favorite meatballs, each as small as a baby's fist, made from finely chopped lamb spiced with herbs and garlic. They nestled in a bed of grapevine leaves, which Brax ate, relishing the grease that clung to them. Polydora popped one meatball after another into her mouth, wiping her fingers on her tunic. I had thought that after the incidents of the past two days I wouldn't be hungry, but I ate as much as she did, silently thanking Eurykleia for making something she knew I would relish.

I pulled a flask of wine from the folds of my clothes, where I had concealed it so that Polydora and I would be assured of a share before Brax discovered it. I passed the flask to her, and she poured out a few drops as an offering to the gods. She took a long pull, and then I did, and then I passed it to Brax.

"You know about my father's leg?" Poly asked abruptly. Brax and I nodded. "So you know that Damon can't leave until he gets better." The words "*if* he gets better" hung, unspoken, in the air between us. We nodded again.

She lay back and pillowed her head on one arm. "Damon's going to sell me to Sophonisba." Behind her matter-of-fact tone I heard hurt and bewilderment.

"Oh no," I protested. "No, Poly, he told me he wouldn't." But she was shaking her head.

"You just wait until the winter. Wait until he sees Father still laid up and Bito and Sotera hungry, with nothing in the storehouse. And wait until he tries to find three dowries. What will he do then?" She sat up and grabbed the wine before Brax realized what she was doing. When she had taken another drink and dangled the flask between her knees, she reached for a pouch of olives. "Damon will sell me, all right. And if he waits too long, I won't fetch as good a price, because Sophonisba will see he's desperate and will offer less. He knows it, so he'll do it sooner rather than later. It's what I'd do in his place," she added as she saw me starting to object.

"But I'm not going to let him," she continued, "and I'm not going to starve my sisters by staying. If I'm not there, he has one less person to feed and one less sister to marry off. So when I saw the boats taking provisions to your ship, I hid under a pile of blankets. Getting into the hold was easy. The men loading the boat didn't even see me." She tossed an olive pit onto the sand. "You don't have to worry about me," she said, although I didn't think I had shown any sign of concern. "Wait until we get to Pylos, and I'll get everything sorted out. It's a big city, my father says. I'll find something to do." Her confident tone almost fooled me into thinking that she wasn't worried, but then I saw her wrinkled forehead and her downturned mouth. I knew that she would rebuff any attempt at comfort, so I kept silent.

I made two trips back to the boat, fetching provisions for the night. We argued briefly about whether to make a fire. I was still nervous about our encounter with the Zakynthian sailors and the knowledge of how close we were to their island; Brax and Polydora thought a fire would keep animals away. They won, and I fetched the firebox from the boat. The embers were somehow still alive, despite all the upset we'd had earlier with the sea creature. We warmed our hands and feet by the flames as the sun sank.

I wrapped up in one of my mother's blankets and stretched out next to Brax's warm side. His familiar horsey smell almost made me forget how far I was from home.

Polydora was huddled in a cloak on the other side of the fire.

"Come over here where it's warm," I said.

"No." She didn't look at me.

Brax propped himself up on one elbow. "Come on, Poly. You'll be cold over there by yourself."

She looked at us stonily. "My brother would kill you."

"What?" I felt myself redden as I realized what she meant. "You're like my little sister, Poly."

"But I'm not your sister. I'm Damon's sister, and he's twice as strong as you."

I didn't need reminding that Damon's shoulders were half again as broad as mine and that his beard had been in for some months now.

Brax snorted and settled himself on his side again. "You said he was going to sell you to Sophonisba."

"Shut up, Brax," I said.

"That's different," Poly said hotly.

"Oh, if there's money involved, it's different?" he asked.

"Shut up, Brax," I said again, but he was already snoring.

"Anyway, I'd kill you." Poly wrapped herself more tightly in her cloak and turned her back to us. *True,* I thought, remembering certain incidents from our childhood when I had felt her wrath.

I lay awake staring at the fire. Sparks leaped from a branch that had burned almost through. I watched it, only half awake. The branch fell into the embers. A flame sprang up and seemed to take the form of a girl, dancing and twisting among the glowing coals. She paid me no notice at first, but curved and bent, lifting her arms above her head, her red hair streaming down her back.

Then she turned in my direction, and her eyes gleamed with orange fire. She reached for me, retreated, reached again. I felt myself drawn to her and willed my arms to stretch out, to embrace her, but they refused to move. She leaned toward me, her hair crackling and shooting sparks. I was in a trance, turned to stone, and her glowing face approached closer and closer.

She extended a hand once again. Her long orange fingers disappeared into blue nothingness and touched my shoulder.

"Yaaa!" I cried, and found myself sitting up, the ashes cold and gray in front of me. My shoulder stung where the flame girl had touched it, but when I pulled down the neck of my tunic to inspect it, I saw nothing.

"What?" Brax muttered, half asleep.

"Bad dream," I mumbled, and stretched out again, my back against his warm one. I lay awake until the sun rose.

CHAPTER 15

"The place that is not, on the day that is not—" Poly looked at me questioningly. It was the afternoon of the next day, and I had just finished telling her of my meeting with Daisy. We were facing the open ocean, and the wind made the loose hair around her temples and forehead flutter.

"Bearing the thing that is not," I finished for her. Then I waited for the barb: *You're making this up*, or *She addled your brain like poor old Kleandros*. But instead of teasing me, she nodded thoughtfully and traced the grain of the wood in the railing with her finger.

"I've thought and thought, and I can't imagine what she could mean." I was bolder now, almost daring her to say something about how it was no wonder, with the kind of thoughts that usually occupied my mind. But still she continued to run her fingertip along the rail. I suddenly noticed how slender her hands were, brown from work and with weaver's calluses, but almost elegant with their long fingers. I looked away.

" 'The thing that is not' must mean something that wasn't in the world when she spoke but that will appear sometime," she said. "What could that be?"

"In stories it's always something like an egg. The person who's been challenged brings back an egg, and the king or whoever was the challenger says that's not new, and then it hatches, and the baby bird is something that no one has seen before because it was out of sight."

She chewed on her lower lip, her dark eyebrows drawn close to each other. "Maybe." A pause. "That seems too easy, though. And how can there be a day that is not, or a place that is not?"

"A new island that rises from the sea?" I hazarded. I had heard of such things. But the day that is not? How can there be a day that is not a day?

"How far down the coast *is* this place?" Brax called over to us. He was leaning on his elbows on the other side, looking down the shore. As he shifted his weight, his hooves made a hollow *thunk* on the boards of the deck. The long hair hanging down his back moved in the breeze that was blowing us in a southerly direction. Poly glanced up at the sail, evidently saw something she didn't like, and climbed up the mast.

I was wondering the same thing myself but didn't like to admit it. "Not much farther." I tried to sound sure of myself. "Sebastos said he couldn't tell us how long to go down the coast because he didn't know for sure where we'd touch land. But he said it shouldn't take us more than two days or so to get there."

"That's if the boat is piloted by someone who knows how to sail," Poly called down from the rigging. I ignored her. She slid down the mast and landed lightly next to Brax. "There's a cove a little farther on. I say we pull in there for the night."

I tried to think of some objection just so I could tell her no, but I couldn't, so I sent her back up to call directions down to us. Brax took the oars as I hauled the sail in.

This cove was surrounded by tall pine trees that cast a cool shade over the water. Their smell made me think of home, and I tried not to pay attention to it for fear of falling into sadness. The water remained deep enough that we sailed almost to shore. I eyed the short distance to the beach; with any luck, we could prop the long planks we had stored for this purpose between the deck and the land, and tomorrow Brax would walk on board with only a little help. It had taken a long time and a great deal of effort to drag him on board that morning while he cursed and struggled, hauling on the rope that I pulled while Polydora shoved him from behind. He had scraped his knees from the final effort when he spilled over the rail, and was still complaining about it. I kept silent about the bruise on my shin, where one of his hooves had clipped me.

Poly jumped off the boat again and swam around it, testing the depth. "I think you can stand over here," she called from the shore side, and "But it's deep over here," from the side facing the open water. I dived in, relishing the feel of the clean water on my body and the taste of salt dripping into my mouth when I came up for air. In a few minutes, a splash told me that Brax had followed on the other side. I swam around to where he was, and together we waded to the beach.

I was still uneasy about our encounter with the Zakynthians the day before. "Pull in the boat as close as it'll come," I ordered. When they had done so, I said, "Now we have to gather branches and cover it." They looked at me blankly. "We don't know where we are or who lives here. What if a big ship comes and sees us?"

"Oh, I don't think we need to—" Polydora was beginning, but

I cut her off. I was groggy from lack of sleep, and my muscles ached, and although I didn't want to haul branches any more than she did, I certainly didn't want to have to fight off attackers.

"I don't care what you think," I said. "This is what we're doing. Brax?"

He was looking from one to the other of us, hands on the join between his man-waist and his horse-body. "Whatever you say, Captain." He trotted into the woods. Polydora followed, dragging her feet.

By the time they came back, I had secured the boat. We piled branches up the mast and dangled some off the sides. I stood back and surveyed it. Polydora joined me.

"Well, you were right," she said. I waited for the follow-up, knowing better than to trust in the sincerity of her praise. "Nobody would know there was a boat here. Nobody at all. They'll think that a big clump of branches fell into the water and instead of floating away they all piled up on each other. Yes indeed, that's what they'll—"

"Do you *ever* shut up?" I asked.

"No," she said promptly, but she stopped talking, much to my relief.

Our meal was a gloomy one. This time I stood firm about not lighting a fire, although the evening was damp and cool. We were hungry, but we had already eaten the best of what Mother and Eurykleia had packed. We had finished the meat first thing, since we had no way of keeping it fresh, and of course the honey cakes were long gone. Poly and I had tried to catch some fish that morning, but we didn't know what to do and wound up tangling the nets and swearing at each other. At least a stream ran into the sea near where we had anchored, and we dumped out the stale contents of our goatskins and refilled them with fresh water.

Brax was in better shape than we were, because the land around the cove was covered with soft grass. This wasn't his favorite meal, but at least it was plentiful and would fill his large belly.

The sun was setting, and we were trying to make ourselves comfortable when suddenly, Polydora said, "Fire!"—sounding more surprised than alarmed. Brax and I scrambled to our feet, tripped over each other, stood again. Brax's hoof came down hard on my instep. I swore and pushed him off.

"Where?" I asked. Poly pointed to a dancing light down where the shore curved away from us. Relief made me weak, and I sat down next to her. "I thought you meant the boat." Then I stiffened again. Who would be making a fire on the beach?

Poly and I looked at each other. We rose to our feet.

"Where are you going?" asked Brax, already stretched out on his side again.

"We have to see who that is," I said.

Brax raised his head a little and looked in the direction of the fire. "Why? Nothing to do with us."

Poly and I exchanged glances again. "You stay here, Brax," I said. "We'll come back and tell you what it is once we find out."

I waded to the ship. The water felt cool now that the air was losing its warmth in the evening. Once on board, I shivered in my soggy clothes as I pulled armor and weapons from the hold. I lowered myself into the water again, holding them above my head while making my way back to Polydora. Silently she strapped on the chest armor and pulled on a helmet. I did the same. We each took a sword and started out toward the lights, walking in silence.

As we neared the fires, I heard music and drums. I paused. Pipes were weaving a repetitive tune, and the rhythm of the drums was simple and heavy, like a dance beat.

"Some kind of festival," Polydora said, and I agreed silently.

We continued walking, keeping our footfalls as quiet as possible. When we came to the end of the curve where the cove met the straighter shore, I stopped and strained my eyes and ears. Was that the thud of feet on sand I heard, or just the waves pounding on the shore? The wind shifted to our direction and briefly I smelled a wood fire and cooked meat. I jumped when a burst of laughter met my ears.

"Well, whoever they are, they don't sound very warlike," Poly said. She was standing so close to me that her breath moved the hairs on my upper arm.

I hesitated, chewing my nail. We could pull out to sea again and row farther down the shore, waiting until the morning to approach this area and find out if we were near Pylos.

On the other hand, whoever was on the beach was roasting what smelled like both sheep and ox. And the revelers might tell us the way to Pylos. Maybe they had been drinking enough that, even if they were unfriendly, they wouldn't be able to gather their forces in time to do anything to us before we fled. If we did, that would be the second time I had run away since we had left Sami, and I didn't like the idea.

"Let's keep going," I said. I wasn't surprised when Polydora promptly started walking in the direction of the fires again. I had never seen her fear anything. When we were children, she'd suffered many bloody noses and even a broken finger once when she picked a fight with someone larger than she.

We moved together cautiously. We stopped behind a boulder and Polydora peered over it.

"Poly, I don't think you should—" I was starting, when a huge hand reached around the rock and grabbed her arm. She let out a squawk and then was dragged out of my sight.

If I had been prudent, I would have hung back until I saw what had seized her. But before I could even think about prudence, I leaped out from behind the boulder.

"Yah!" I yelled, brandishing my sword and taking the martial stance that Eurymachos had taught me. Not that it did me any good. A big hand—matching the one that had come around the boulder—swatted the sword from my fist. I caught a glimpse of a bulky form and shaggy hair, and then a cloth bag was forced over my head. Even as I struggled, strong hands bound my wrists together in front of me.

CHAPTER 16

Where's Poly? I thought. Then I heard a stream of curses coming from my left. The thwack of a hand hitting something interrupted the flow, which quickly resumed, but at a lower volume. Someone had hit Poly? I tried to break free and flatten the person who had done so, but a kick to the backs of my knees brought me down. *At least they haven't killed her,* I thought as I struggled to my feet again, but this was not much comfort. Who knew what their plans for us were? Death might have been a mercy.

"Shut up," said a gruff voice, and when I started to say something it added, "You too," the words accompanied by a sharp blow to the side of my head. Someone seized the leather cord between my wrists and yanked me forward. I took a stumbling step, and then two, and then I was trotting down a beach of smooth, hard-packed sand. The gasping breaths next to me told me that Poly too was being propelled along.

"Where are you taking us?" I managed to ask, but the only

answer was another blow, this time between my shoulder blades. *Ah,* I thought, *so someone is behind me as well.*

We moved more swiftly than I would have thought possible along unfamiliar ground, blind, and with no hands. Every time I stumbled, the bond around my wrists was jerked upward and I was kept on my feet. The smell of smoke and cooked meat grew stronger, and I began to hear snatches of song and laughter.

Once, Poly tripped over something and collided with me. In the instant before she was jerked back, she whispered into my ear, "Where—?" Even if I had known where we were going, I would have had no chance to reply. My head was still ringing from the blow our captor had dealt me, and I did not want to risk another one.

I strained to see through the bag, and I thought I made out some light. It must be the fires we had spotted from far off. *Where's Brax?* I thought, and then shook my head. There was nothing he could do against armed men, even if he had the courage to attack. Better at least that one of us should stay alive.

The forward tug on my wrist bonds ceased, and the gruff voice said, "Hold!" I stumbled to a stop. Someone was panting next to me; in the hope that it was Polydora, I shifted my weight a bit to that side, and was rewarded by the warmth of an arm, too small to belong to one of our captors, against mine. I took comfort in the pressure.

A new voice spoke in front of us. "What did you find, Stolos?" It was a man who sounded as though he had taken more than his share of wine.

"Two offerings, sir," said the deep voice, and from behind me someone added, "Poseidon isn't satisfied with your bulls, Father— he sent us something more to sacrifice!"

My mind's eye saw the animals that had been sacrificed for my voyage, their throats slit, their knees buckling, their eyes turning blank. Was that what the second speaker meant? That we would be killed like the goat and the pig my mother had offered to the gods? My stomach wrenched as I tried to banish the image of Poly's dirty tunic soaked in her blood, her eyes rolling back in her head, and then of myself being led to the altar, where a shining blade awaited my throat.

Silence, except for grunts and then shuffling footsteps. I guessed that the person whom they had been addressing had risen to his feet and was inspecting us.

"Were they alone?"

The voice that had addressed the man as "Father" said, "We didn't see anyone else. But these two were armed."

"Unhood them," said the voice. The big man complied, none too gently. I thought he would take off my nose along with the bag. I blinked in the sudden glare of the fire, unable for the moment to see anything in its dazzling light. Then the heavy hand descended on my shoulder again, squeezing until my knees began to buckle.

"Are there more of you?" asked the man who had ordered us to be unhooded. I saw that he was tall and round-bellied, with a mild face and curly pale hair. I couldn't tell in the firelight if it was blond or gray, and his face didn't betray any particular age.

"Any more of you?" repeated the big man, who I assumed was Stolos, and he shook us.

"No!" I said, but at the same time Polydora said, "Yes!"

"Which is it? No or yes?" The tall man sounded impatient.

Silently, I cursed Polydora. It was bad enough that we were caught by this giant. At least we could have kept them from knowing about Brax, so that *he* might escape, anyway.

She looked at me with a stricken face. *Too late to think of Brax now,* I thought.

"It's yes." I was surprised at how easily the lie rose to my lips.

"We've come with a fleet of ships. We're the advance party, scouting to see if you're friendly or not. If we don't come back, they'll send a larger force to find out why."

The big man shifted his weight, and his hold loosened—not enough to let me escape, but the pain of his grip eased.

"Is this true?" the pale-haired man asked.

Stolos shook us again. "Is this true?"

"Oh yes, absolutely, it's true," Polydora babbled. *Shut up,* I thought to her.

"Yes," I said. "It's a fleet of long ships, each with a dozen oarsmen. We're here on a trading mission and the two of us were sent ahead, as I said. We mean no harm. If you don't want us, we'll leave and find another place to spend the night."

I felt them looking at one another.

"Just where are these ships now?" asked the curly-headed man, who appeared to be the leader.

I gestured vaguely toward the sea. "Out there. Circling. They're going to pick us up tomorrow morning."

"Did you see any ships?" he asked the man who was holding our shoulders.

"No, only the one boat. Small enough for two or three to sail. Down in the cove."

The leader pulled at his lower lip thoughtfully. "Still, you never know. Send some scouts to take another look as soon as it's light. Meanwhile, tie these two up and keep an eye on them."

Soon Polydora and I were lashed to separate trees. My wrists were still bound together, as were my ankles now, and I was secured to my tree, sitting down. "Pol—" I managed to say before a leather strap was forced over my head and between my teeth.

So began the longest night of my life, at least thus far. My hands soon cramped from their confinement, as did my feet. I could neither sit up well nor lie down, and the way my lips were held open rapidly dried out my mouth. A knob of bark dug into my back and I couldn't wriggle out of its way. The wound on my face from Daisy's claw, still not completely healed, opened again, and blood trickled down my cheek, causing unmerciful itching. Once or twice I thought I heard a whimper from Polydora. *Better you had stayed behind with Sophonisba,* I thought, and I wondered if she was thinking the same.

Worse than the pain to my body was the pain in my mind caused by two questions: *Where's Brax?* and *What are they going to do to us?*

I was so exhausted that despite my cramped limbs, my twisted position, the knob in my back, and the thirst, I dozed off near dawn. I woke to see a small child, his big eyes staring at me, standing nearby. When he saw me looking at him, he turned and ran, round heels kicking up sand as he went.

I straightened up as best I could. The camp was stirring; I heard muffled voices and the sound of men pulling on clothes. Oatcakes, or something like them, were being cooked on a fire out of my sight. A groan behind me told me that Polydora was awake. I wished I could say something to her, to find out if she was hurt or merely uncomfortable and frightened, but the gag prevented me from making any intelligible sound.

The light grew stronger, as did my thirst and now a need to urinate. I had almost made up my mind to relieve myself right there where I sat when I saw motion a little way off. The pale-haired man came out of a brightly colored tent, stretching like one who has spent a good night on a comfortable bed. The sight made all my muscles ache in longing.

Two armed men went up to him and, in answer to a question, said a word or two. The leader glanced our way, as did the two soldiers, and they shook their heads firmly. The world darkened before me. These must be the scouts giving their report. I had foolishly, ridiculously hoped that they would see the nonexistent ships I had told them would be looking for us.

The three men approached. The leader loomed over me, his hands on his hips. Now I saw that he was in late middle age, his face lined from the sun, his hair gray. His expression was still mild, and I caught myself thinking he looked like a sheep.

"I nearly believed you, boy." He sounded sorrowful at my deception. "But as I'm sure you are aware, there are no ships. Just one small boat—a nicely built one, tied up in the cove. It was a good story, though, and told convincingly."

"What do you want us to do with them?" one of the soldiers asked.

"Untie them." The world lightened, only to plunge even further into darkness when he went on, "And take them to the altar and slit their throats."

I made a strangled sound and heard a squeal from Poly. "A good story, that about the ships," the man said conversationally, as one of his soldiers cut the thongs tying my wrists to the tree trunk. My hands prickled painfully as blood flowed into them. The man turned to face me when the soldier hauled me to my feet. "Yes, a good tale, and well told, too." He laughed as though in surprise. "You might be as good a liar as—" He stopped. Out of the corner of my eye I saw the other soldier leading away a stumbling Polydora.

"Stop there." His voice had changed. "Bring them to me." I started shaking. What had made him change his mind? What was he going to do?

The soldiers complied. Poly was red-eyed, wild-haired. Blood trickled down the inside of one calf. Yet she held her chin out and glared up at the man, who paid her no attention.

"Look at me, boy," the curly-haired man commanded. I lifted my face to find him gazing at me intently. Anything sheeplike I had seen in his pale eyes was gone.

"As good a liar as my old companion Odysseus, I was about to say." I tried to answer, but the gag got in my way. He nodded curtly at one of his soldiers, who reached up toward my face with his knife. I flinched, expecting to feel the cold steel at my neck, but instead I felt pressure as the blade pulled on the strap and then sliced it open.

"What's your name, boy?"

I croaked, my dry throat keeping me from making any sense.

"Wine," he ordered, and a man hurried up with a leather cup. He offered it to me, but my hands were too numb to take it, so he held it to my lips and I drank.

I swallowed and tried again.

"Telemachos," I managed to squeak out. "Son of—" My throat closed again.

"Telemachos," the man repeated. "Telemachos. The very name Odysseus gave his newborn son. 'Distant battle,' he told me on the ship as we sailed to cursed Ilios. 'A good name; it will remind him of why his father had to leave him.' And your mother?"

"Penelopeia, daughter of Ikarios." My heart began to stir in my chest. The man nodded as though I had confirmed something. "I am come from Ithaka, sir, seeking King Nestor of Pylos."

"You have found him," the man said.

CHAPTER 17

This time my knees gave way completely, and I would have fallen if someone hadn't caught my elbows from behind. He lowered me to the ground, where I sat with my head bowed until the world stopped spinning. Then I found, to my shame, that the front of my robe was soaked through.

The person who had supported me was squatting at my side. With the hem of his tunic he mopped the cold sweat off my face. "Better?" he asked. I nodded, and he helped me to my feet, keeping a steadying hand on my upper arm.

"Thank you." I fixed my eyes on him in the hopes that he would look back at my face and not at my sopping robe. My helper resembled King Nestor so closely that I blinked and glanced from one to the other. This man was younger, only a few years older than myself, I guessed, but he had the same pale, curly hair, the same mild, sheep-like face, the same light-colored eyes as the man who had ordered first my bonds and then my throat to be cut.

Poly's eyes darted from me to the king. I was about to ask for her release when Nestor barked, "You!"

I began to say, "Me?" but before more than "M-m-m—" was out of my mouth, Stolos, the giant of the night before, had flung himself on his belly, his hands clasping the king's ankles.

Nestor kicked at the huge man's face, and I winced. Stolos loosened his grip, but remained prone on the ground. "What do you mean by treating my old friend's son like this?" the king asked between his teeth, aiming a kick at the man's side. I winced again as Stolos yelped.

"But you ordered—"

Nestor kicked again, and Stolos squealed and then fell silent. "I ordered you to bring me the pirates who had sailed into the cove," the king said. "These two aren't pirates. They are the son of King Odysseus and—" He seemed to notice Poly for the first time. "Who are you?" he asked her, apparently not noticing that her gag was still in place.

"Polydora," I answered for her. "My—" I paused. What *was* Poly, anyway? My friend? My friend's sister? "She's my neighbor, recently orphaned, come to Pylos to look for work." Nestor apparently lost interest. He turned back to berating and kicking his servant.

"Come on," the young man said, his hand still on my arm. "Let's get you cleaned up."

"But I need to talk to him," I said, pulling away. "I've come all the way from Ithaka to ask him—"

"My father will be busy for a while. Come with me and have a bath and a rest."

"And Poly?"

He glanced back at her. "Of course," he said with a smile. "And Poly." He pulled a knife out of his belt and sliced the leather straps from her face and hands. She worked her jaw back and forth, holding her chin and grimacing. "I'm Pisistratos, son of Nestor," the young man added, turning and heading inland.

I hesitated, longing to stay and ask Nestor what he knew about my father, but the king didn't appear to be in a conversational mood, so I joined Polydora and followed Pisistratos down the shore. Poly whispered to me hoarsely, "Orphaned?"

I felt my face flame. Lying was coming to me as easily as telling the truth, it appeared. "I didn't want them to know you were a runaway," I whispered back. "Harder to find work. They might even sell you in the slave market." That shut her up.

The sand turned to pebbles and then to rocks. Long grasses grew among them, their edges sharp where they scraped against my bare shins. Seabirds wailed overhead and a troop of pelicans swept by, their wings barely moving above the waves as they stared straight ahead of them. Mingled with the fresh salt scent of the ocean came the heavier smell of rotting seaweed and dead fish, and under it all the smell of smoke and roasted flesh from the sacrifices of the night before.

We turned away from the shore and climbed along a rough path between the grasses. In front of us, a wider area opened out, revealing a group of perhaps half a dozen tents, most of them faded blue, some brown, with the remains of cooking fires between them.

Ahead of us our guide called out, "Mother!" and a heavy-set woman emerged from the largest of the tents. Poly and I waited while they conferred. The woman went back inside and then re-emerged with a younger version of herself, then another, and another, and another, until four broad-shouldered girls with stolid, sallow faces and long dark hair were standing in a row looking in our direction. They were silent.

"My mother," Pisistratos said, waving a hand at them, "and my sisters."

I stammered something about what a pleasure and an honor it was, but they ignored me. The woman spoke to the largest of the girls—she appeared to be about my age—and they went back into the tent, all but the littlest, who stood looking at us, twirling a lock of hair in her finger, and the second oldest, who knelt and blew on the embers of a fire over which was suspended a large pot.

"No brothers?" I asked.

"My mother bears sickly sons, except for me!" He flashed us a smile. "The last two boys died as infants. My oldest brother died at Ilios, and the second one drowned in the well in the palace court-yard the morning of the day he was to be married." He shook his head sorrowfully. "A great tragedy."

Without looking at us, the girl called from the fire, "The water's ready." She beckoned to Poly, who glanced at me. I shrugged, and she hesitated a moment before following the girl into the tent. I watched her duck through the opening and tried to banish any uneasiness. Surely she would come to no harm there with those silent women.

The smallest sister remained outside and Pisistratos called after her to go in. Still she didn't move until he took a step in her direction, and then she scrambled after the others.

Pisistratos laughed. "Bath?" he suggested.

I dropped my sodden and reeking tunic on the sand and stood while Pisistratos ladled water over me. I scrubbed myself with soft lye-soap and he talked. I learned that I had arrived at the end of the Pylians' annual ceremony honoring Poseidon.

"We sacrificed black bulls," he said. "Nine big ones." I whis-tled. "I know." He scrubbed my back with a sea sponge. "It seems extravagant. But the ground has been uneasy lately. My father's concerned about earthquakes, and he thinks that we should keep the Earth-Shaker happy. Don't you sacrifice to Poseidon in your kingdom—what did you say it was called, Ithaka?"

I thought, *How can he not have heard of Ithaka? We're only two days' sail away!* But all I said was "Well, yes, of course we do. But nine—I don't think there are that many bulls in the entire kingdom!"

"Small, is it?" He dumped the last of the warm water over me and then handed me a strigil. With its curved blade I scraped off the remaining soapsuds and most of the water.

Yes, Ithaka was small, and it was rocky, but suddenly my heart yearned for my home until I thought it would burst.

Out of the corner of my eye I saw the flap of a tent open. It wasn't the same one that the girls had emerged from, but a gaily striped orange-and-red affair, larger than the others, and set back a little. I caught the flash of dark eyes turned in our direction, and then the flap dropped.

I jumped when I felt my new friend's hand under my chin, but Pisistratos was merely turning my face to look at the marks that Daisy had left. The three on the bottom had healed cleanly with no festering, but they still felt raw. The top one oozed blood after it had broken open the night before.

"Wild beast?" He handed me a pad of wool, and I held it to the wound. I nodded, not wanting to explain about Daisy (how could anyone explain about Daisy?), and felt myself grow hot and red from toe to scalp, mortified that I had started at his touch. I wished there was a way to keep from blushing every time I felt flustered.

Pisistratos didn't seem to notice my embarrassment. He handed me a gleaming white tunic and picked up my old one with a long stick. He was about to throw it on the fire when I said, "Stop!" He halted and looked at me with a quizzical frown.

"My mother made that," I explained.

"We'll have one of my sisters wash it, then." The warm smile returned. He turned toward the tent. "Kaste!" he called. A heavy-browed face poked out of the opening of the tent that his sisters had entered. "Wash this." He pointed at the tunic. The sullen face disappeared again.

"Come on," he said, but I hung back.

"What about Polydora?"

"Who? Oh, the girl?" He laughed. "You know, I didn't even know she *was* a girl until you introduced her. She'll stay here with the other women. They'll take care of her." So I followed him down to the beach, glancing back through the silent tents at the dark trees behind them. Where was Brax? Would he come trotting into the camp, or would he have found new friends among the forest people? I could imagine him in a shady spot in the pine woods, drinking wine and laughing with a satyr or a troop of nymphs.

The cooked flesh left from the sacrifice of the day before had cooled. Bull meat is tougher and stronger in taste than that of oxen, but I was in no condition to care. I turned my attention to a meaty shank dripping with fat. There was also plenty of wine, and I found a platter of flat rounds of bread. It was spongy and it tasted more of barley than what Eurykleia made. I commented on it.

"This?" Pisistratos was lying on his back, picking his teeth with a spine of a sand plant. He turned over a loaf, examining it. "Tastes as usual to me."

"I suppose we do some things differently in Ithaka," I said. I hoped he didn't think I had been criticizing the bread, which, though different, was not worse than what I was used to.

Pisistratos propped himself up on one elbow. "That's what we hear about islanders—that you do things differently. Do you really eat fish every day?"

"Not *every* day." I was getting anxious about Brax. Maybe the prince could help me search for him. "I wanted to ask you—"

"Not every day?" He sat all the way up now. "I thought you islanders ate nothing but fish, and you allowed hairy-backs into your houses."

Hearing him say "hairy-backs" startled me, and I didn't answer.

"Do you?" he asked.

I knew I should say something in defense of Brax and the rest of them, but I couldn't bring myself to be thought an ignorant islander. So I said nothing.

"You do!" he exclaimed.

"No, we don't," I protested weakly, but he obviously didn't believe me, for he said, "I don't see how you stand it. I would have to burn down my house if one of them came inside."

"Some of them aren't so bad. Some of them—"

"Oh, some of them might be all right," Pisistratos acknowledged. "And a nice little nymph or centaur filly can be . . ." He smacked his lips. "But to allow them in your house!" He lay back down, pillowing his head on his folded arms. "It wouldn't happen here," he said with finality. "No hairy-backs in a human house. Not ever. Not on the mainland, in any case."

I put down the long bone I had been gnawing on, my appetite driven away by his words. How would I find Brax now? And what would I do with him when I found him? Would Pisistratos mock me for our friendship?

No matter. Forest people had a way of finding each other. He would be fine, I told myself.

I was about to wipe my greasy hands on my robe when I remembered its shining newness, so instead I dug my fingers into the sand to clean them. There was a pause during which my companion seemed about to doze off. I made patterns in the sea foam with my fingers and watched a long-legged bird search for oysters. The wind picked up, and little grains of sand stung my skin. All the while, I burned with impatience. Did Nestor know something about my father and his whereabouts? When could I ask him?

Before I could think of how to approach the subject with Pisistratos, he chuckled. "I saw my wife looking you over earlier."

"Your wife?" I felt myself turn red yet again as I realized that the large striped tent must belong to Pisistratos, and that I had not been wearing a stitch of clothing when the flap had opened. I didn't know what to say, but he went on as though merely amused.

"She's my second. The first one brought me some good vineyards. This one is for breeding. She's already working on her third brat. The first two were girls." He threw another stick into the sea. "Girls do seem to run in my family."

"Your second wife?" He didn't seem much older than I. Why did he have two wives and I none?

As though reading my thought, he asked, "You married?" I shook my head. "How many wives did—does your father have?"

"Just my mother." At his look I added hastily, "He was going to take a second when the call to arms came." I didn't want him to think that my father was too poor to support more than one wife.

"So you have no brothers?"

I shook my head. "Or sisters."

Eurykleia had told me that when my father was newly king of Sami and Ithaka, he looked to the daughters of Ikarios of Sparta for a bride. He chose my mother, Penelopeia the Dutiful, over her two sisters, Iphthime the Fair and Aglaia the Witty. I had always wondered if they called her "witty" because "wild" or "disobedient" showed a lack of respect for the king's daughter. He must have been planning to find other wives later to provide him with beauty and entertainment once he and my mother had gotten settled, but shortly after I was born, along came the summons from Agamemnon.

Somebody was heading down the shore toward us. The figure was unclear against the bright sun, but I saw that it was moving with an odd, lurching gait. Could it be Brax? I shifted my weight on the sand. I told myself that I didn't care what Pisistratos thought about humans' being friends with forest people—I couldn't call Brax a hairy-back, even in my thoughts—it was just that a meeting between him and my new friend right now would be uncomfortable.

As the figure drew near, I realized that it wasn't Brax but Stolos, the big soldier who had captured us last night. I hoped he wasn't coming to seek revenge for his beating. I hadn't really been the cause of it, but I knew that this wouldn't make much difference to a man who had been kicked so savagely.

I was starting to scramble to my feet when Pisistratos opened one eye. He chuckled. "The last time I saw Stolos with a face like that was the day after his wife caught him in the tavern with two girls," he said. I kept my seat, since Pisistratos didn't seem concerned. Still, I remained alert. The man's wife must have a powerful fist, I thought, if she had done as much damage as the king's feet. Stolos' nose appeared broken, one eye was swollen shut, and surely he hadn't been missing a front tooth last night.

When he reached me I tensed, despite Pisistratos' reassurance. But instead of exacting revenge, the giant dropped to his knees in front of me. "Please forgive me," he lisped through the gap in his teeth. "I'm stupid, I know. The king said to seize the pirates, and I was too stupid to see that you were really his friend's son and not a pirate."

"Think no more of it." I was unsure of how to handle this. "There was no way you could have known." I glanced at Pisistratos, but he was gazing out to sea and yawning as though our conversation was of no consequence.

"So you forgive me?" Stolos asked.

"I do." He bent farther, clearly in pain, and kissed my foot.

"What is it you want?" Pisistratos asked. He stood up and brushed sand off his arms and the backs of his legs. "Surely you didn't come hobbling out this far merely to beg forgiveness."

"I was sent by the king." Stolos turned to me. "He bids you to attend him in his tent." I looked at him wonderingly.

"There," the big man continued, "he will tell you about your father."

CHAPTER 18

I sat on the ground in Nestor's tent as he droned. The air was musty, despite the sweet scent of the king's carved-cedar throne, and details of the embroidered cushions and draperies were difficult to make out in the dim light slanting in through the flap. My head was fuzzy from lack of sleep, my bones still ached from being tied to the tree all night, and most of all, I was worried about Polydora and Brax. I didn't expect to see Poly here, in the men's part of the camp, but nobody had even mentioned her. *She's fine,* I told myself firmly. *And so is Brax. I'll find them soon.*

When would Nestor get around to talking about Odysseus? He seemed determined to tell me everything that had happened in Ilios, starting with his own disembarkation on the shore. But his was not the exciting tale that even as poor a bard as Phemios would have made it. It was all about the difficulty of finding provisions, the bickering among the men, the daily cleaning and polishing of armor.

Then I heard my father's name. I sat up straighter. "What did you say?"

"I said, then Odysseus thought of bringing a horse up to the walls of Ilios—" Either Nestor had skipped to the end of the war, or I had fallen asleep during his recital of the battles.

"Why a horse?"

"Oh, not a real horse," he explained. "A *horse*."

What was I missing? "I'm sorry, sir, but I don't—"

"Not a horse with hair and legs. A siege-horse. It's like a"—his hands sketched out something vague—"like a stairway, or a ladder—yes, actually more like a ladder, but it's enclosed in a wooden box and it's on wheels, and you fill it with soldiers and roll it up to the wall of the city. Most of the men who move it get killed by archers on the city walls, but the enemy can't harm the soldiers inside the horse, because they're protected by the box, you see?" I nodded, impatient for him to go on. "And then the soldiers climb up the ladder and they come out the top and go over the wall. If you do it in the daylight, the enemy knows what you're up to and the first soldiers out get killed too, of course, but the rest keep coming, and some will eventually make it to the city gates and let in your main force. None of us had ever heard of a siege-horse before, but Odysseus was crafty." He laughed, but I chilled at the word "was." Did he mean that my father had been crafty when alive but was now dead, or merely that he had been crafty when he thought of the ruse with the horse?

"We kept the horse hidden while we were building it. When it was complete, we rolled it up to the walls one moonless night." He spat and motioned to his servant to refill his gleaming wine cup. He took a swallow. "I don't think they would have noticed us any-way, even if it had been broad daylight. The Ilians no longer kept a strict watch—didn't feel the need to. They never thought we'd find a way in. You could stand three men on each other's shoulders and the top man still couldn't see over their wall. And we'd been camped there for so many years that they'd become accustomed to us. Anyway, all forty of the men who had been hidden inside the horse made it over without being noticed, and one of them opened the gates, and the rest of us came in. And that's how we took Ilios." He rose and stretched, evidently finished.

"But—" I started, and then stopped.

"But what?" He shot me a look of annoyance.

"But what of my father?" I swallowed. "What of Odysseus? Was he at the sack of the city? Did you see him alive afterward?"

He drained the last drops of wine from his cup, tossed it to the ground, and then spread out his arms. The waiting servant slid a robe over his shoulders, and the king shrugged to settle it.

"Go to Sparta, boy." He belched. "Ask Menelaos. He was with Odysseus after the war ended. If anyone knows what happened to your father, it's Menelaos." Nestor ducked through the tent flap, leaving me with his servant. I would have followed him, but he seemed annoyed at my questions. After what I had seen of how he treated a man who displeased him, I thought better of it.

"Wine, sir?" It was the servant with the jug. He was young, and his face was scarred. Had Nestor given him those scars? I shook my head at the wine, but then realized that the man was going to stay with me until I left the tent. You never know if an ignorant islander is going to make off with the king's bronze wine cup, after all. So I followed Nestor through the flap and stood outside, un-sure what to do next.

The sound of hooves pounding on the sand made my heart leap for a moment as I thought, *Brax!* But then I realized that whatever was making the sound was much larger and heavier than my friend. In a moment, a shining vehicle drawn by two gray horses appeared from around a bend in the shore.

I had never seen a chariot before, but one of my mother's black-and-red wine vessels showed one whose painted driver held the reins of two horses, their eight legs twirling under them. In that scene, an archer stood with his bowstring pulled taut, aiming at an unseen enemy behind him. But the reality of thudding hooves and creaking harness leather and the glistening chariot with the tall man guiding it was much more splendid than that vase.

It pulled up near me. The driver was Pisistratos, and he tossed the reins to a servant who came running up to the high wheel. The prince jumped down and I went to greet him. I stroked the soft gray nose of one of the two matched geldings. Despite the speed of their approach, I saw they were eager to move again, stamping their feet and tossing their beautiful heads. The smell of horsehair gave me a pang as I thought again of Brax. Where had he gone? I leaned my head against the animal's warm side and closed my eyes for a moment, imagining it was my friend.

But I couldn't keep my eyes shut for long with such a lovely thing to look at. The chariot was small enough for Pisistratos to drive alone but large enough to hold two men comfortably, as long as they were not too bulky. It was painted a glossy black; without thinking, I reached out and touched it, leaving a smudge on the polished surface.

"Sorry," I said and in my haste to wipe off the smear with my tunic I only made it worse.

Far from being angered, Pisistratos asked, "Want a ride?" At my mute nod, he took his place again and motioned me to join him.

"Your first time?" Pisistratos asked. I nodded, ashamed to

admit it, but he said, "I envy you," and my heart swelled with gratitude that he hadn't scoffed. "I don't remember my first chariot ride. They say my father had me in one before I could walk, and after he returned from the war he gave me my own, pulled by a fat little pony." He smiled. "I thought she was a noble steed, and I called her Iris, after the swift messenger of the gods." I smiled too.

The sun was high overhead now, and in the distance dark thunderclouds hung low over the sea. The waves kept up an insistent beat on the sand as our wheels rolled over it.

"We break camp today," Pisistratos said after a while. "It's time for my father to go home."

"Oh." I felt awkward, like a child unsure of his welcome. "He said I should go to Sparta."

Pisistratos nodded. "Good idea. Menelaos knows everything."

"Sparta," I said. "That's where my mother was born. I never thought I'd go all the way there." *I never even thought I'd cross the sea,* I added mentally, *much less be taken for a pirate, or ride down the beach in a racing chariot. If only Damon and Brax could see me—* A sudden panic seized me. How would Brax find me if I left for Sparta?

"What is it?" Pisistratos asked.

"What about—" I stopped, still unwilling to mention Brax.

"What about your little neighbor, you mean?" he asked. "Polyhymnia?"

"Polydora."

"My mother has promised her as much weaving as she wants. The queen is hard to please, but she expressed only satisfaction at the girl's work." *Mother taught her well,* I thought. "She'll come back to the palace and will be given a place to live with the other royal loom-girls."

"Well, that's taken care of, then." I tried to sound cheerful. I couldn't imagine Poly living in a palace, but I didn't know what else would become of her. Finding work in the city was what she wanted, after all. I hoped she would be content. *And what a relief it will be not to have to put up with her teasing. I won't miss her at all,* I told myself. *Not at all.* Now I had only Brax to worry about.

"Where *is* Sparta, anyway?" I asked, changing the subject. I was fearful Pisistratos would somehow know what my real concern was.

"Don't worry." His hand descended lightly on my shoulder. "I'll take you there."

I tried not to show how thrilled I was at the thought of a trip with my new friend in this gleaming chariot. "Where were you thinking of going now?"

"I thought you might like to take some things off your boat. There's no point in leaving the food to rot or the iron to rust."

When we reached the boat, I saw that someone had been there before us. The sand was churned with the deep marks of small hooves, and every scrap of food or wine was gone. Boxes were broken open; goatskins had been punctured as if the thieves had been too eager for the wine within to drink through the openings but had let it pour into their mouths from the gashes.

Yet, when I rummaged through the straw, I found the store of bronze my mother had provided me to use for trade and offerings. I sat back on my heels and inspected it. It all seemed to be there. I piled the pieces onto a cloth and tied it into a bundle.

I glanced over my shoulder. Pisistratos was nowhere to be seen. Quickly I pried open the secret compartment where I had hidden the iron goods and pulled out the heavy packet, still wrapped in wool inside oiled cloth. I spilled the contents onto my lap and was relieved that I could see little rust. I retied it and slid the bundle under my tunic, next to my skin and the sharp little knife. The iron lay against my belly, feeling cold and heavy. There was so much of it that I could give most of the bronze to Nestor as a guest-gift and still have enough iron to present to my mother's cousin, King Menelaos of Sparta.

Pisistratos came up behind me. "Hairy-backs," he said with disgust, and spat as though in the presence of uncleanness. "Must have been. They took the food and wine, but they have no use for metal. If it had been men, they would have taken the bronze and left the rest." He sniffed the air. "I can still smell them."

"No matter." I was anxious not to inflame him further against the forest people. "There wasn't much left. And at least I have this." I opened the sack, allowing him to see the bronze pots and plates and knives I had gathered. I was tempted to show him the iron, sure he would be impressed at the skill of our island smith, but I had promised my mother that I would keep it hidden, so I said nothing about it.

We returned to the encampment more slowly than we had left it, and by the time we arrived, most of the tents had been struck. The giant Stolos was directing operations, yelling at men to pull harder, to fold the tents more tightly, to put one more sack onto an already top-heavy wagon. Each wagon was pulled by two large mules that stamped and flicked their long ears as our chariot passed them.

I was going to jump down and help, but when I saw that Pisistratos made no move, I held back. Perhaps it was not seemly for the prince and his guest to labor alongside servants and soldiers. I would remember this when I went back to Ithaka and was pressed into service at harvest time.

Nestor rode up in another, larger chariot, and once more I

noticed the resemblance between father and son. Was that what people who knew Odysseus saw in me? Pisistratos pulled to a stop and tossed me the reins, going over to speak with his father. I held the leather straps, proud that he trusted me and hoping that the horses would not take it into their heads to start running down the beach again. I tightened my grip. Fortunately, the two grays merely tossed their heads to loosen my hold and tore at the sea grass with their teeth.

Pisistratos exchanged a few words with the king and came to stand next to the chariot. He leaned one arm on its edge and looked up at me. "You have nothing to worry about," he said.

"Worry about?" I hadn't realized that my concern over Brax was showing.

"About those thieves." Oh. Not Brax, then. "There's a nest of hairy-backs—centaurs and satyrs and I don't know what else—in the woods behind the cove where your boat is, er, hidden." His eyes twinkled, and I flushed. Poly had been right; piling brush around the boat had only made it more visible. "I've wanted to get rid of them for a long time, but my father has a certain fondness for some of the nymphs and has always refused. But when I told him about their despoiling of a visitor's provisions—" He shook his head. "My father holds hospitality as his most sacred duty. Some of his soldiers are on their way to exterminate them right now. And about time too, I say."

"No!" I exclaimed so loudly that my voice cracked. He would kill whole families of satyrs and nymphs and centaurs for taking some half-rotten food and sour wine from my boat?

"No what?" Pisistratos raised his eyebrows.

"No, don't exterminate the—er, the thieves," I said, feeling hollow.

"Why not?"

I couldn't say that my best friend was a centaur and that I didn't want any of them killed on my account. Pisistratos would never have anything more to do with me.

"Among my people . . ." I paused and wondered where my words were going to lead me. "It's customary, at the end of a voyage, to make an offering to the local forest people. I forgot to do so when I landed yesterday, and what they took should stand in for the offering. If you were to kill them, I wouldn't dare take another trip until I had made it good, and I have nothing left to give them." He was still looking at me, his pale eyes expressionless. "There wasn't anything decent left to eat there, anyway."

Pisistratos turned to the soldiers. "Never mind!" he called. "We'll take care of them another time." With relief, I saw them unbuckle their greaves and pectorals as the prince leaped back into the chariot. "Banquet tonight," he said. "We leave for Sparta at dawn."

CHAPTER 19

I rinsed off the dust and sand of our ride and fell into a deep sleep on a pallet that a silent servant pointed out. By the time I woke and approached the banquet tent, the meal was in full swing. I stood on the edge of the crowd of diners, feeling awkward.

"Telemachos!" Someone was calling me. I looked around and saw Pisistratos, gesturing at me to join him. I approached a long bench filled with young men. "Move over," the prince said to one of his bench-mates. The man obliged, and I slid into the space he left. A serving girl poured water over my hands as Pisistratos introduced me to his companions.

Men and boys were carrying around large flasks of wine, those flat rounds of barley bread, and bowls of meat and vegetables. I smelled roasted fowl and herbs, and my hunger sharpened into almost a pain. A juggler tossed golden balls so fast they turned into a shimmering oval in front of him, while three girls bent over and around themselves and one another to the applause and calls of the crowd. I craned to see over the heads of the diners.

"What are you looking for?" Pisistratos asked.

"Poly," I said. Pisistratos looked blank, and I flushed at my use of the familiar-sounding nickname. She was a servant now, after all. "Polydora," I amended, but that didn't help. "You know, the girl I was with."

"Oh," said Pisistratos. "She's not likely to be in here unless she's displeased my mother. She's a weaver, not a table servant."

They had so many servants that they divided them up by the kind of work they did? It was hard for me to imagine such luxury, but I tried not to act impressed. I kept looking for a short girl with black braids, and was surprised at the depth of my disappointment when she didn't appear.

I ate and drank, and ate and drank some more. Every time I emptied a bowl it was replenished, and my wine cup was always overflowing. Just when I thought my belly would explode like an overstuffed sausage, silence fell. Everyone stopped eating and looked toward the king's high table.

"Ah!" Pisistratos said softly, leaning in so close that his breath ruffled my hair. "Now we'll have a treat. I wager you've never heard a singer like Homeros."

Wondering what he meant, I looked toward the door, where everyone's attention was fixed. A man, heavy-set and stoop-shouldered, long gray curls dangling over his ears from the edge of his shiny pate, was being led in by a handsome black-haired youth. The man's left hand rested on the boy's shoulder, while in his right he held the most beautiful lyre I had ever seen, each of its four strings as long as my arm, its two horns decorated with gleaming gold and ivory.

Nobody spoke as the boy stopped and the man reached forward, feeling for the stool that was placed behind the king and to his right. The man settled down, and as he turned to face the company I saw that his eyes were shut and his eyelids were dented inward, as though concealing hollows.

The bard bent over his instrument, his sparse locks falling forward across his cheeks. Both he and all the company remained as still as the statues I had glimpsed in the courtyard, and then his hand descended, he struck the strings of the lyre, and he began.

"Hear this," sang the blind bard, his voice nasal but rich. He sang of the valor of Nestor at the walls of Ilios, of the king's wisdom, and especially of his prowess as a charioteer. As he sang, I lost all sense of time and place. His voice disappeared; in its place I heard the snort of the king's chariot horses and the cries of the people of Ilios meeting their death at his sword. I smelled the blood of Nestor's enemies, not the food that was growing cold in front of me. Instead of the rather short, sheeplike king, I saw a valiant Nestor standing as proud as Ares in his war chariot. My concern about Brax and Poly melted away until all I could think about was the war at Ilios and the great victory of the forces under King Agamemnon.

The song came to an end with the customary "And now my tale is told," and my senses abruptly returned to my surroundings. Diners tapped their spoons on the table in approval, and several beckoned servants over, handing them choice pieces of fruit and cheese to take to the singer.

The bard started another song, and I leaned forward.

"Hear this," he began again. "The shining boat pulled up to the shore, and the company disembarked, led by the godlike youth. He strode with eager step to where the noble charioteer Nestor sat upon his throne and was made welcome along with his crew, feasting on rich fat and roasted meat." *A warmer welcome than the one I received*, I thought sourly. *This godlike youth was lucky that a brute didn't tie* him *up to a tree all night.*

The singer went on, telling of the great feast and the games that followed it, all in honor of the godlike youth.

"All the sons of Nestor gathered around the king," Homeros sang. So this festival must have taken place years ago, while some of the other princes were still alive. "And they made welcome the godlike youth, the noble Telemachos." I started. I had thought my father had made up my name. But Homeros was continuing, "Noble Telemachos, son of crafty Odysseus, stood and returned thanks."

I turned in surprise to Pisistratos, who, along with everyone else, was paying rapt attention to the bard. I nudged him and he turned toward me, the flash of annoyance in his eyes quickly replaced by a question. I said under my breath, "What's he talking about? I wasn't welcomed like that, and there weren't any other princes there."

Pisistratos leaned in to whisper, "Of course not. Nobody expects a poet to tell the truth. It's a better story this way. Have you ever heard a poet who sang like this one? And to make a tale such a short time after it happened—well, none but Homeros could do that, and do it so beautifully."

All too soon, Homeros sang, "And now my tale is told," and struck a final note on his lyre. I sat in silence. To say anything about Phemios after that performance would have been like mentioning a firefly in the presence of the sun-god. I came to myself enough to see that the boy who accompanied the bard was circling the room with his bowl, into which the diners were dropping choice portions of their meals. I blurted out to Pisistratos, "What happened to his eyes?"

He took a swig of wine and wiped the back of his hand across his mouth, leaving a red streak on his knuckles. "Oh," he said. "My father put them out."

"*Why?*" I was unable to hide my shock.

"To keep him here. A blind singer can't travel far, and my father was unwilling to share him." And Pisistratos turned back to dip his bread into the bowl of stew that a perspiring servant had placed on the table.

CHAPTER 20

"Want to drive?" Pisistratos asked as I mounted the chariot beside him the next morning. I nodded, afraid to speak lest I sound childishly eager.

Trying to imitate my friend's gestures of the day before, I slapped the horses' backs with the ends of the reins. They continued pulling up clumps of weed, although one flicked his hide as though in annoyance at my attempt to make him move. I looked at Pisistratos. He looked back at me without speaking, so I tried again. Still nothing.

Finally, he took pity on me. "Keep hold," he commanded, and stood behind me, his arms reaching around and his hands gripping the reins near where my white-knuckled fists were doing the same. "You're too tight. Loosen up." I obeyed. "Now pull their heads up smartly." He tugged sharply, and as though by magic both horses lifted their long necks. "Now really slap them with the reins." To my relief, they started forward this time.

We rode like that for a while, Pisistratos' breath warm on the back of my neck, his strong arms controlling both my movements and those of the horses. After a time he asked, "Ready to do it on your own?" I nodded, and he let go and moved next to me.

So we left. I had barely had a chance to stammer thanks to Nestor and to present him with most of the bronze I had carried, carefully concealing the iron. A gleam had come to his eyes at the sight of the precious metal, and he thanked me graciously enough, presenting me with a gold ring set with a large red stone in return.

I didn't get a chance to say good-bye to Poly, who was well on her way to the palace to begin her new life as a weaver. I reminded myself that I would see her again on my way back from Sparta. I would bring news of her to Damon and their father, and they would rejoice to know that she was alive and doing well.

Somehow this didn't make me feel any better.

I didn't know where Brax was, either. He must be with his new companions in the forest. Centaurs are fickle, but somehow I had always assumed that Brax and I would remain friends, no matter what happened. Apparently he had other ideas. I tried to tell myself that this was the way it had to be, that Pisistratos was a prince like me and more fit to be my friend, and that I had outgrown my childhood companions.

But for some reason, despite Pisistratos' company and the jokes he told, despite the promise that I was soon to meet relatives who would welcome me in their palace, I felt more alone than I ever had in my life.

Once, long ago, a foreign trading-ship anchored in our harbor. Its brown-skinned sailors told us in a musical accent that they had come from the land of Aegyptos, far to the south, where the kings were buried in huge pointed tombs and the people worshipped snakes and jackals. They had with them a strange kind of animal they called a *qat*, which resembled a weasel but had a long tail held straight up in the air, pointed ears, and soft mottled-gray fur. My mother bought me a *qat* from an Aegyptian trader after I had worn her down with my begging, and I carried it around and took it into my bed at night and fed it from my plate until, one day, I played with it too roughly and it made a rasping noise and scratched me. Then I became wary of my *qat*, although I still loved it and still sometimes cautiously lifted it onto my lap, where I stroked its back to try to make it rumble like miniature thunder, deep in its throat.

The Aegyptians told us that their people too loved these beasts, and that when their kings died their bodies were tanned like leather and buried with their richest belongings, including their *qats*. When our old dog Argos killed my pet, I mourned. I tried to preserve it like the Aegyptian kings so it could join its family in their afterworld. But my tanning process turned out not to be effective, and the small linen-wrapped body began to stink, so Eurykleia threw it on the garbage heap.

The Aegyptians told us other strange things about their homeland: the great heat in the summer and the wide, slow river that rose every year to bring fertility to their land. But the stories that interested me most were about the ocean of sand all around them, with its own waves and tides and storms. *That would be an ocean I would not be afraid to cross,* I thought. *No water to drown in, no ships to sink.*

I remembered the tales of the ocean of sand now as we passed, hour after hour, over a landscape nearly as desolate as the one described by the Aegyptian traders. True, there were no blowing sands here, no hump-backed horses with flat hooves that went for days without water, but it was still a barren, waterless waste. Shriveled bushes and gray, broken trees showed that it must have at some time been a more hospitable land, but now the brown mat of what had once been grass was so parched that it turned to dust under our wheels, making me sneeze and slowing the horses.

Our chariot was built for speed rather than comfort. For the first part of our journey, we drove along a broad road of packed earth flanked by low boundary-walls. The chariot's large wheels went over rocks easily, although I soon felt as though my teeth would be jarred out of my head, and the shaking opened the wound in my cheek again. On both sides of us lay fields, some of them planted with grain whose tall heads nodded in the breeze, others with vines whose small leaves showed that the ground beneath was poor. Goats raised their heads to stare at us as we drove past, their evil-looking eyes following us, the flesh under their chins swinging.

At first we passed groups of men and women laboring, some bent over spades and hoes, others tending to olive trees. The farther we drove, the more sparse and brown the fields became. I thought with longing of the green farms of Ithaka. The workers in these Pylian fields looked at us as we drove by, but their eyes seemed dead and flat. I noticed, as we passed one group that was shuffling along the side of the road, that their ankles were chained together.

"Slaves?" I asked Pisistratos. He turned and looked over his shoulder as though he hadn't noticed them.

"Or debtors," he said indifferently. *No wonder the farms look so poor,* I thought. Forced laborers would never do as good a job as someone whose own land was under the plow.

Soon afterward, we turned off the road and onto the plain.

The fields grew thinner and the landscape more barren, until now it reminded me of the wasteland described to me by the Aegyptian traders so long ago.

Two goatskins full of water and one of wine hung off the chariot's sides, and at our feet were sacks containing enough food to see us to our destination. My pouch of bronze valuables was stowed along with the food. The iron was still strapped to my waist under my clothes.

"Why did we leave the road?" My voice shook along with the chariot.

"That road leads to Messene," Pisistratos said. "They don't like Pylians there. We have to go overland for a while."

So for hours we had been crossing the land of pale rocks, where only a few stunted trees grew, and I saw no animals but the large birds overhead. The sun was strong, and with no shade anywhere, I felt as though we were baking in my mother's bread-oven. The horses seemed to be feeling the heat too, and their pace slowed.

We stopped once. The horses drank most of the water and we most of the wine, and we ate the tough dried meat. Only some olives and a bit of bread and hard cheese remained. Pisistratos seemed unconcerned, reminding me that we were due to arrive in Sparta, famous for its hospitality, early the next day.

We bumped along the hard ground as the wind picked up bits of the sandy earth and threw them in our eyes and teeth. I gripped the edge of the chariot when we hit a particularly large rock, and even my eyes rattled in their sockets. The sun was getting low, and I knew that the next day I would ache all over from the strain of staying upright and fighting to keep from being tossed out of the chariot.

"How much farther today?" To my shame, my voice squeaked like that of a little boy.

Pisistratos glanced at me, and the corner of his mouth rose in a smile. "Tired?" I nodded, not wanting to trust my voice again. He pulled up the horses and they stopped, lowering their heads a bit and puffing.

"So are the horses," Pisistratos said. "We might as well stay here tonight. No one from Messene would pass this way."

This spot had nothing to recommend it, but it was no worse than anyplace else we had passed since leaving the hard-packed road. We cleared the larger stones off an area to spread out our travel blankets while there was still light. It was just as well that we did so, because it turned out that the firebox had been upset and the coals were cold. We spent a miserable half-hour lighting a new fire, neither of us being very adept at it, and the night coming on fast. I had heard that there were lions and wolves on the mainland; I had never seen either and wasn't eager to make their acquaintance at night on a plain far from help.

"Finally!" exclaimed Pisistratos as the wood shavings he had made caught under the spark of my flint.

I gathered dry brush and wood, and after we ate the last cheese and olives with the strange Pylian bread, we sat by the fire, tossing in fuel whenever it began to burn low. I was too tired to talk much, and my muscles were starting to stiffen. I was rising to unroll my blanket when I saw Pisistratos looking at me fixedly but with little expression.

"What?" I asked.

"We're not in my father's kingdom anymore." I nodded, but his statement—and even more, his stare—made me uneasy. Why was he telling me this? I didn't feel threatened; we had seen nobody, not even a farmer or a wandering shepherd, since a short time after we had left the palace. We were still far from the road, and there was very little to draw someone, either thief or hostile Messenian, out into this waste.

"You agree that we're not in my father's kingdom and that we have eaten the last of the food from the palace," he said. I hadn't noticed that the food was gone, but we were due in Sparta tomorrow, so what did it matter? We could fast for the early part of the next day, and the Spartans would certainly feed two strangers, as would anyone receiving guests. The fact of my being related to the Spartan king would even ensure that we would dine well. So I nodded. "That means we are fellow travelers now, not host and guest," he continued. From somewhere deep inside of me a little wiggle of fear disturbed my stomach. I nodded again, and he seemed satisfied.

"There's enough wood on the fire to last till morning," Pisistratos said. "Let's go to sleep and get an early start tomorrow." I didn't object. I wrapped myself in one of the blankets and pillowed my head on my old tunic. Despite my uneasiness, I fell asleep almost instantly, shifting the small bundle around my waist to settle down.

Even with the night chill and the hard ground, I slept well, as usual, and woke, as I had known I would, with aches all over. I lay for a few minutes with my eyes closed, not wanting to move on the hard ground.

I waited to hear sounds of the fire being rebuilt—we might have at least a cup of hot water before leaving—but Pisistratos must still have been sleeping, for there was silence. I didn't even hear the heavy breath of the horses. I rolled over with a groan and opened my eyes.

The realization that it was full daylight made me sit upright. I had thought we'd be getting an early start, and instead we had overslept.

"Pisis—" I was beginning when I realized that he wasn't there. Neither were the horses. Or the chariot.

Something was wrong. Even before I clapped my hand to my waist, I knew what I would find.

My precious iron was gone.

CHAPTER 21

For a moment I stood frozen as still as a temple statue, my hand foolishly clamped to my hip where the iron should have been, my mind blank. Then I bent down and scrabbled in my blanket, forgetting my aching muscles, and searched long after it was clear that the small bundle was not there, had not come untied in the night and gotten tangled up in the cloth.

"Stupid!" I dug my hands into my hair. "Stupid, stupid, stupid!"

Pisistratos had stolen the gifts that I was planning to give to my mother's family, and then he had driven off, leaving me to fend for myself in this unfamiliar and desolate place. I cursed whatever it was that always made me sleep so heavily. This was my punishment, I thought, for abandoning Brax and for not taking my leave of Polydora. It was small consolation that Damon would never know how discourteously I had treated his sister, for my bones would lie here polished by the wind while he lived out his life on Ithaka.

My first impulse was to shout for help. But who would hear

me? I looked at the plain that stretched away in all directions. A light wind came up, lifting the hair off my forehead, but there was not a branch to stir or a bush to rustle. I was alone, without food or water, barefoot, with no idea of where to go. I grew lightheaded as I pictured myself wandering through this wasteland until I died and the crows came and plucked the eyes out of my lifeless head. Mother and Eurykleia would never know what had happened to me. My father would never come home.

Despair was replaced by rage. Was it for this that I had conquered my fear of the open sea? Had I gone to Daisy's lair and emerged alive, had I survived nearly being swamped by a sea creature and being threatened by Zakynthians and being seized as a pirate, only to die in this forsaken spot, my body unburied, my spirit wandering through eternity?

"No," I said aloud. I considered. Even my knife was gone, as was the firebox. I tried not to think about what would happen when night fell and I was alone and defenseless, with neither weapon nor fire to keep away any beasts or wild forest people that scented me. Dark, after all, was still a long way off, and I had a more pressing need right now—namely, finding my way to a city or a shepherd's hut. Surely even out here the laws and customs of hospitality applied, and someone would take me in. But which way should I go?

I pressed my thumb knuckles into my forehead and concentrated. Pylos, to the southwest, was much too far to return to, especially barefoot, even though I burned to tell Nestor about his son's treachery. His wrath at this treatment, I was sure, would be terrible. South lay the sea.

Where, then? The road to Messene had pointed northeast, and Pisistratos and I had traveled due east ever since leaving it.

This meant that Messene must be somewhere to the north and Sparta to the east—if Pisistratos was to be believed. If I headed toward either one, surely I would soon come upon cultivated fields and vineyards and eventually houses or even the city itself. But which was closer? And would I find a welcome in either? The Messenians had no reason to treat me better than any other lost traveler. They were probably civilized enough not to kill me and might even feed me for a day or two, but it was beyond reason to hope that they would help me reach my destination. Even if I did find my way to Sparta, the people there might be reluctant to believe me when I said that I was the son of Penelopeia. I no longer had anyone to vouch for who I was, and no gifts.

I needed a sign. I looked around, but everything was dry, gray, and nearly lifeless. Not a single ant crawled by to lead me in one direction over another.

Then Kleandros' voice spoke in my head: "Always go the hardest way." Sometimes fools and madmen speak with the words of the gods, but I had often seen Kleandros in the marketplace, babbling earnestly to bored-looking dogs, sleeping infants, uninterested satyrs, and whoever else he was able to trap. I couldn't trust that he spoke with divine inspiration.

He had been right in the case of Daisy's lair. Still, I didn't know if he was talking only about the hardest way among the paths in the cave, or if he really meant *always*. And of course it was possible that I had found Daisy by chance, not by following Kleandros' vague advice.

I chewed my nail as the questions whirled through my head. "Oh *gods*," I muttered. But I knew I had no choice. I had nothing else to guide me but those words, and if I didn't go somewhere I would die.

East—to my right—rose slightly, as though the land was about to become hilly. Hills would be difficult, certainly. Though north—straight ahead—was flat, the terrain was more uneven, with large boulders strewn about as though by the hand of a giant. *An earthquake, more likely,* I thought, remembering how Pisistratos had mentioned his father's concerns about Poseidon the Earth-Shaker.

I made up my mind. East it would be, toward where I hoped I could convince my mother's family to take me in. That I could also ask for news of my father no longer seemed important.

I rolled up my blanket and my old tunic and tied them to my back. I set out, trying to avoid the bristly plants and sharp stones that lay scattered among the flatter stones. Although my feet were hardened by long use on the beaches and fields of Ithaka, these rough rocks would make for difficult going.

I walked for hours, glancing at the sun as I went to make sure that I was still heading east. The sun rose higher, bringing warmth with it, and with the warmth came thirst. I tried not to think about it, though I scrutinized the landscape for any sign of a spring. But there was nothing green that would indicate water. I saw only huge black boulders sticking out of the hard earth, a few dried-up bushes, and now and then a bird high overhead searching for something to eat.

After I had walked nearly to exhaustion, I stumbled and cracked my shin on a boulder. I groaned and lowered myself to sit on a flat rock. I had already bloodied a toe on a stone I had not avoided neatly enough, and blisters were forming on both my heels. My thirst was maddening. I knew I couldn't go on much longer without provisions. If I didn't reach a habitation soon . . . I glanced up and saw three birds circling. I couldn't tell at this distance if they were looking for something live to catch or something dead to feast on. I shuddered.

Fool, fool, FOOL, I mentally cursed myself. When Pisistratos had made sure I understood that he was no longer bound by the laws of hospitality, I should have seen it as a warning. He could steal my iron and leave me out here to die without violating the customs that he said his father held most highly. But how was I to know that he was aware of the treasure I was carrying under my cloak?

I lay back, and tears oozed out of my closed eyes and trickled down my cheeks. In my mind I heard Pisistratos' voice again, talking about retrieving my possessions off the boat: "No point in leaving the iron to rust." *FOOL!* I told myself again. I had never mentioned my treasure to him. No doubt one of his father's soldiers had searched my boat while we were on the beach and had found the secret compartment. Pisistratos wouldn't steal the metal while I was under his father's protection, but at his first opportunity he had done so. I was lucky he hadn't slit my throat.

I was lying so still that I clearly heard the thump of something landing behind me and the rustle of feathers. Had the crows decided that it was time to start eating me? Maybe slitting my throat would have been a kindness.

"I'm not dead yet," I said, and I expected to hear the flap of wings as the startled bird took flight.

Instead, a scratchy voice said, "Not yet, no."

I suppose I should have been surprised at the sight of the man-bird perched on the rock behind me. I had never seen one before, although of course I had heard of harpies and the like. We didn't have any on Ithaka, though, and it hadn't occurred to me that I would see any here on the mainland. But I was too weary and discouraged to feel anything.

The creature was about the size of a large hawk, its greasy-looking black feathers reflecting the sun as it shifted from one wrinkled foot to the other. Only its small face and ears looked human. In fact, it was almost all bird, which was a bad sign. The less human, the more difficulty in understanding.

"Will you be dead soon?" it asked hopefully as it hopped a little closer. It was impossible to tell if this was a male or a female or even how old it was. Its facial features were tiny, with piercing black eyes that had hardly any white around them, a thin, straight nose, high cheekbones, and the darkened skin of one who spends a great deal of time outdoors.

"Of course not," I said. It cocked its head, and a look that might have been disappointment—or perhaps skepticism—crossed its face. It lifted a scaly foot and scratched under its chin, its eyes half closing. It opened them again and stared at the gash on my left cheek. Its tiny, human tongue flicked out and licked its lips.

The bird-thing remained silent, and I had made up my mind to start walking again—to escape its cold little eyes, if nothing else—when the scratchy voice said, "Why are you in this place?"

"I don't want to be. I'm trying to leave it. I'm looking for a city or a palace or something."

No answer, so I stood up, but once again it spoke.

"Palace?" Again the bird-thing hopped in my direction. "Big house?"

"Yes," I said eagerly. "Big house. Is there one near here?" I was counting on the creature's not being intelligent enough to figure out that answering me would deprive it of a meal.

"Near," it said as though considering, and looked over its shoulder toward the south. "There."

I followed its gaze but saw nothing. "How far?"

Instead of answering, it flapped its wings and took to the air.

With its flat face it reminded me of an owl. It flew upward in great spirals, then wheeled in the sky and came back, landing next to me with a thud. It settled its wings with a dry rustle.

"There."

"Do you mean you saw the palace—the big house—from up there?"

"There," the creature said again.

I considered. The bird-thing had flown high, but not so high that I lost sight of it. If it could see the palace from where it had flown to, perhaps I might be able to reach it before nightfall. *If* the bird-thing was telling the truth, and *if* I had correctly understood what it meant.

"Which way?" I asked. No answer, so I took a step in the direction where it had looked earlier, to the south. "This way?"

"This way." I couldn't tell if the bird-thing was mocking me or agreeing with me. "Will you die soon?"

"Hope not," I muttered. I also hoped that this repeated question wasn't a warning about what I might find in the palace. Was this a creature of omen telling me of my doom, or was it merely hungry and hopeful?

"What do they eat in that big house?" I asked. The creature fluffed its wings and looked away. "Do they eat men in that big house?"

It looked back at me. Its little eye gleamed coldly. "Not men."

"Boys?"

"Not boys."

"What, then?" I was getting exasperated.

"Hot sheep." The bird-thing flew away, this time out of sight.

CHAPTER 22

I slept poorly, inside a hole in a sun-warmed rock that quickly lost its heat. My den was so small that I couldn't shift position, and the pain in my feet and my cramped muscles woke me several times. My sleep was further disturbed by images of Brax hunting for me without success and Poly hunched over a loom, her fingers raw with the heavy work of stringing the warp lines. In my dreams they turned eyes full of reproach on me. I tried to explain to them why I had left so suddenly, but they looked at each other, shrugged as if dismissing me from their thoughts, and turned away.

"Don't go!" I croaked, and my own voice woke me. I lay for a few moments with my heart pounding, and then gave up trying to go back to sleep. I pulled myself out into the open, waiting for enough light to enable me to see my path and avoid the sharpest of the rocks. I tore half of my old tunic into two pieces, wrapped them around my feet, then covered my head with the other half and set out again before the sun had fully risen.

Dawn spread across the sky in pinks and oranges, but I was in no mood to admire it. What did catch my attention, though, were the birds. They were back, and there were more of them—five now—and they circled closer. I walked and walked until I found a rock to sit on and catch my breath. The birds' spiral tightened.

How could they tell that I was weak and thirsty and crippled? I rose, attempting to stand straight and tall, and started walking, grimacing with the pain but planting my feet as solidly as I could bear. I tried not to look up at the birds but I couldn't stop myself, and each time I did, they appeared larger and closer. I fixed my gaze on the ground in front of me, watching my feet wrapped in their red, blood-spotted rags stepping one in front of the other. I hoped the birds would wait until I was dead before they perched on my face, plucking out first one eyeball and then the other, and then . . . I shuddered.

I hobbled along for what felt like a long time, although the progress of the sun in the sky seemed slow. My swollen tongue clove to the roof of my mouth, my eyes felt sandy, and my nostrils were as dry as the landscape around me. I stopped to rewrap my feet. Dark blood was caked between my toes, and a chunk of flesh was missing from my left heel. Blisters had formed and popped, new ones forming under them. My face was cracked and sore, and my eyes were swollen from the sun and the wind that had started blowing this morning and now blasted gritty dirt into them.

I sat down for a rest. I had never in my life been alone for more than a half-day at a time. I hugged my knees to my chest and remembered how much I used to relish a few minutes alone in my bedchamber when Grandfather was out on one of his infrequent errands, or a visit to the privy. I would willingly have listened to him now, even his babbling, even his pathetic questioning of my identity, if I could only hear someone talking. I tried to say a word to break the silence, but the croak that came from my parched throat frightened me and I clamped my lips together.

On and on I walked. Once, a small lizard darted in front of me, but other than that there was no motion, no sign of life anywhere. Except straight overhead, where the birds spiraled ever closer.

When a blurred shape began to keep step with me, for some reason I wasn't surprised. I gritted my teeth and walked on. After a while, I glanced to my left and saw what appeared to be a girl made of swirling, whirling sand, the grains shifting so quickly that they nearly blended together to make a solid form. Nearly, but not quite, for I saw the rocks and scrubby plants through her as she moved, her pace still matching mine.

I stopped, and she did too. "What do you want?" I croaked. She merely looked at me without speaking, her expression not changing. "Are you the thing that is not?" I tried to seize her arm, but my hand passed through it, the grains of sand stinging. My touch didn't seem to hurt her, and she continued looking at me. I turned to resume my trek, but my foot caught on a rock and I fell as straight as a tree falls.

Though it wasn't the first time I had fallen that day, it was the first time I couldn't summon the strength to rise. I lay there hoping to feel some energy return, but instead what little force I had left drained out of me until I could not even raise my head. The world receded around me, and then I knew no more.

I don't know how much later I came to myself enough to become aware that something was moving nearby. Soft sounds, as of something brushing against the dirt and dust. *Those birds,* I thought dully. *Vultures or crows or whatever they are.* I lay there passively and thought, *I hope it's quick.*

"Is he dead?" someone asked. *Cruel bird,* I thought, *to speak in Poly's voice.*

"No, not yet," said another voice. The words were the expected ones, but the second bird too—surely a crow, to have such a gift for mimicry—used a voice not its own, this time Brax's.

I heard a thud, as of bony knees hitting dirt. *BIG bird,* I thought. Something brushed my cheek, and I thought, *My eyes! They're going for my eyes!* My hands flew up and covered my face.

"Stop it, idiot," said the first voice, but I clamped my hands down hard. Something forced them apart, and I felt liquid dripping onto my lips. My tongue jutted out and tried to capture it. My mouth opened of its own accord, and more drops fell in.

I let my eyelids separate and saw Polydora, her face dust-stained, her hair tumbling in dark curls around her shoulders. I struggled to sit up, but another hand—Brax's, it turned out—pushed my shoulder gently, and I lay down and let Poly dribble water from a goatskin into my mouth.

Later, I found the taste of that same water bitter with the pine resin that coated the inside of the pouch, but now it seemed sweeter than clover honey. As I sipped at it, my strength began to return, and I tried to reach up to squeeze the skin, to hasten the flow of the drops, but Poly said, "No you don't," and moved it out of my reach. "You drink this too fast and you'll puke it all up, and we don't have any to spare."

"She's been keeping me on short rations ever since we left Pylos," Brax said, his sun-reddened face coming into my field of vision. "Stingy little thing."

Poly snorted and resumed the dribbling. "At least *I* thought to bring water," she said. I wished I could leap up and embrace the two of them, but I lacked the energy even to thank her. A tear gathered slowly in the outside corner of one eye and it slowly, stickily oozed down my temple.

Of course Poly had to let me know she'd seen it. "Don't waste water," she said, wiping it off with her fingertip. Despite my weakness, I felt myself smile a little. She smiled back.

After a while, I sat up, supported by Brax. The world lurched when I turned my head, so I looked around cautiously and saw that the sun was now nearly set. Poly was seated beside me, bent over my bloody feet. She unwound the bandages, pausing when one stuck and I flinched, and resuming when I had recovered. After a muttered "Idiot," she moistened the end of her tunic and dabbed at the blood that was crusted between my toes. She pressed the peeled skin back into place with a gentleness that surprised me and wound fresh cloth, taken from the pocket of the weaver's smock that she wore, around them.

"You came for me." I hadn't known I was going to speak until I heard the words in my hoarse voice.

Poly didn't answer, but finished wrapping my feet and straightened. "Where are we going to spend the night?"

"Who are you asking?" Brax said.

"Nobody, I guess. He"—she nodded at me—"is in no shape to help, and you don't have enough sense to find anyplace useful. Give me a minute." She stood and shaded her eyes with her hand. "There." She pointed. "There's a little overhang. Two of us can fit in at a time. You and I will take turns watching."

"Watching for what?" Brax asked, reasonably enough, but she ignored him and helped me to my feet. I could barely hobble, but the water was doing me good. My tongue seemed less swollen and it no longer stuck to the roof of my mouth. I looked at the half-empty skin with yearning, but Poly didn't let me slow my creeping pace until she lowered me to sit next to the rock. Then she emptied a small amount of water into a cup and handed it to me.

"That's all for now," she said. I drank it at one gulp, leaned back, and closed my eyes. In a few minutes I opened them again. Brax was kneeling on his front legs, his hind legs straight and his long-tailed rump in the air. His face showed unusual concentration as he struck flint and steel together. So we would have a fire tonight, if Brax could manage it.

Poly was rummaging in a pouch. She pulled out a flat loaf and a handful of something brown that I guessed was dried meat. My stomach wrenched. She must have noticed, for she tore off a piece of the bread and handed it to me. I swallowed it, wondering how I had ever found the taste of Pylian bread strange. Ambrosia of the gods, it was.

The spark took—Brax had always been more skilled at fire-building than I—and he settled down, holding his hands out to the flames. Just in time too, because as I leaned forward to feel the warmth on my face the sun dipped below the horizon.

"Why did you come after me?" I asked, while Poly divided the food among us, giving Brax a larger portion of the bread to make up for not having any meat. *Even after I abandoned you*, I thought but did not say. I looked at Polydora, who was busily working a shred of meat out from between her front teeth with a fingernail.

Brax too turned to Poly. She must have felt our gaze on her, because she looked up, the tip of her finger still in her mouth.

"What?" she asked.

"Why did you come after me?"

She and Brax looked at each other. "That wasn't the plan at first," Poly said. "I was just trying to get out of there."

"Why?" I asked.

She pulled her finger out of her mouth. "That's a *bad* place, that kingdom of Pylos." Brax nodded vigorously in agreement. "The weavers are treated like slaves," she said bitterly. "They have to work through all the daylight hours—even in midsummer, when the sun sets so late—and they only get fed once, in the middle of the day, and they can't leave. Ever. There was an old woman there who said she was my age when she came to earn a little money to get married and they never let her go."

"Surely not!" I said. My mother had the reputation of being an exacting mistress, but she would never force service out of a freewoman.

"Surely yes," Polydora snapped. "All of them told me to run away before very long, because once the queen saw how skilled I was she wouldn't let me go. I slipped out of the palace the same day that we got there. I don't think they missed me, at least not for a while, because nobody followed me. And then—"

"And then I found her." Brax took up the tale. "I was leaving too. There's a spy in the palace, a nymph named Rinn who's a favorite of the king, and she got word to the forest people that there was a plan to kill everybody who lived in the cove where our boat is, and where I was hiding."

"I know!" I blurted before I thought.

Brax looked at me, his brow furrowing. "You *know*? You mean, you knew? And you didn't warn me?"

I felt my face grow hot. "I didn't know where you were, and anyway, I stopped them. I told the prince—"

Brax heaved himself to his feet and clopped away. Not far; his hoofbeats stopped in a very short time. But far enough that I couldn't see him in the darkness.

Poly maintained silence for a few minutes, either out of tact or, more likely, to make me wallow in my embarrassment. Then she continued.

"We hadn't gone far when we saw the prince come galloping back in his chariot. I'd heard that he was taking you to Sparta, and I don't know how far away Sparta is, but I knew he couldn't have gone all the way there, spent a night in the palace, and come back. It made me suspicious, so I told Brax we should look for you."

"How did you know where to look?"

"The vultures," she said simply.

⟨HAPTER 23

"**N**o," I said. "We'll think of some other way."

It was the next morning. Poly had reviewed our food and water situation. She announced that we couldn't wait for my feet to heal, and that the only way to continue was for me to ride on Brax. Except for the return from Daisy's cave, I hadn't done that for years, not since we were children and I sometimes flung myself on him in a wrestling match and he took off running to unseat me. I didn't want to make the mistake of treating him, a forest person, like an animal, especially now that he wasn't talking to me.

But in the end I had to agree with Poly. My feet were in a sorry condition, and she was too small to help me for any length of time.

"Brax, I'm sorry," I said as I hoisted myself up on his rump with Poly's help. He grunted and started walking. It wasn't any bumpier than riding my donkey at home. What was uncomfortable was the silence.

Finally, I could no longer take it. "That Pisistratos was talking about hairy-backs"—Brax flinched a little—"and saying things about islanders, and so I was embarrassed and didn't tell him about you. I'm sorry," I said again, lamely. "But I did stop them from exterminating—er, killing everybody in the cove."

Brax was silent. His hooves clopped on the rock.

"That's all right, brother," he finally said. "I denied you too. The forest people in Pylos hate humans so fiercely that I thought they'd kick me out"—at the word "kick" he gave a little hop with his back end that nearly threw me off—"if they knew we were friends, so I said you had kidnapped me and forced me to go along with you. I wasn't going to admit that I offered. Not to them." The reminder that he had volunteered to accompany me stung, but I knew I deserved the rebuke and I accepted it in silence.

Poly trudged beside us, her stout shoes making easy work of the rough terrain. When we stopped for a rest and a drink of water, I remarked that the landscape seemed less severe than before. It was true; the grit underfoot was giving way to what looked more like dirt, and occasional patches of green brightened the landscape.

And then we stumbled on a road. It wasn't much of a road, to be sure, but it was broad and flat, and marked with recently made wheel ruts and hoof marks. We turned onto it with lighter hearts.

By mid-afternoon, a cart had stopped and its driver offered us a ride. "But not him," the carter said, pointing a finger at Brax.

"Why not?" I asked, insulted for my friend and ready to refuse.

"Too heavy," the man said, and Brax rolled his eyes at me. I had always been more sensitive than he to suspicions of insult, sometimes seeing them where they were not intended, and it appeared that this was one of those times.

"I don't need to ride," he said. "Just having you off my back will make the way easy."

The cart was empty; the man explained that he had taken a load of sheep pelts to pay off a debt and was now returning to his farm on the other side of Sparta. Poly and Brax helped me in, the carter tsk-tsking in sympathy at the sight of my feet. Brax shook his horse-shoulders, trotted into the shrubbery that now lined both sides of the road, and stopped to pull handfuls of leaves and grass to eat. Poly settled next to me. Whenever we hit a bump in the road, she was thrown against me. I didn't object.

Poly was asleep, her head pillowed on my thigh, and I was dozing when I felt the cart come to a stop. "Why aren't you going on?" I asked the carter.

"Thought you'd like to see this." I sat up straighter and looked out past him. Poly roused herself and joined me.

There, famously on a plain and not on top of a defensive hill, spread out in a green and fertile valley, lay the city and its palace. Through the gathering dark I saw broad fields and a wide river that moved in gentle curves. And in the middle stood an enormous building with a gate through which two chariots could have driven side by side.

"Sparta," Poly breathed.

The stone gateway loomed above us, topped by carved and painted images of twin eagles, each clutching a dead soldier in its claws. I leaned heavily on both Brax and Poly. We had to keep moving aside as people went in and out through the gate in twos and threes, sometimes shouting at one another, sometimes weeping, sometimes laughing.

"What's going on?" I asked a man who was bidding farewell to a companion.

He looked me up and down, and I suddenly realized how I

must appear. My feet were wrapped in blood-soaked rags and if my condition mirrored Poly's, I was grimy from the road. My face felt dry and sunburned. I didn't remember when I had last bathed.

"Justice day," the man said briefly and turned away, exchanging a joke with his friend.

"Good," Polydora said. "That means we can get in to see King Menelaos."

"But we don't have a dispute to argue," I said.

"He doesn't need to know that," she answered. True. Once we were in there, I could make my case as the king's relative and the son of his old comrade-in-arms.

A guard barred our way at the palace door. He took us in at a glance—the exhausted centaur, the ragged girl, and me with my feet wrapped in bloody rags—and evidently decided that we were no threat to a well-armed Spartan soldier. He lowered his sword.

"What do you want with Spartan justice?"

It was a good question. I looked at Brax. He looked at me. So did Poly. It appeared that I was the one who would have to answer.

"I must see the king. I have urgent business with him."

"What is the nature of your business?" he asked, but from inside a voice called out, "Let all petitioners enter," and the guard stepped away from the door.

Brax and Poly moved aside as though to let me go in by myself. I shook my head and said, "No, you come too."

"Are you sure?" Brax raised one ginger eyebrow. I nodded.

The high-ceilinged room was glorious. The floor was made of a pale stone so highly polished that our shapes preceded us at our feet as we made our way to the throne. The walls were defined by sparkling white columns with wide openings between them, through which lay the green fields of the valley. Rolls of cloth at the top of the gaps appeared to be blinds that could be lowered when required. Brightly painted statues of the gods stood between the columns, posed and pointing so as to lead the eye to the end of the room, where a squat man sat on a tall chair. He stared straight ahead; bristly reddish hair streaked with gray fell in waves past his shoulders. Even at that distance I could feel the strength that emanated from King Menelaos. I breathed deep at the sweet scent of cedar.

A man on his knees in front of the king appeared to be finishing an argument. "He was my only son." His voice was thick with emotion. "Peritas knew that the bull was mad when he told my son to go into the paddock." He stopped as though to recover himself. "When his mother and I got the body back," he went on in a lower tone, "we would not have recognized him if it had not been for the clothes he wore."

Menelaos addressed another man standing next to the kneeling one. "Is this true?"

"I didn't intend for the boy to die." This man twisted the hem of his robe in his hand. "I was just trying to scare him. He was paying altogether too much attention to my daughter—"

"Is this true?" the king repeated, a slight edge to his voice.

The second man bowed his head. "It is true." He raised his face to look at the king. "But I promised blood payment to Lykos. I can't pay it all this year, but I can give him some now and the rest when the harvest is in—"

"Do you have a son?" the king interrupted.

"Yes." Even though I saw only his back, I could see that the man was suddenly tense.

The king turned to the kneeling man. "Take his son and kill

him. You may not mutilate his body as your son was mutilated; that was the fault of the beast, not of the man. But you may kill the boy. Slit his throat and return his body to his parents."

A murmur came from the people clustered on both sides of the room, and the kneeling man rose to his feet and bowed. As he stumbled past us, I saw that his face wore a mixture of misery and a kind of triumph. The other man shouted and would have run at the king, but he was held back by his companions. They led him out, still shouting.

Silence fell.

I now saw that behind the king stood several people, one of them shrouded in black that covered even the figure's face. A tall, slender man standing next to the king's high chair beckoned to me. I gathered myself and tried to walk straight without leaning on my companions, but my bound and bloody feet were awkward. People turned to look at me.

The slender man stepped forward as we reached the foot of the chair. "Your name?" he asked in a bored tone.

"Telemachos, son of Odysseus, son of Laertes." I watched for a reaction from the king, but he didn't stir. His arms were stretched out on the arms of his chair. Gold hoop earrings hung down almost to his shoulders, and a gold band circled his brow. I realized that his brightly colored and bulky cloak was made of the wings of birds stitched together. A scar ran down the side of his face and under his jaw.

"Purpose of your visit?"

"I need to speak to King Menelaos." My voice faltered.

"Yes," said the tall man with exaggerated patience. "Of course you do. And for what purpose?"

"I need to ask him something."

"What do you need to ask him?"

"If . . ." I hesitated. It sounded so odd, so unlikely in this glorious stone hall. "If he knows what happened to my father. If he knows what happened to Odysseus and where—"

The slender man motioned at me to be quiet, and I obeyed, breathing as hard as though I had run a race. "Boy says he's the son of Odysseus," he said, apparently to the king but in a voice pitched loud enough to reach the knots of people standing nearby. They tittered, but the king still showed no reaction.

Poly swung to face the nearest group. "What's so funny?" Her brows were drawn together in her fierce glare.

"Wants to know what happened to his father," the man went on, to the further amusement of the waiting crowd. "Most likely he'll ask the king for a gift to make up for his loss."

"What are you talking about?" I was bewildered. "I don't want any gifts. I only want to know what happened to my father. I want to find him and bring him home."

The man turned to someone standing behind the throne, next to the figure shrouded in black. "How many sons of Odysseus have come seeking news of their father?"

The other man stepped forward, a grin on his ugly face. "Three or four."

"What?" I was shocked. "My father didn't have any other sons. I'm the only one."

"So you say," the tall man said. "So they all say. Why should we believe you?"

I cast my mind around for an answer. "Well, everyone says I look like him."

The slender man turned to the crowd. "Anyone here ever see Odysseus?" Silence.

"You, sir." I took a step toward the king. "You must remember him well. I'm taller than he, and my legs are straighter, but—"

He raised his head and turned his face in my direction. Before he let it fall again, I saw that the centers of his eyes were as gray as the streaks in his long hair. King Menelaos was blind.

CHAPTER 24

All the air left my body, as it had once, years before, when Damon's head had slammed into my belly while we were wrestling as children. But I wasn't going to give up now, not after all that I—and Brax and Poly—had gone through to reach Sparta. I cleared my throat. "I swear to you, sir, that I don't want a gift. I don't want anything except to know what happened to Odysseus. The last anyone saw of him was when he boarded his ship at—"

"Hush!" The tall man raised a warning hand, but I finished my sentence, "—at Ilios."

The black-shrouded figure behind the throne started as though someone had pushed it. A wail rose from it. I took a step backward, and Brax's hooves scrambled on the stone floor as he stumbled toward the door. Polydora grabbed my sleeve and I put my arm around her shoulders, holding her tight, whether to protect her or to feel the comfort of her strong body, I don't know. Was this Death itself that lurked behind Menelaos' gleaming throne?

The figure stepped forward. A long white hand protruding from the black garment dragged a little girl with it. The child, about the size of Poly's sister Sotera, was of an unearthly, fragile beauty. Her head was shaved, as my mother had told me was the custom with Spartan girls. Stubble the color of ripe wheat covered her delicate skull, and her skin was honey-gold against the dead white of the hand that clutched her. Her full lips, as red as the gills of river fish, were perfectly shaped. But they were still, and her light-brown eyes looked as flat as those of the same fish. She seemed not to hear the wail that came from the figure that gripped her so tightly.

The figure's other hand reached up and tore the black cloth from around its head. And despite the ravaged face, the mouth set in a grim line, the large pale eyes ringed with red and staring wildly, I knew that I must be gazing on the famous beauty, Helena of Ilios, wife to Menelaos, cause of the great war that my father had joined and from which he had never returned.

Her wail rose to a scream, and that scream was one word, *"Ilio-o-o-os!"* I looked at the king, but he didn't move. The queen advanced toward me, pulling the little girl along with her, until she was mere inches away, staring up into my face.

"Ilios." With a trembling hand she pushed the child in front of her. "It was in Ilios that they killed my husband." I looked at Mene-laos, puzzlement warring with fear in my heart. Her husband? Was this not Helena, wife to Menelaos? Still the king did not move. I looked at the courtiers, but the expressions they all wore said they had heard this many times before.

"They—they cut his throat. Where he lay in bed. With me. And with our baby." She shook the little girl's shoulder. The child winced but made no move to get away. "Our baby was bathed in her father's blood before she was one moon old. I scrubbed her, I scrubbed her, but I never could get the blood off. It clung to her. I can smell it still. Can you smell his blood? The blood of my beautiful husband, of Paris?"

I tried to stammer something, but she didn't wait for an answer. She wailed again and fell to her knees, clutching the girl to herself in a way that must have wrenched the poor child's back.

"She has no name," the woman spat, looking up at me fiercely, as though I had asked. "Her father was to have named her. But he didn't have time. They killed him the day of her naming ceremony." She buried her face in the little girl's neck and sobbed.

"I'm sorry," I said. "I didn't know." I should hate this woman, the cause of so much suffering and death and of my father's absence, but all I felt was pity at her destroyed mind and ruined beauty. Poly made a little sound of sympathy, and Brax came and stood by me again. The three of us watched as the woman squeezed the child and wept over her. Nobody made a sound; nobody except Brax moved a muscle. The king stared with his sightless eyes into the far distance. Why was no one comforting the queen?

I stepped closer. "I'm sorry, ma'am," I said awkwardly, and Helena reached toward me. I tried not to recoil as her fingers clenched and unclenched rhythmically, like the claws of the brightly colored bird that one of the Aegyptian traders had carried. She clasped my tunic, let it go, and clasped it again, all the while staring at me blankly, as though unaware of what her hands were doing. Her talons gripped again, this time around the shreds of the old robe that I had worn from Ithaka, which I still carried tied to my waist. It came off in her convulsive grasp.

"That's mine," I said, even though the queen was clearly past hearing me. I tried to pull the tunic away from her, but she gripped it with her free hand as though it were a treasure. "I need that," I tried again. "My mother made it. I need to keep it." It was like talking to a statue.

The tall man had been watching with a sour expression, and now he said to a servant, "Send for the queen's woman to accompany her to her apartment." The man hurried off and soon returned with a short woman swathed in widow's black like the queen. She trotted to Helena and spoke to her soothingly, gently unwrapping her mistress's long fingers from the cloth. This woman's sweet face held no fear, no shame, nothing but concern for her mistress, who was cradling my tunic like a baby.

"Come, now," she said. "You need a rest, and the girl wants something to eat." She continued to talk until the queen relaxed her grip. "Here." The short woman extended the tunic to me. Then she stopped.

"Where did you get that?" She stared down at the blue stripes with an odd expression on her face.

"My mother made it for me," I said stiffly, not wanting to hear anything she had to say about its condition. "It's worn, I know, but that's not the fault of the cloth. I've had it a long time."

She paid me no more attention than the queen had. "Look at this," she said to another woman, who had started leading Helena away. This second woman looked back over her shoulder at the cloth, and then glanced at me.

"Spartan work." I heard a question in her voice.

"How can you tell?" asked the tall man, and the two women flew into a discussion of warp tension and how the knots were tied and other matters that I didn't follow.

"And made by the second daughter of a third daughter," said the woman in black, pointing to the blue stripes at the edge. The queen pulled at her attendant's arm, and the two women left with the child.

"Is that what that means?" I asked. I had never thought to wonder why my mother always wove two and then three rows in blue.

"You didn't know that?" Poly's scorn was inevitable. "That's why your mother taught me to weave one, then two, and Sotera to weave two, then two. Our mother was the second daughter, and I'm her—"

"My mother came from Sparta," I said to the short woman. "Her name is Penelopeia, daughter of Ikarios. Do you know her?"

She looked down and stroked the cloth as though it were fine silk. "Penelopeia," she murmured. "She was always so skilled at weaving. So dutiful. Not like me. Our mother had to tether me to the loom." She looked at me again and her eyes were wet.

"You are Telemachos." It was not a question.

I bowed. "And you are my aunt Aglaia."

Before I stepped into the bath, my aunt gently unwrapped the bandages from my feet, moistening them to loosen them where they stuck. She handed me a loincloth and then turned her back on me, busying herself with heating water, while I stripped off the filthy Pylian tunic. I lowered myself into the tub, hissing through my teeth as the warm water stung the sores on my feet. Now I was leaning back, letting her pour herb-infused water over my head and shoulders, while a silent maid trimmed off dead skin and cracked toenails with a sharp knife and skillful fingers. She rubbed a soothing lotion into my blisters. Another maid brought me a wooden plate heaped with roast mutton. *Hot sheep,* I thought as I chewed on a succulent piece and washed it down with unwatered Spartan wine, as dark as squid ink.

My aunt kept up a constant stream of chatter. I thought she was trying to distract me from the discomfort of what was happening to my feet, but I later learned that she was habitually as talkative as my mother was quiet. She told me that both her parents, my grandparents, were long dead, as was her sister. My aunt Iphthime had left several children, who lived a day's journey away. *My cousins,* I thought. It sounded strange. I, alone of all my friends, had never had cousins. I allowed myself to feel some hope. Cousins now, perhaps a father soon?

Aglaia herself had been widowed when her husband was killed, early in the war against Ilios. She had not had children and now lived in the palace at the charity of her relative and mine, King Menelaos.

"Do you think he can tell me about my father?" I asked.

She was working lather into my hair. "If he knows something, he'll tell you." Something in her voice told me that she didn't hold much hope. She carefully sponged my cheek, clicking her tongue in sympathy as she dabbed at the wound that Daisy had inflicted on my face, the one that refused to heal.

"Where did you get that?"

"Clawed by a beast," I said, as briefly as I could. "It left four scratches. Three of them healed quickly, but this one . . ." I broke off as she smeared some foul-smelling but comforting ointment into the gash.

She rinsed my hair and held out a large towel. I stepped out of the tub onto a lambskin, which cushioned my still-tender feet as I stood dripping the sweet-scented water. I let my aunt wrap the soft woolen cloth around me, feeling as I had when Eurykleia had bathed me as a child—relaxed, drowsy, warm inside, but with a chill on the skin where a draft touched me.

"She—Helena—said Paris' throat was cut while he was in bed," I said. "I thought he was killed in combat."

She turned me around and briskly rubbed my back. "That's what the poets say. It sounds better than the truth. He was a prince, after all. What really happened—or at least what sounds most like the truth—is that the Ilians killed him in his sleep."

"The *Ilians*? But he was their prince!"

"Their prince who led them into an unwanted war. Their prince who caused the death of many of them. No," she said, "they didn't love him. They wanted to send Helena back here and get on with their lives."

"What's wrong with her?" I couldn't shake those horror-stricken eyes from my memory.

Aglaia sighed and pulled my head down to rub it dry. "She's been that way ever since she returned. It's understandable, I suppose. Being dragged off to that barbaric country—"

"Ilios? But she went there of her own accord with Prince Paris."

"Who's to say how much was choice and how much was force? Whatever it was, after she and Paris had fallen in love she had to leave. Menelaos would have killed her if she'd stayed, and the prince too, for all that he was a guest."

"But the king now lets her live."

"He does," she replied, "even though she has begged him many times for death, her own and that of the child too. He has guards watching her night and day to make sure that she harms neither herself nor that poor little witless girl." She paused and then resumed her rubbing of my back, although it was now dry. "They say—some of the maidservants who come from Ilios and knew the family—they say that the child is the image of her father."

"But why doesn't Menelaos have the queen killed?" I'd have thought he would be glad to be rid of the reminder of his shame.

"It is her punishment." I looked a question at my aunt, and she explained, "Living is her punishment."

CHAPTER 25

It was well that I held low expectations for information from King Menelaos, because that way my hopes had less distance to fall. The king called me to his chamber after I had rested and told me stories about my father's bravery in battle. He said that he'd seen Odysseus take ship at Ilios, but that neither he nor any of his men had been heard from since.

"Stay here as long as you wish," the king said. "You and your friends. When you've rested and healed, I'll send you to Pylos in a swift chariot. Tell Nestor of his son's treachery. A king needs to know. From there you can sail back to Ithaka."

"No!" I said before I thought, and then amended hastily, "I mean, do you really think so, sir? I haven't found out anything about my father, and that's why I came here." I had faced death more than once on this quest. If I were to go home now, it would all have been for nothing.

"There's no one left to ask." Menelaos sounded bored. "If

Odysseus were alive, he'd be home by now. Unless he doesn't want to go home. You should go back."

So that was it, then. My mother would marry one of our neighbors. I would have to watch a stepfather preside over meals and give orders to Eurykleia and tell me how and with whom I could spend my days. I didn't know which made me feel more sick—my mother being forced into a marriage with one of those men, or my having to get back on a boat and cross the open sea. But suddenly the thought of home—of Ithaka with its rocky shore, of Mount Aenos standing sentinel over it, of the other islands crowding near it like piglets around a sow, of my mother and grandfather and Eurykleia, of Damon—the thought of home pained me like a toothache.

"Perhaps you're right," I said. "Thank you, sir."

So I rested, staying in the women's chambers, where my aunt Aglaia could tend to me more easily. Poly visited a few times, standing in the doorway under my aunt's watchful eye and telling me that Brax had made fast friends with a satyr whom she described as slow-witted. She also said that she was showing the Spartan women an Ithakan technique of twisting together a new strand of wool with an old one to make a smooth join. When my aunt was called away once, Poly came in and unwound the bandages that Aunt Aglaia had bound around my feet and redid them in a fashion more to her liking. Her touch was even more soothing than that of the servant who had dressed my sores the first day.

On the fourth day, I was feeling well enough to be restless. I was also tired of using a chamber pot and decided to look for a privy. I limped out of my chamber and into the cool, dimly lit hallway. I paused. Which way out?

A passing servant, carrying a jug in each hand, paused. "Help you, sir?" he asked. I stammered out my need. "This way," he said. He placed his burden on the floor and led me past marvels I had never imagined: clay pipes that brought water into the building, or so claimed the servant; walls painted with scenes of banquets, of men engaged in sport, of grapevines twining up into impossible shapes.

Cunningly arranged windows and shades allowed cool breezes to sweep away the odors made by so many people living together. But in a short time a disagreeable smell reached me. I wrinkled my nose. "What's this?" I asked the servant.

"The privy, sir."

"Inside the *house*?" Why keep such a filthy thing in the building where they slept and ate? But when the servant showed me its wonders, my disgust fled. The suction caused by the water running in the pipe below, he explained, removed what was left there. I didn't really understand it, but I had to admit that the smell was not nearly as strong as I would have expected, and when I thought of the convenience of not having to run through the rain to use a privy, I agreed that an indoor one was a very fine thing.

The man returned to his work, and when I emerged from the small room I realized I had no idea which way to go. I hesitated, looking first one way, then the other, but it didn't really matter. Soon I would find either a familiar room or someone to direct me.

The palace was even larger than it had looked from outside and was as confusing as a puzzle maze. As I rounded a corner, I came upon a long hallway that looked promising. Doors led out of it on both sides. Surely one of them would take me back to where I had started from. I had followed it for a few yards, hoping to find a room or a passageway that I recognized, when I heard a soft whirring sound coming from a chamber whose door was covered by a thin cloth of undyed linen. I stood outside, hoping for a clue as to what the sound meant, but it merely repeated itself every few seconds, growing neither louder nor softer. Finally, I pushed the cloth aside.

Seated at a low stool was a woman. I knew instantly that this was no servant, from her tunic of bright white linen and the gold band encircling her long hair, which was the color of a fox's pelt. A gold armlet reflected the light with a rich, dull gleam. Her arm moved up and down, up and down, as she rhythmically twirled a drop spindle, turning a thick hank of wool into yarn.

I was about to slip away when she paused to wind the yarn she had made onto the ball she held between her knees, and in the process she saw me standing there.

"Ah." She nodded as though in recognition and turned back to her work.

"Excuse me," I said. "I didn't know anyone was in here."

"No matter." Her arm moved up and down again, and the yarn grew. "You're the son of Odysseus, are you not?"

I nodded. "I'm come to try to find out whether he is alive or dead, and if alive, where he is."

"Why?"

"So I can find him." What an odd question! "So I can bring him back."

"Why?" she asked again.

Was this some kind of test? She stopped her work and looked me full in the face. I realized that she must be the king's daughter. Her wide cheekbones resembled his, and his hair could at one time have been the same color as hers. Her eyes were Helena's, though. They looked at me with a blackness so deep that the pupils were invisible.

"You're Hermione," I said. Everyone said that the princess was as beautiful as her mother, and for once the poets were not lying. How old was she? I wondered. Was she married?

"Why do you want your father to come home?" she asked as though I hadn't spoken. I said nothing. "At first I wanted my mother to come home." She did not take up her work again, but sat with her hands idle in her lap as she looked at the wooden tool and the yarn. "I refused to believe it when they said that she had left. *She wouldn't leave me,* I thought. Especially not for our guest. I thought Paris had come courting *me.*" A pause. Oh. Much too old for me, then, despite her beauty.

"I told myself that they were lying, that she had drowned in the river or been eaten by wild beasts. When they finally convinced me that she had gone to Ilios with Paris, I lay awake and prayed for her return every night. I went to the temple and sacrificed to my grandfather Zeus so that he would bring her home. I used to think that if I worked hard, that if I was a dutiful daughter, that if I behaved myself perfectly, she would return. And so she did." She picked up the spindle but still didn't go on with her work. "I wish she had not. Do you know, when she came back she didn't recognize me? She had to ask which of the girls was me."

My feet ached, and I shifted my weight from one to the other.

"You've seen her?" My silence answered for me. "So you know what she is." She fed wool into the spindle again, twisting it into yarn. "It didn't really matter that she had lost her mind. She had already done enough damage."

"What damage?" I asked.

Her black eyes bored into me. "Do you think anyone would marry the daughter of Helena, the woman who ran away with a foreign prince? Though any man I wed would be the king of Sparta, nobody would have me. Even Pisistratos of Pylos refused me. I was supposed to wed his brother. I had gone to Pylos, had been dressed in my wedding gown, my golden bracelets. And then—" She bit her lip and looked away.

"Then the brother died," I finished for her. "He fell down the well, didn't he?"

"Fell?" She grimaced. "He didn't *fall*."

"Yes, he did. Pisistratos told me—" I stopped as I remembered his words. *The last two boys died as infants. My oldest brother died at Ilios, and the second one drowned in the well in the palace court- yard the morning of the day he was to be married.* My blood chilled. Had Pisistratos killed his brother? Had he coveted the throne of Pylos that much?

"And then my father sent word that I should marry Pisistratos instead, but he refused me," she said. "He didn't say why, but I knew. It's because of *her*. Even that murderous hound didn't want a woman who might disgrace him the way my mother disgraced my father. He prefers to wait for my sister. He knows that she is too witless ever to run away." I didn't know what to answer, so I sat in silence as the spindle made its soft whir.

"Nobody else would have me. None *I* would have, at any rate. Men are so scarce since the war that those remaining take three or four wives, even the small farmers. But no one wants a wife whose mother ran off with a foreign prince. So I will live out my days here in the palace with my blind father and my crazed mother and my witless half-sister, at least until she is wed and goes to Pylos to bear witless children for Pisistratos."

She stood and gathered up her work. "You should reconsider. You might be better off returning home and forgetting about your father." And she was gone.

CHAPTER 26

What a sour spinster, I thought, but her words made me uneasy. I gave up on finding my room and climbed out a window. I would go to the front gate and ask directions of the guard.

But then I stumbled upon a pig yard. The familiar smell of well-kept swine and their cozy grunts put me in mind of home, so I settled down outside their enclosure and leaned back against the fence post, enjoying the afternoon sun.

I was feeling pleasantly drowsy and had decided to allow myself to drift into sleep when through my half-closed eyes I saw a figure in front of me. I looked up and for some reason felt no surprise when I recognized Mentes, the Taphian sea captain who had visited Ithaka and encouraged me to seek my father. The sun must have been lower than I thought, for it hit him full in the face, and his gray eyes flashed sparks at me.

"What are you doing, young prince, lying there in the sun?"

I sat up straighter. "Resting."

"From what Heraklean labors?" What did the man mean? "Have you forgotten why you are here?"

"Of course not!" How could he accuse me of such a thing? "I'm looking for my father."

"But you already know he's not in Sparta. Why have you not gone home?"

Who was he to quiz me as if I were a child caught stealing sweets? I mustered all the dignity I could gather. "I'm wounded," I said. "I hurt my feet walking through the desert, and my face won't heal, and I think I have a touch of sunstroke."

He ignored these complaints. "Do you even remember what the Titan's daughter told you?"

"You mean Daisy?" How did he know about Daisy? I had visited her cave days after his departure from Ithaka. I sat up straighter, suspicion hardening my heart and shortening my breath—although what I suspected, I couldn't say.

He frowned. "So that's what you call her?" I nodded. "Well, do you remember?"

"Of course." I cast my mind back and felt a moment of panic until her words returned to me. "She said to return to the place that is not, on the day that is not, bearing the thing that is not."

He waved a dismissive hand. "That's not important. I meant, do you remember what she said about kings?"

Not important? How could the prophecy that was driving me not be important? And I wasn't sure that I remembered exactly what Daisy had said about kings. I remembered her counting off a list on her long claws, starting with the smallest toe—or finger, or whatever it was. I squeezed my eyes shut. "She wasn't the one who said it. *I* said it, and she agreed with me. Wait!" I said as he started to interrupt. I heard the gravelly voice again. *The king is*

the strongest, the bravest, and the most generous. . . . I think there's
something else. Something else that a king is.

I looked up at Mentes, who was nodding as though he had heard my thoughts. "Yes," he said quietly. "Yes. There is something else. And you already know what it is. You know the fourth thing that a king is."

"I'm sorry, sir, but I don't."

"You do." *I did?* "Why did you let the sea creature live?" he asked abruptly.

"The sea creature? You mean that thing tangled in the net our first day out?" He nodded. How on earth did he know about that? "Have you spoken with Brax?"

He shook his head impatiently. "I've spoken with no one but you. What about it? Why did you spare the thing's life?"

"Well, he wasn't really trying to hurt me," I explained. "He was trapped and was going to die."

"And why did you allow Damon to stay home? He would have been much more help than your centaur friend."

"How do you know about that?"

He didn't answer, but his voice grew more urgent. "Don't you know what is happening on Ithaka?" My mouth dried. What *was* happening at home?

Then I felt my heart shrivel in my chest as the sea captain's stocky form elongated and changed; his short robe lengthened, and the rough cap perched on his grizzled curls turned into a sparkling helmet. Not Mentes, but the goddess Athena, stared gravely at me. Only the gray eyes remained the same. I tried to speak, but my mouth wouldn't obey me.

A sharp blow struck my shoulder from behind. I shot to my feet and spun to see Brax holding a handful of pebbles, taking aim at me with a second. "Hey!" I said, and then I looked back to where Mentes—or Athena—had stood. But the pigsty was empty, save for the grunting hogs. I swung around again to Brax. "Where did he go?"

"Who?"

"Mentes." Brax raised his ginger eyebrows in a question. "You know, that sea captain who came to Ithaka—"

"He left." Brax launched another missile at me. I ducked it easily. "He got on his ship with that other one, and they left."

"No, dolt. I don't mean where did he go when we were at home—I mean where did he go just now?" At Brax's blank look I explained, "He was here just now. We were talking."

Brax threw the whole handful of pebbles at me. "You weren't talking to anyone, except if you count snoring."

I shook my head. "No. I was talking to Mentes. And then he—" I stopped. *Had* it been Athena?

"You were dreaming. I heard you snoring from all the way in the stable," Brax said as though answering my unspoken thought. He flopped to his knees and stretched out full-length on the grass. He rolled onto his back and wriggled, scratching an itch, his legs flopping in the air. "And dreams that come in the daytime mean nothing, brother. Best forget it."

Could that be true? If I had been dreaming, that would explain why I thought I saw the sea captain here, and how he seemed to be able to read my thoughts and claimed to know all about what had happened to me since I'd left home. People in dreams can do all sorts of things.

On the other hand, if it had been Athena, that would also explain how she—or he, as Mentes—knew all those things.

"Brax." I sat up. "Come on. We're going home."

Menelaos protested that I had not yet partaken enough of his hospitality, but I knew that he was merely preserving the formalities and had no great desire for me to continue my visit. My aunt's objections were stronger; she shed tears, told me that I was not yet healed, that I had not made the acquaintance of my cousins, and why did I want to leave so soon after nearly dying to reach Sparta? I said only that I missed my mother and wanted to leave before the autumn storms began.

My farewell banquet was held in the great dining hall. Brax and Poly were present, although far away from the high table, where I sat at the king's right hand. Helena did not put in an appearance, nor did her little daughter. On the king's left sat the stonily beautiful Hermione. She said not a word to me or to anyone else, and after picking at a roasted dove she bowed quickly to the king and left.

While we ate the meager food that the few men remaining in Sparta could provide, a bard entertained us with tales of the loves between gods and mortals. When he related the story of Helena and her sister Klytemnestra, I thought it a poor choice. I looked at Menelaos out of the corner of my eye, but he continued eating his chickpea-and-onion stew, his spoon moving slowly from bowl to mouth, the rhythm unchanging even when the bard praised the beauty of the naked Helena, newly hatched from the egg laid by her mother, Leda, after Zeus had visited her in the form of a swan.

The bard finally ended with "And now my tale is told" and came around with a bowl. When he got to me, I dropped in the leg of a crane I had been gnawing on without much appetite. He muttered his thanks and moved on. Other diners added portions off their plates until his bowl was full, and he settled on a three-legged stool in the corner.

Without the bard's song, silence settled in the hall. A servant refilled the king's wine cup. I tore a piece of bread into shreds and then into crumbs, wondering how soon I could leave without being discourteous.

I was making up my mind to stand and deliver the speech I had composed and committed to memory, telling Menelaos how the glory of Sparta, which was spread even as far as Ithaka, westernmost of the islands, would be increased when I told everyone of the magnificence of his palace and his generosity, when the king himself stood. Everyone looked at him in silence.

He motioned, and a servant handed him a leather sack. The king reached into it and pulled out a large bowl suitable for mixing wine. "Take this. It was made in my grandfather's time and is of pure silver with a band of gold around the rim. It is a guest-gift for you, kinsman." I stammered out my thanks.

"And this," he said, as the servant gave him a rough cloth bag, "is barley to sacrifice to Poseidon, to ensure a safe trip back to your kingdom." He seemed to have forgotten the name of my kingdom.

I launched into my farewell speech. I couldn't read the king's face, so I didn't know if he was bored or merely inattentive, but he made no answer, and I had barely finished when he bowed in my direction and left the room. I was relieved that he didn't seem to expect a gift from me in exchange, since my store of iron now lay in the thieving hands of Pisistratos.

My aunt packed a great deal of food for our journey across the desert, which should take no more than three or four days, she said. On my way to Sparta, I had wandered so far off the road that I had spent much more time than necessary. She also put in a small pot of salve for my nearly healed feet.

All that remained was to say farewell to Polydora. Brax found her by her scent. She was sitting at a loom in the women's quarters with a little girl on her lap, guiding the child's small hands to cast the shuttle back and forth. Poly appeared to have found what she was looking for when she ran away from home and stowed herself on my ship. How long ago now? It seemed a lifetime. She had pleasant work and was no longer, as she thought, a burden on her family.

Polydora looked up as Brax and I poked our heads through the window. We were not, of course, allowed inside the women's quarters. I had been sent to share a room with some of Menelaos' sons the day after I had decided I no longer needed my aunt's care. I looked at Poly in silence for a moment. I would probably never see her again, never see those familiar black braids, those snapping eyes, that red mouth that looked too sweet for the words that sometimes came out of it.

"We're leaving tomorrow," I said. She whispered something to the little girl and set her on the floor, then came to the window.

"What do you mean, leaving?"

"Going home." The word suddenly made me ache with longing. "Back to Ithaka. The king is lending us a chariot and driver to carry me back to Pylos, where we'll take ship." The thought of the sea still gave me a chill, but my homesickness was stronger than my fear. "Brax will keep pace near the chariot, and then the two of us will leave for home."

"The three of us," Poly said.

"What?" I asked.

"I said, the *three* of us."

"You're coming with us?" I tried to subdue the wild leap of my heart.

"But what about everything you said on the boat?" Brax asked.

"About Damon selling you, and there not being enough food for your sisters?"

"I should never have left," Poly said. "I know that now. I should have stayed. I could have helped Damon with the girls and with some of the farming. I doubt that Sotera can mend clothes and take care of Bito. And who's tending to my father?"

A tension that I hadn't known I had been feeling was lifted from me. I had thought that I was going to leave Polydora here, never to see her again. *You're being ridiculous*, I told myself. *She should stay; you should convince her to stay where she has work and where there's no danger of her becoming like Clio and Sophonisba.* But I didn't say anything. I wanted her to come home, back to Ithaka, with me. I told myself that it was because I would be ashamed to face Damon without her, but I knew it was more than that.

And so the next day we departed.

CHAPTER 27

"I suppose someone's taken the boat," I said. "I'm sure Nestor will give us another one." Menelaos' charioteer had left us on the beach, as I requested, and not at the palace. I wanted to find my boat and clean up from the journey and get a good night's sleep, so I could make a dignified entrance in the morning. It wouldn't do to come straggling into the throne room to denounce Pisistratos with the dirt of the road stuck to my sweat. Custom demanded retribution. A king was bound by custom as much as any of his citizens. My mother and Eurykleia had always taught me that, and Menelaos himself had encouraged me to report the crime to Nestor.

But we had not been able to find the boat. I thought we were missing it in the gathering dark, but Brax, who could see by the light of even a single star, said that it wasn't anywhere near where we had left it. Poly looked at me with an expression that I recognized well, and sure enough, the next words out of her mouth were ones that I had heard endlessly when we were children: "Told you."

I didn't answer. She persisted, "I told you all along that the boat wouldn't be here, but you wouldn't listen." We'd been arguing about this almost before we had driven out through the gates of Sparta. "The king took your boat, just as I said he would." Polydora's tone was one she would have used with little Bito. "He never thought you'd come back from the desert after his son stole your iron. I would wager that he told Pisistratos to kill you but the prince lacked the nerve."

"No!" I protested. "He's a king—he upholds the laws and customs. He—"

"Brother, do you think he didn't know what Pisistratos was going to do?" I turned in surprise. It wasn't like Brax to come up with a thought like this. "Once he finds out that you survived the attack, he'll have you killed. He certainly won't give you a boat so you can go home and tell people about his son."

"King Nestor would never do that. I'm his *guest*."

They both cast pitying looks on me. "He'll find some reason to kill you," Polydora said. "He'll say you attacked Pisistratos or something."

"But Pisistratos is a thief," I said.

"He is," Brax agreed. "But he probably told a different tale. Who will people believe?"

"Nestor will give back my boat. Or he'll give me a new one." I ignored his snort and Poly's snicker. "In the meantime, let's find a place to camp. We'll go to the palace in the morning."

"But—" Poly began.

"Quiet," I said, and she shrugged without answering but with an expression that meant she knew better than I did. We continued hunting up and down the shore. I ignored the glances that I could feel my companions throwing to each other.

The scent of the sea, pungent, salty, and wild, was borne up to us on the wind that was throwing waves onto the beach. They slammed the hard sand and then withdrew with a hiss that made me think of my long-dead *qat*. The moon was hidden in the gathering clouds. Strands of seaweed, black in the moonlight, tangled around my feet, and I nearly tripped.

"Careful, brother," Brax said, his hand gripping my upper arm. I shook it off, having no need of a nursemaid. He took the rebuff with his usual good humor and continued down the beach. Then he paused. "What's that?" Something about his tone made my ears prick and the skin on the back of my neck twitch.

"I didn't hear anything."

"Nor I," said Poly, but she too stopped.

"Nor I," agreed Brax. "But I smell something."

"The sea, a dead fish, the—" I said, but Brax was shaking his head. His nostrils flared, and I saw that his eyes were ringed with white.

"No. Something flesh, but plant too." His head tilted to one side, and I heard the *whiff-whiff-whiff* of his nostrils. "I don't like it. Now I smell fear. And death."

"Oh, stop it." Poly started walking again. "You're just trying to scare us, Brax."

I wasn't so sure. "Where's it coming from?" Brax raised one arm and pointed into the woods. I hesitated, jiggling the sack of barley as I shifted from one foot to the other. I knew that after what Brax had said about fear and death, I wouldn't be able to sleep until I put my mind at ease that all he smelled was a dead dolphin or the remains of an animal's prey.

"Come on." I turned toward the woods.

"You two go ahead," Brax said. "I'll stay here."

"By yourself?" Poly looked pointedly at the dark sea. In the pale light, the waves heaved and crashed, heaved and crashed. Their foam looked like huge paws creeping up the shore.

"Never mind." Brax gave a little snort and a jump. "I'll come with you."

We made our way through the undergrowth, trying to avoid the thornbushes, and pausing occasionally to untangle our hair from the branches that were whipped around in the wind. Brax guided us with his nose, but soon I too picked up the odor, and my gut wrenched.

We stepped into a clearing just as the moon came out from behind a cloud. It stayed out only the length of a few breaths, but that was long enough.

Strung up between two trees, one hand tied to a branch of each, dangling with her slender toes pointing toward the ground, was the body of a wood nymph. Her dark hair, which I knew would be green in the daylight, hung down her back almost to her knees, and her face was turned to the sky. I caught a glimpse of hollows where her eyes should be, before the merciful clouds covered the moon again. I moved closer to Poly, and she took my hand.

Brax whimpered. "Rinn. That's Rinn, the favorite of the king, the nymph who lives—lived in the palace."

"The one who warned the forest people before Nestor could have them killed?" I asked. Brax nodded. We stood in silence.

"We should go," Poly finally whispered. "This is a bad place."

"Not until we take care of her." My voice was firm.

"Telemachos—" Poly whined, but I shook my head.

"No. She saved Brax and the others. We can't leave her here. Her spirit will never find peace until her body returns to the ground. That would be poor thanks for the way she saved the forest people."

The soil was soft and damp, and easy to dig with the broad pieces of driftwood that Brax brought up from the shore. Soon we had Rinn's body returned to the earth that had given it life. We stood a few minutes by her grave without speaking.

Polydora broke the silence.

"Still think that Nestor will just *give* you a boat?"

⟨HAPTER 28

The sky was pale, but any sun or moon was hidden. I couldn't tell if it was day or night. *The day that is not?* I shook my head. If it was, then I had failed, for I was far away from Ithaka and would not be returning that day. What did it matter? I hadn't found anything that was not, and I couldn't return both to Ithaka and to a place that was not.

"We tried to wake you, but you just said something about Mentes and Athena and rolled over." Brax lay curled next to the small fire we had made the night before. He told me that a few hours earlier he and Poly had heard fishermen down the coast readying their boats for the day's work. Poly had left in search of a trader or a fisherman to trade the silver bowl, my guest-gift from King Menelaos, for a boat. I wanted to object that it was up to me, not them, to decide what to do with my gift, but since the bowl was already gone (and since it was a good plan), I let it pass.

A drizzle started and stopped, then started again. As the

feeble sun reached its height behind the clouds, Poly appeared, trotting toward us along the path. She was accompanied by a man not much taller than she but twice as wide, with the rolling gait of a sailor and the broad shoulders of someone used to rowing. When Poly was within hailing distance, she called out, "We've bought his boat." Her triumph was unmistakable. "Come and take a look."

I followed her up the beach, leaving Brax to keep an eye on our meager supplies. The black boat lying tilted on the sand was barely large enough for the three of us. The man stood by as I pretended to inspect its bottom, not sure what to look for except obvious holes and rot. I saw none. I looked at Poly.

"This boat, a sail, two sets of oars, and three days' worth of provisions, for that bowl," she said.

"Is that all?" I turned to the fisherman. He was cross-eyed and had drawn his thick black eyebrows together in a suspicious scowl. "The bowl is silver, and it's this big." I sketched a shape with my hands.

"You're taking my livelihood." The man spoke for the first time. "I'll need something to live on until I can build a new one. And you have good food in here—bread and cheese and wine enough to get you to Zakynthos and beyond."

Behind the man's back, Poly nodded at me. I sighed. I pulled the bowl from inside my cloak and gave it to the fisherman. His dark eyes widened, and I regretted not holding out for more than three days' worth of food. I watched its silver luster disappear inside a sack, and he departed.

"All right." I glanced at the dark woods. "I don't want to stay here any longer than we have to."

Brax had let our fire almost go out. Poly fed it with twigs, looking smug about her purchase. The flames weren't large but should be enough to toast the barley that Menelaos had given us for Poseidon.

"Where's the barley, Brax?" I asked while fanning the fire to keep it alive long enough for the sacrifice. When he didn't answer, I repeated, "Brax?" Still no answer. I looked up. The half-sheepish, half-smug look on his face made my stomach drop.

"You ate it, didn't you?"

"You brought along plenty of food for the two of *you*," he said. "Nothing for me."

"Brax . . ." I let it drop. He had been well fed when we left the fertile valley of Sparta, and we had crossed the plain in a short time, not long enough to justify his plundering of the grain intended for the Earth-Shaker. But the barley was gone, and there was nothing I could do about it.

Poly got up and stomped to the boat, muttering that she would find something in the stores to sacrifice. I was not optimistic about the sailor's generosity in stocking his larder, but I wasn't prepared when Poly let out an indignant squawk and came running back.

"There's nothing in there!" she fumed. "That thief! He took our bowl—"

"My bowl," I said.

"—and didn't leave us a single crumb to eat. And nothing to sacrifice. What are we going to do now?"

Good question. Poly stood with her hands on her hips and a scowl on her face, glaring at me and then at Brax.

"Go after him?" Brax hazarded.

"Oh yes," she said. "Think I'll do that. And he'll say we're lying, and he and his friends will sell us as thieves. Any other ideas?"

"I guess we'll have to find something," I said. "Maybe a hunter left a snare and we can find a rabbit, or we can borrow some grain from a field—"

"Too early for this year's grain," Poly said. "There might be some berries or something. I'll go look. You keep the fire going." Before I thought to tell her that I was the one making the decisions, she strode off into the woods.

"Angry, isn't she?" Brax asked, but when I turned on him, furious about the barley, he looked so crestfallen that I didn't have the heart to scold him.

I had to get up once or twice to find more wood. I wished Poly would return so that we could make whatever poor sacrifice she had found, but the day wore on and she didn't appear. A drizzle was falling again, and our skimpy fire almost went out more than once. I nagged at Brax until he roused himself and helped build a shelter over it, but I couldn't shake my anxiety.

The sun was low behind the clouds, and still Poly hadn't re-turned. The tide had turned and was leaving more and more damp sand exposed. "I'll go look for her," Brax offered. I grunted. It was little enough compensation for what he had done. He left, and after only a very few minutes I heard human footsteps, not the *clop-clop-clop* of his hooves, coming from the woods.

"Finally!" I said. "Where have you—"

But it wasn't Poly. It was a well-armed soldier, and he ad-vanced on me with his sword drawn. Before I could make a move or say a word, he grabbed my arm.

"Hey!" I said, startled, and tried to shake him off. His grip held firm. "What are you doing?"

"Aren't you the boy who attacked our prince in the desert?" His eyes narrowed as he tried to make out my features. "That fisherman was right. First you attacked our prince and now you've stolen the fisherman's boat."

"What? I didn't attack anyone. Pisistratos was the one who stole—"

"You're coming with me. Ho, there!" he called in the direction of the woods.

"What?" I said again. "No, I'm not going anywhere. I bought this boat, and I'm leaving as soon as my friends get back." He paid no attention, and continued pulling me with him. Again I tried to break away, but his grip was too strong, and although I struggled he was too big for me. *"No!"* I cried, but he dragged me farther away from the boat and home.

"Brax!" I called frantically. "Poly! *Brax!*"

A thudding of hooves, and then Brax burst from the woods and shot toward us, his brown hair whipping behind him. His face was grim. He reared to a stop in front of us as the man gaped; then he pivoted and shot his hind legs back, his hard hooves cracking the soldier on the chest. The hand flew off my arm, and the man fell as a stone falls through water.

"Come!" Brax shouted. Needing no encouragement, I fled after him back down to the shore. When I caught up, Brax was already straining against the boat, trying to push it toward the water. The muscles in his back and upper arms bulged.

"What are you doing?" I gasped.

"Look back there." His words came in grunts. Down the side of the hill, past the forest, poured a procession of lights like a string of fireflies. I uttered an oath. It had to be soldiers carrying torches, coming in response to their comrade's shout or to the sailor's treachery.

I joined Brax and leaned my whole weight against the boat. It barely moved. "Wait!" I said. Brax kept shoving, but without my help it stopped moving. "We can't leave without Poly!"

"Telemachos." Brax's voice was hard. "We'll die if we stay. We'll probably die even if we leave. We *can't* wait for her."

I peered through the rain. The lights were getting closer, and now I heard men shouting.

"Poly!" I called. Nothing. I lifted two fingers to my lips and blew a blast. Still nothing. Despair made me dance frantically, trying to catch a glimpse of her. Where could she be? How could I leave her behind?

Brax's fear must have given him strength, because the boat rasped on the sand. "Help me," he grunted, but I couldn't, not with Poly out there somewhere.

Before I could whistle a second time, Polydora burst out of the thicket, her braids streaming behind her and a dead rabbit tied to her waist, bouncing on her hip. She flew down to where we stood, and now the three of us turned to the boat, shoving with all our strength.

As soon as the prow hit the water, it lightened. "Brax!" I bellowed. "In!" He hauled himself up, Poly shoving at his hindquarters until we heard the knock of his hooves on the deck. "Poly!" She leaped, and Brax's brown hand reached down and yanked her on board as I continued pushing.

I didn't dare take the time to look behind me, but I heard footsteps pounding on the beach. Good; if they kept running, their aim would be poor. It was when the footsteps stopped that I would begin to worry. I reached up for the boat but it was already too far away. A rope came down and clouted me on the side of the head. I grabbed it and swarmed up the side and spilled onto the deck.

Brax was already hauling at the oars. Water foamed around

the blades as they chopped into the water. I threw myself on the bench and grabbed an oar from him. I pulled at it until I thought my shoulders would pop out, but it felt as though we were barely moving. All I could think of was the sea, the huge sea, where we would lose ourselves. Why had I ever feared its sheltering vastness?

"Pull!" Poly screamed. *"Pull!"*

What do you think we're doing? I thought, but I didn't spare the breath to say it.

An arrow zinged over my head. I ducked. Brax tried to do the same, but his big horse-chest got in the way. We were almost out of range, and by the time they found boats, we would be swallowed by the night, if the moon kept her cover. Another arrow whined past my ear. Just a little way, just a little farther—

And then Brax stopped rowing. "What are you doing?" I gasped, reaching for his oar. He looked at me wordlessly and then down at his chest. I followed his gaze even as I pulled on both oars. Something was wrong. The end of a black shaft stuck out from below Brax's right man-shoulder. I thought wildly of the thorn I had removed from his belly so long ago—when we were children, it now seemed—and as if in a dream, I reached to pull out the arrow in the same way. But before I could touch it, a stream of blood, black in the dim light, gushed out from around the vicious Pylian arrow, and my friend fell.

(HAPTER 29

"No!" I bellowed. "No!" I turned in my seat but Poly shoved me aside. "Keep rowing," she said between her teeth as she dragged Brax back, out of the way of the oars. Instead of tending to his wound, as I had expected, she left him and returned to where I sat, unable to move. She elbowed me aside, slid onto the bench, and grasped the oars.

"No!" I said. "Brax! Go to Brax! He'll die if—"

"We'll all die if they catch up with us." She leaned into her task without a further word. I glanced at my motionless friend. His legs were bent at odd angles. But then another arrow whirred past me and I grabbed one of the oars from Poly and pulled at it until my hands tore and bled.

We rowed and rowed, I don't know for how long. When I couldn't move the oar any longer, I slumped. My arms shook and shuddered. Poly stopped too, and bent over her oar, her breath rasping in her throat. After a moment, I heard her slide from the bench and make her way back to Brax.

When I was finally able to raise my head, I crawled to where he lay on his side, his long legs splayed out against the floor of the boat, his torso twisted so that he faced nearly upward. Poly had wadded up some cloth torn from her tunic and was pressing it into his shoulder around the arrow. Brax's brown eyes darted from my face to Poly's and back again. He writhed, and every time the boat bucked on a wave he groaned.

"How bad is it?" I asked Poly. I flinched in anticipation of her answer. He looked half dead.

"I don't want to stop and look. He'll start bleeding again." She pressed steadily on the wound, her face serious, her braids swinging with the motion of the boat.

I stifled a sob and laid my hand lightly on my best friend's shoulder, trying not to disturb him.

"This is all my fault," I said miserably. "If I'd waited for Damon to come with me, Brax wouldn't have even been on board ship."

"You couldn't wait." She raised the pad and peered under it and then slowly lifted it away. The blood had slowed, at least for the moment. "You know you couldn't wait."

I shook my head. I should have been able to think of some way to escape without killing my best friend. It was my fault we had been caught there in the first place too. "If I hadn't insisted on going back to Pylos," I said thickly, "if I had only tried to find some other way home . . ." A sob cut off my words.

"It's done now." Poly's words didn't provide much comfort. "Why don't you put up the sail?"

Glad of something to do, I gathered the sail together, my arms still shaking, and barely managed to hoist myself up the mast and tie it on. It was a clumsy job, but as I came down a breeze caused the heavy cloth to belly out. I went back and stood next to Brax. I shuddered to see the deck dark with his blood. Poly still knelt over him, holding the pad tight against his chest. She had removed the arrow. That must be why she had sent me away—so I wouldn't have to watch her do it. She could lean her weight more directly on the gash left by the vicious barb now.

I pulled the last remnants of my worn tunic from the pouch at my waist and tore it into strips. Poly helped me knot the pieces into a long bandage, and together we wrapped it around Brax's chest, trying to shift him as little as possible.

When we were done, I said, as much to myself as to Polydora, "We'll see either Zakynthos to our left or the mainland to the right. Then we'll know which way to go." The clouds made me more uneasy than I liked to admit; if I couldn't locate the North Star, I wouldn't be able to steer, and we might turn completely around and land back at Pylos, where the soldiers were waiting for us. But for the moment the star twinkled from between wisps of fog, and I set our course while I could still catch glimpses of it.

As the night wore on, Brax's groans turned into snores. *At least he's alive,* I thought, and my heart felt bitter as I wondered how long that would last. The breeze was still pushing us mostly toward the north, minor adjustments with the rudder keeping us on the course I had set.

After a few hours, Poly came and sat on the deck at my feet. "How's Brax?" I asked.

"Still sleeping." *Or unconscious,* I thought. As she leaned back against the side of the boat, her hair brushed my knee. We sat in silence for a few moments, and then she said quietly, "You should have left me."

"What?"

"Back there. On the shore. If you'd left earlier, he wouldn't have gotten shot. The Pylians would have taken me in. I'm sure the queen remembers my weaving."

"Be quiet," I said. "We wouldn't leave you." *I* couldn't *leave you,* I thought, but did not say.

As the night wore on, the wind dropped and the mist thickened into fog. Soon we were drifting without aim. I didn't pick up the oars. What was the point? I had long ago lost sight of the North Star, and even the moon was such a faint blur that I couldn't trace its path in the sky. Wherever the waves took us was as good a destination as any, as long as it wasn't Pylos. Or Zakynthos, of course.

Brax slept on, groaning occasionally. Poly too fell asleep, but after a few hours she roused herself. She rubbed the back of her hand across her eyes. "Sail still up?"

I nodded, and then realized that she couldn't see me. "Yes."

"I'll take it down." She stood stiffly and stretched her arms above her head. "It's getting wet in all this fog. It'll get so heavy it will break the boom." She started up the mast. I watched her climb, a slender outline barely darker than the sky behind it. I heard her tugging at ropes. The ox-hide tether that held the sail in place must have swollen in the damp air. An occasional oath drifted down to me.

We passed through a thin spot in the mist and the light became a bit brighter. The moon was now a disk, fuzzy around the edges but clearly a circle, not the blur it had been. I strained to catch a glimpse of the North Star.

"Telemachos." It was Poly. I didn't answer, not wanting to wake Brax, but then her voice came more urgently. "Telemachos! What's that?"

She was pointing forward and to the left. A huge, unmoving

shape loomed out of the water. I seized the rudder, but with no wind and no one rowing, steering was impossible. I strained my eyes. Was it a low-lying thundercloud? A sea creature? Or—a shiver ran from my belly up to my head, causing my hair to bristle—was it Poseidon rising from his realm to put an end to our voyage as punishment for our failure to sacrifice to him?

Then I remembered. "Poly," I called in a voice pitched just loud enough to reach her. "That's the rock near Zakynthos— remember? We went around it on our way out. Come on down and row, and I'll steer clear of it." She was motionless. Then I saw her nod, and she started her descent.

As she was swinging a foot free from the rigging, a roar came—from the rock, it seemed. The huge shape appeared to jump, as did the land that was now becoming visible behind it. I cried out, no longer worrying about waking Brax, and grabbed wildly for something, anything.

Without warning, the sea rose around me and shook the little boat the way Argos would shake a rat. As though in a dream, I saw Poly fly off the mast and land in the water with a splash that I saw rather than heard.

"Poly!" I shouted. Should I jump in after her? How would I find her in the sea, as dark as Spartan wine? I looked wildly at Brax— could I leave him?

He stirred and groaned as the boat rose on a wave and landed with a crack. Yet another giant wave rocked us, and Poly's head dis- appeared beneath it. Without thinking, I released my hold and dived headlong into the churning water.

Instantly I recognized my folly. Even if I found her, what could the two of us do that one could not? The boat was being swept away, too far for me to swim to alone, much less while towing a girl behind me. But I could not bear to stay on board while the black waters closed over Polydora's head.

"Poly!" I called again and again. "Poly!"

Nothing answered but the wail of a solitary seabird protesting the disturbance that had interrupted its sleep.

CHAPTER 30

I swam in circles, calling Poly's name. Then I stopped and floated, moving only enough to keep my head above water. I don't know how much time passed, because the heavy fog returned and swaddled the moon out of sight. I lost any idea of where the huge rock was, or the island behind it. The boat—and Brax with it—had disappeared; whether it was a few yards off or at the bottom of the sea or miles away, I had no way of knowing. I fought back the image of his body being eaten by sea creatures or wrapped in seaweed. *No time for mourning now,* I told myself sternly. But the picture kept rising to my mind, despite my best efforts.

I tried to take off my cloak, but the strings holding it closed around my throat had knotted. I swallowed so much seawater that my stomach rebelled and I vomited. *There's your offering,* I thought grimly to Poseidon. If my mother had not consecrated a sufficient sacrifice to him on our departure, and if he had been displeased that we hadn't managed to toast the Spartan barley to him on the shores of Pylos, the Earth-Shaker should have been patient. He should have waited until our return to see if we would make reparations before loosing the power of his earthquake upon us. Now, with Poly and me drowned, and Brax gone and sure to be dead soon, Poseidon would have to go without any gift from us.

My arms were as heavy as iron, but when I tried to rest I pictured my legs dangling down toward the endless stretches of cold water below, while creatures with strange faces and long teeth reached up, up, up—I shuddered and tucked my knees to my chest, wrapping my arms around them. I lifted my face and gasped a breath of air, then bent my head back down again.

How long this continued, I do not know. I finally let my legs hang again. I was going to drown. My mother would never know my fate; Damon would never know that his sister had run away with me and saved my life in the desert; Poly would never know that I had sacrificed my life for her. Why not let myself sink?

Then I felt something brush my ankle. I shrieked and churned my legs, trying foolishly to clamber out of the water as something long and cold and slippery wrapped around my waist. I pushed down on it with both hands, but it held me fast.

This is it, I thought as I kicked and struggled. *This is the end.*

Something huge shot out of the sea, throwing water in my face. In front of me loomed an enormous gray-green torso. When I reared back, treading water furiously in an attempt to escape from it, I saw that it was topped by a head covered with blue-green hair. A snaggle-toothed mouth gaped wide in a grin. It was the creature we had met on the voyage out, the one who would have drowned in the net if I had not cut him free of it. I was too stunned to feel fear or even surprise. "Do what you will with me," I told him.

"Shammizé!" he boomed, although I don't think he heard me.

"Oshammi shammi!" He twisted away, and the top, man half of the creature dived into the sea. I saw now that what was holding me aloft was a pale pinkish-gray tentacle. Many more below me—I barely made them out under the surface of the water—undulated and churned, shooting us forward at a speed that I was sure no man had felt since the days when Iason and his Argonauts flew between the Clashing Rocks.

Then the creature changed course, whipping me in the air as he turned until I thought my neck would crack. One of his tentacles burst up out of the water to my right, and in its grip was yet another sea creature, this one with a mop of what looked like black sea-weed plastered on its top. The thing's dinner?

But then a curse spluttered out of the smaller creature, and two fists pummeled on the tentacle that was clutching it.

"Poly!" I cried.

She twisted and stared at me open-mouthed, and even in my terror I felt a spark of satisfaction that for once she had nothing to say. I wished the tentacles would come closer together so I could touch her and satisfy myself that it was really Polydora and not some vision created by my weakened mind.

We sped through the water, both of us held up in the air enough to keep from drowning but low enough that I occasionally got a cold slap of seawater to my face. "Where are you taking us?" I called foolishly to the creature. Even if he spoke human lan-guage, his head was under water and he couldn't hear me. His long gray-green arms raised a wave at each stroke, and he lifted his head only occasionally to take a breath, diving back down almost immediately.

Despite our speed, we traveled for a long time. The fog thick-ened so that the sun, when it rose, was visible only as a slightly paler patch in the clouds. That spot moved across the sky and was nearly at the western horizon when the creature finally slowed and then stopped. I felt the tentacle around my waist loosen, and the blood flowed back into my cramped legs as I slid down through the pinkish coil. What was he doing? Had he brought me all this way only to let me drown?

Then I saw through the mist that we were near land, or at least a pile of rocks. The creature let go of me, and I sank, but almost immediately my feet touched sharp stone. I struck out feebly and swam a few yards farther, and this time when I dropped my feet my head stayed above water.

I looked back. Poly was struggling to follow me. I reached out and hauled her close. Her cold arms circled my neck, and I staggered to the shore. The rocks were unstable and shifted under my feet until we reached land. I pitched forward. Poly loosened her hold on me, and we lay side by side, gasping for breath.

When I could, I raised my head and looked out to sea, but the creature had disappeared. "Thanks," I called, hoping that he was still within earshot.

Poly was stretched out next to me, shivering. I moved close to her and wrapped us both in my cloak. Being wool, it held some warmth even soaking wet. I couldn't believe she lay in my arms and not at the bottom of the ocean, wrapped in green seaweed, being nibbled by fish.

"Where are we?" she asked when the chattering of her teeth had slowed. I looked around. Nothing was familiar, but then, I had seen so few lands, thanks to my nearly lifelong refusal to board a ship.

"I don't know. It looks like there's been a landslide here recently. The earthquake that knocked you off the boat must have shaken these rocks free." I saw land on both sides of us, but in the dark, and with the shifting nature of newly fallen boulders, I didn't want to risk breaking an ankle exploring. "When the sun comes up, we can go in search of help."

"What if it's Zakynthos?"

I shook my head. "Not likely. We were next to Zakynthos when the Earth-Shaker struck, and we traveled for a long time before landing here. This must be a different place, unless the creature was taking us for a long ride to amuse us."

"Like Bito on Brax," she said with a shaky laugh.

Brax. What had become of him? Tears rose to my eyes, hot and stinging, and before I knew it I was sobbing, my face pressed into the warm crook where Poly's neck met her shoulder. Finally, my tears slowed and I lifted my head. She turned to me, and her solemn dark eyes flecked with gold fixed on mine.

When I kissed her, I tasted the cool salt of the mermaid, and felt the heat of the fire girl and the rough prickling of the sandstorm girl. I smelled the forests and ponds of the wood nymph and the water nymph, and something else, something so human, so Polydora, that I forgot that I was cold and bruised and frightened, that Brax had disappeared, that we were lost, and that I had not fulfilled Daisy's prophecy.

⟨HAPTER 31

I woke alone to the light of the sun. It was still pale and milky, but at last the mist was starting to burn off. I stood, every bone in my body aching—it seemed that some part of me had hurt since the day we'd left Ithaka—and walked down the beach. Small waves lapped ceaselessly around my feet as I strained my eyes for a glimpse of Brax.

A dark shape huddled against a rock caught my eye, and I ran toward it, not knowing whether I hoped or feared to see my friend, but it was merely a tree trunk wrapped in seaweed, whose ends wriggled in the water as the waves came and went, came and went.

Once more I cursed the sea. It was treacherous and murderous, and didn't care who it swallowed up. What did it want with Brax? What is more a land creature than a centaur? I remembered how difficult it had been to get him on and off the boat, and how awkwardly he always swam, his long legs churning the water madly, his body lurching as he struggled to keep afloat. I hung my head at the memory of how I had teased him about it.

I gave up for the moment and retraced my steps. As I approached the place where we had spent the night, my face flamed. How would I greet Poly when I saw her?

As if in answer to my thought, she appeared, teetering on rocks as she made her way back from where she must have been bathing. I rose to meet her and extended a hand, but she ignored me and hopped down, landing lightly. She seemed to be avoiding my eyes. I didn't feel like meeting hers either. The only other time I had felt this uncomfortable was when I had realized I was naked in front of my mother's suitors back home in Ithaka.

Before I opened my mouth, she said, "This is a bad place. It's bewitched or something."

"What do you mean?"

"When I was over there, I saw a hill that looked just like Mount Aenos. And the coastline farther down looks familiar too. I think something is bewitching this place to make it look like home."

"Like Ithaka?"

"Of course like Ithaka."

"Come on." I was seized by an idea, and without waiting to see if she'd follow me, I clambered over the nearest boulders, not caring that I bruised my knees and feet as I went.

It turned out that the shore where we had spent the night was very narrow. If we'd only had a little moonlight, we would have been able to climb over the rocks and sleep on a much softer surface of pine needles and earth. I stopped, and Poly caught up with me. "Where are you going?" She rubbed a toe. "My legs aren't as long as yours. I can't keep up."

I stood, hands on my hips, and surveyed the area. Then it was as though the gleaming ribbon tossed by a juggler slowed and turned back into flashing balls that dropped one by one into his hands, and I understood what I was looking at.

"Poly," I said. "We're home."

"What?"

"This is Ithaka." I pointed to my right. "See? That path there. It goes to my father's farm. And there's the way to Daisy's cave."

She looked to the right and then to the left. "But we don't have all those rocks on the shore at home. And there isn't a bay on the west side of—" She stopped, and I saw that now she understood.

I nodded. "That earthquake knocked all those rocks down off the hill and into the strait between Ithaka and Sami. It joined them, so what used to be the strait is now a bay, and the two are one island. It's—" It was my turn to stop talking. *It's a place that was not.*

I had no time to find an offering for Daisy, much less light a torch, but this time I knew the way. The tunnel took its first twists, and once again I was instantly in darkness so deep that I seemed to have entered the land of the dead. I felt my way along the wall until I reached the spot where the three trails diverged. I had no need to pause. The hardest way was imprinted on my mind's eye.

The stench still hung in the air, even more putrid than before. Had another luckless person blundered down the trail to rot in Daisy's chamber? For an instant I faltered. Maybe I should go back and catch up with Poly, who would be most of her way home by now. Then I shook my head. I dropped to all fours and crawled forward.

But not for long. I was groping on the floor of the chamber, trying to avoid stepping into a crevice and twisting an ankle or, worse, getting my foot stuck. So I was not looking in front of me and had no warning when the wall opened and, as before, I nearly fell into Daisy's large chamber.

The dim, greenish light was so welcome that I let out a sob. I turned, feeling with my feet, and climbed down, finding toe- and finger-holds as I went. When first one foot and then the other touched the damp floor, I closed my eyes and leaned against the wall for a moment, thanking whatever god had led me here and asking him to return me safely to the outside world when my task was complete.

Then I turned. For a moment I felt the same disorientation as when the shapes of the hills had informed me that I had arrived home to Ithaka. The cave was familiar, yet somehow not. It took me the span of only one eyeblink to realize what was different: Where I expected to see Daisy stood a huge boulder.

I drew near to it, stopping and pulling my tunic over my face as the stench nearly choked me. I moved forward again, breathing shallowly through my mouth. Once at the boulder, I squatted, trying to make out what lay under it. The glowing creatures on the walls and in the water didn't shed much light, so I reached out one hand, the other still clutching folds of cloth around my face.

I felt something cold and leathery. It took all my strength not to jerk back my hand but I forced myself to touch it lightly all over.

It was a hand—or a paw—with four long claws. Their points were still sharp. Poseidon's earth-shaking had reached all the way into Daisy's chamber and had dropped a stone on her. As punishment for helping me? I sat back on my heels. It was impossible to free Daisy's body. Nothing smaller than a Kyklops could lift that boulder, and a Kyklops would never fit down the passageway.

She was entombed here forever, in the rock of Sami that was her father.

But I was not. I made my way back out through the rocky passageway and then along the smoother one that led to the outside world. As I emerged, my first thought was that Daisy would never know that I had fulfilled at least part of her prophecy: When I had returned to the place that was not, the sun was so hidden by mist that it was truly a day that was not.

I still didn't know what she meant by bringing home the thing that was not. I had nothing but the Spartan tunic and cloak that my aunt had given me. Could that be what Daisy had meant? Perhaps the cloth had not been woven at the time that she spoke, so it *was not* at that time but it *was* now? No; somehow I knew that *the thing that was not* was more than new clothes, fine though they were. And even if something new and special had been on the Pylian boat, it now lay at the bottom of the sea, with the body of my best friend. But Daisy had admitted that she wasn't sure of the prophecy. Maybe I had already fulfilled the requirements. Maybe my father was home.

I hastened toward the palace, feeling Ithaka under my feet again, breathing its air, smelling its smells. *I'll never leave you again,* I promised my home. *Never.*

CHAPTER 32

I stood in the doorway, unobserved by the crowd, and tried to see if my mother was in the hall. Six of our neighbors were present tonight—feasting and drinking, as usual. The last time I had been in this chamber, the day before my departure, Brax had been with me. *Never again,* I thought, and I didn't know if I could bear home without him.

In the corner huddled four beggars, two of them—Iros and Pylenor—known to me. The others were the only men in the room that I didn't recognize. Was one of these tattered men Odysseus, the great hero of the Ilian War? But my father wouldn't come back dressed as a beggar—he would announce who he was and chase our neighbors from his home. Wouldn't he?

One man—I couldn't tell who—was already passed out under a table, and Eurymachos, even balder than when I had left, was fighting with his brother Ageleos, apparently over a piece of meat. The rest were eating or drinking or both. Smoke drifted in from the kitchen, bringing with it the fragrance of roasting fowl, herbs, and apples.

I longed to run to my mother and tell her everything that had happened, but she wasn't there. Had something happened to her? No, the household would be in mourning if she had died and silent if she were ill.

My stomach rumbled so loudly that I was sure everyone would turn to look at me, but their own noise drowned out any my body might make. I surveyed the crowd. I had not fulfilled the entire prophecy, but perhaps I had done enough to bring my father home. Had he landed on Ithaka yesterday, the day when I had returned to the place that was not on the day that was not?

I held still even as I strained to see more clearly through the smoke of the mutton-fat torches. I had no desire for Antinoös and the others to catch sight of me now. They would not be pleased at my return, of that I was sure. They must be hoping that I lay at the bottom of the sea.

I inspected the beggars. All were men. One was old Pylenor, but he was an Ithakan born and bred, not some newcomer. The arrogant Iros, standing beside Pylenor, was also familiar. Next to Iros was a younger man, one I didn't recognize, but he was far too young to be my father. His skin was covered with sores, and the others appeared to take care not to brush against him.

The fourth was lowering himself onto a stool. I peered through the smoke-thickened air to make out his features. His straight black hair was streaked with silver, but he was not elderly, and he had broad shoulders and thick legs. I couldn't tell from where I stood if they were straight, or bowed as my father's were said to be. The beggar settled his chin to rest on his hands, which clasped the round knob of a wooden staff. He gazed down at my old nurse,

Eurykleia, who began washing his dirt-stained feet in a large earthenware bowl, the one that my mother told me they had used for my baths when I was a baby.

Without warning, Eurykleia flung herself backward with a shriek, her hands in the air, the water from the bowl splashing up and over the man's knees. I had to grasp the doorframe to keep myself from running to her aid. If the man had harmed her—

Two younger women flew to Eurykleia and helped her to her feet. They led her from the room and out the door, supporting her, since she seemed about to faint. I ducked into the courtyard and raced around to the back of the house, where I sped to the side entrance of the women's quarters. Ahead of me, the three women were entering my mother's room. I slid into the shadows and waited until the two younger ones came out, chattering.

"Whatever did she mean when she told the mistress, 'I saw it—I knew it—the boar's tusk'?"

The other one shook her head. "Who knows? Poor old thing. She's too feeble to be mixing with company, especially young men like these." They hurried away down the hall before I could hear any more. When I was sure they were gone, I slipped into my mother's room.

The two women stood clutching each other. They turned toward me as they heard my footsteps. My mother looked at me, and her eyes were those of a hunted deer. She said, "Telemachos." Eurykleia loosed her hold, and my mother stumbled forward and buried her face in my shoulder. I held her as she sobbed, repeating my name over and over. She drew back a little and looked up at my face. Her eyes darkened as she touched my face, her fingers stroking my cheek and my chin. "Oh no," she whispered, and she began to cry again.

Eurykleia gently removed my mother's arms from around my neck and mouthed to me, "Wait outside," so I retreated through the doorway. In a few moments, the old nurse followed me. She held me to her and murmured, "Praise all the gods, you've returned in one piece."

"No thanks to Poseidon if I did."

"Oh, were you caught in his earth-shaking?" I nodded. "Then all the more praise to whoever it was that kept him from killing you."

Eurykleia stepped back and looked up at me. She touched me under the eye with a withered hand. "It still hasn't healed."

"What? Oh, this?" I felt the gash that Daisy had given me in her cave. "No, it keeps opening. What's the matter with Mother? Why did she seem upset at my face? Surely this wound isn't that serious."

"No, no; it's not the wound. It's what Odysseus told her as he was leaving for Ilios. He said that the war was bound to last many years and many men were going to be killed, but that Penelopeia shouldn't despair of him until he had been gone so long that 'the boy' had a beard. If he didn't come back by then, he said, we were to believe him dead. And when you came in and we saw . . ." Her voice trailed off, and I put a hand back to my face. It was as she had said. I felt soft hair on my cheek, my chin, my upper lip. *Finally.*

"Do the others—our neighbors—do they know that my father said this?"

She nodded. "They've joked about it for years." And all this time I had thought they were mocking my lack of hair. Instead, they had been eagerly awaiting its appearance.

"There's nothing to worry about now," I said. "Nothing at all. She won't have to marry one of them. Let me in to tell her the news. My father has returned—or at least I think he has. I hope he has. I'm *sure* he has."

I had no need to tell my mother. She was standing in the doorway, holding on to it with one hand as though she didn't trust her legs to support her. Her lips were white and her eyes were red; for a moment I thought of the wild-faced Helena. "Mother—"

"No." Her tone was firm, despite her trembling lips. "Your father has not returned, and he never *will* return."

"Penelopeia." Eurykleia caught her arm. "You have to—"

My mother's voice shook as she said, "It's *not* Odysseus. It isn't. It can't be."

"*Who* isn't Odysseus? That beggar?" They ignored me.

"I know, my dear, I know." Eurykleia patted my mother's arm. "I don't want to believe it either. But I saw the scar, and I looked into his eyes. Despite all our prayers and all our sacrifices to Poseidon, he has returned."

"I don't understand." My voice rose, but the women appeared to have forgotten that I was there. My heart pounded. My father had returned? "*Despite* all your prayers? *Despite* all your sacrifices? What do you mean? What are you talking about?"

"That beggar," Eurykleia said. "The big one, the one with the broad shoulders." I nodded, impatient to hear the rest. "He's your father. No"—she stopped my mother's protestations—"he *is* Odysseus. He has returned." My mother moaned another denial. I felt as if I were in a nightmare.

"Mother!" I barked. They turned to me, looking startled. "What is going on? What do you mean that he has returned *despite* your prayers?"

Eurykleia licked her lips and glanced at my mother. "No, Penelopeia," she said as my mother appeared about to speak. "The boy must know." And she told me.

She told me about what she called my father's brutality, about

his heavy hand with her, with my mother, even—they feared—
with me when I was grown older. She told me how my grandfather
had been terrified of my father, but in the fog of his old age he had
forgotten how harshly his son had treated him. In the way of old
people, he remembered only the best parts of his life.

"I went in fear for my life," Eurykleia concluded. "More than
once, Odysseus killed a slave while drunk. The neighbors were
outraged, but he said that slaves were his property and he would
do the same to anyone who objected." All the while, my mother
kept her dark eyes fixed on me.

"It's not true," I said when my old nurse finally, mercifully, fell
silent. But then why did her words fall like lead on my heart?

"It is." My mother's voice was wooden.

"You've always told me that he was brave and strong and
generous—"

"He was. But did you ever hear me say he was kind? Or that
he was loving?"

I cast my mind back and could not find a memory of either of
them saying such a thing. Still, I said, "I don't believe you." I *couldn't*
believe her.

"I didn't want you to know. I hoped that you would grow up
without ever learning the truth."

"But he turned the plow out of love for me." I felt as though the
air had left the room. "You told me—he went to war rather than
harm me."

"Not for *your* sake." Eurykleia's voice was bitter. "No, not for
you. For himself. To have an heir to his property, a son he could
raise to be strong enough to retain the kingship."

"So if my father hasn't returned—if that beggar isn't my father,
and if our neighbors know what he said about me"—I felt myself

grow red at discussing the new hair on my face with these two women—"then you're going to have to marry one of them now."

My mother made a helpless gesture with her hands. "What can I do?" she whispered. "Can I deny him? Pretend I don't recognize him? Would they believe me?" Her voice trailed off. Whether she was addressing me or Eurykleia or some god, I could not tell, but I knew that I couldn't bear to see her despair.

"I'll take care of it," I said. "You stay here, Mother, and you too, Eurykleia. I'll go sort things out."

But how could I? I kissed my mother on the top of her head and made my way back to the banquet hall.

Once again, I stood there without being noticed. By now the men were so drunk that they might not have recognized me even if they had caught sight of me. Ageleos had thrown something at old Pylenor, who was sitting on the floor holding his head in his hands. A trickle of blood ran down his face, and he moaned. Antinoös said something that I didn't hear but that he and the others found uproariously funny. Phemios the bard cowered in a corner, his stubby arms wrapped protectively around his lyre. The beggar with the sores had shrunk against the wall and was inching toward the door, his eyes downcast as though he were trying to become invisible. I let him pass; I was as unknown to him as he to me.

I stopped a maidservant as she hurried by me with a bowl. She started to evade my grasp and then looked more closely at me. "You're back?" She didn't sound pleased.

"Obviously." I had never liked this girl, despite my mother's fondness for her; she was always much too friendly with the men who came seeking the queen's hand. "Where's that other beggar, the new one?"

She grimaced, as if to say that dealing with beggars was

beneath her, and tried again to leave. I held fast, though. The reputation of my home for dealing generously with all guests, beggar or not, was damaged by servants like her. I shook her arm a little—not enough to hurt, just to get her attention.

"Where did he go?"

The girl managed to wrench free. "*I* don't know." She tossed the curls out of her eyes. "Maybe outside?" She slipped away from me before I could seize her again. I swallowed my anger and went out to the courtyard.

At first I didn't see the beggar, but a whine made me look to the dung heap, and there he sat, caressing old Argos' head. The dog's white muzzle lay in his hand, and as I approached, the man looked up at me, his eyes wet. "He knew me. And to think that he's still alive after all these years—" He swallowed. My heart was pounding so that I was sure he could hear it.

"He's always been well fed and cared for," I said.

The man looked at me, and then his eyes narrowed in his broad face. "Who are you?" he asked. When he rose to his feet, I saw that he was bandy-legged. At the sight of that stance, so often described to me, everything around him turned gray and faded. He thrust out his chin at me in a way that looked familiar. I recognized the gesture as one that my grandfather made.

"I'm Telemachos."

A pause. Then, "Are you, now?" He came closer and looked up at me, and before I knew it I was weeping and we were locked in each other's arms.

⟨HAPTER 33

My mother and Eurykleia were wrong, I was convinced of that. Perhaps he had been too firm, but the man who was walking in the garden with me was not the brute they made him out to be. He was my father, and now that he was back, all would be well in Ithaka.

Though I burned to ask him where he had been for all these years, he was eager to find out how things stood at home. I told him about our neighbors and my mother and her trick with Grandfather's shroud (this made him laugh). I hesitated, unsure of myself, when I told him how Mentes had encouraged me to search for him, and my father's quizzical look didn't reassure me.

"Mentes?" He cocked his head to one side and looked at me quizzically.

"Mentes of Taphos." Had my father forgotten him? Mentes—or Athena—had certainly remembered my father.

"Mentes died years ago."

"Then, Father, it wasn't Mentes—it must have been—"

But my father interrupted me to ask for more of my tal
told him how I'd gone to Pylos and then to Sparta, and how we
been swamped by a huge wave in an earthquake, and how I h
leaped overboard to find Polydora. He praised my bravery, and
felt myself turn red.

I told him about Daisy's prophecy and how I had fulfilled two
of her requirements, but not all three of them, but that she had not
seemed certain of them herself, so I was sure it didn't matter, because here he was, wasn't he? He praised my intelligence and my
courage, and again I flushed.

I showed him the gash on my cheek and said that, though
three of the cuts made by Daisy's claws had healed, the fourth
was stubborn. I related the riddle about the four things that define
a king. Despite what Mentes—or Athena—had said in that Spartan pig yard, I still didn't know what the fourth thing was.

"Do you know what she meant?" he asked.

My cheek tickled as a little blood oozed out of the topmost
scratch. I wiped it away and shook my head.

"She was teasing you. Just like a half-Titan. I came home
even if you didn't fulfill all three parts of her silly prophecy, didn't
I?" I nodded. "And there isn't any fourth thing that a king is. Brave,
strong, and generous. That's all it takes."

That's what I had thought, but it still worried me that Daisy
had seemed to think there was something else.

"My mother doesn't recognize you," I said after a minute.
Even though this wasn't strictly true, the lie came easily.

He grunted. "Old Argos knew me, and my nurse knew me.
Even *you* knew me, and you were only an infant when I left."
I refrained from saying that this Argos wasn't the one he knew
and that the dog greeted everyone like a long-lost master. Nor

did I remind him that nothing escaped Eurykleia—surely he was aware of that—and that my grandfather had described him to me so often that I would have known my father even without my old nurse's help.

I also didn't tell him what Eurykleia had said about him. Although I didn't know what lay behind all her falsehoods, I did know, even more surely now that we had talked, that she was wrong. He might have been heavy-handed, but a king has to rule with strength. Women sometimes confuse strength with brutality.

"Why have you come back disguised?" I asked. "Why not reveal yourself and throw them all out? They wouldn't dare stand up to you."

"I had to see the lay of the land," he answered. "Find out what everyone's been up to. You, our neighbors, your mother—I have to know whether everyone's behaved themselves." He grinned, showing a missing tooth. "No problem about *you*. You're just as I would have wanted you." I glowed inwardly.

"Mother too," I said. "She's always done just as you would have wanted." He grunted. I looked at him hard then. His face was difficult to read. "What, don't you think so?"

He shrugged. "She didn't know me."

"She will, I know she will. It's just the surprise. She's been wishing for your return for so long, and I'm afraid she's given up hope." He grunted again. Did he think my mother hadn't behaved virtuously all these years?

"Grandfather!" I sat bolt upright. "He'll recognize you!"

"My father lives?"

I nodded. "And if he wasn't in the banquet hall, I know where to find him." I left him in the orchard and ran back to the outbuildings.

It was dark and cool in the storage room. Was that only a pile of old clothes in the corner? But as I looked at it, it moved.

"Hey!" Grandfather sat up. White wisps of hair stuck out all over his head. He looked even older and frailer than when I'd left. "Did you bring my wine?"

"No, Grandfather—something much better."

He peered at me. "You're not that pretty girl with the wine," he said suspiciously. He hauled himself to his feet and approached me. Then his face began to work as recognition lit his dim eyes. The corners of his mouth turned down, and tears streamed through the wrinkles on his old cheeks and the straggly gray hairs of his beard.

"You've come back." A sob interrupted his words. "I knew you would."

"Yes, Grandfather. And I've brought—"

But he wasn't listening. He fell on his knees. I tried to raise him, but he took my hand and covered it with kisses. "You've come back," he said again. He wept quietly and pressed my hand to his withered cheek. Finally, he allowed me to help him to his feet.

"Grandfather." I swallowed.

He still wasn't listening, and now his face was transformed by a large smile. It was as though he had not wept at all. He grabbed both my shoulders and looked up at my face. "The king has returned." His old voice cracked.

"I'm Telemachos," I said gently. He looked bewildered. "I'm your grandson, not your son."

"My son," he said, as though struck by the idea. "There *was* a son. Where is he?"

The room darkened even more as my father appeared in the doorway. "Here I am. I've come back from the war, after all these years."

Grandfather looked from one of us to the other. "My son?" Bewilderment was plain on his face. He turned to my father, and his eyes widened. He looked my father up and down and then put out a hand as though searching for support. I seized it and wrapped my arm around his waist, holding him up as he croaked, "Odysseus! Odysseus, my son!"

My father and I laid our plans carefully. I was to make sure that my mother and Eurykleia and all the serving women stayed out of the hall. Then we would quietly remove our guests' weapons, so that they could not defend themselves when my father meted out his justice. He and I would equip ourselves with arms that I would bring from the storeroom in case any of them resented his judgment. I was to lock the door that opened to the banquet hall from the courtyard to make sure that none of our neighbors eluded my father's wrath. Next, my father and I would stand in front of the other door, the one that led into the corridor. He would reveal his identity and fine the parasites for the wreckage they had visited on his house and then send them home. My mother would see how wrong she had been in her memories of him. He was my father. He was not as she and Eurykleia had described.

It was a good plan, and my heart floated as I ran to do my part of it. My father was stronger than any of my mother's suitors; that much was obvious once I looked past his beggar's rags. He was brave enough to have gone to fight in Ilios. He would prove himself generous to his supporters, of that I was sure. He was the true king of Ithaka, despite what Daisy had said about the fourth thing.

My mother was still with Eurykleia in her chamber. She hardly looked up when I told her to stay in her room and tend to her spindle, but nodded agreement, so I left and returned to the hall.

Our neighbors were by now so drunk that they didn't notice as my father slipped knives and even a few spears and a sword out through the door to me, where I crouched out of sight. The blood buzzed in my ears as the metal clanked; how dare they bring such things into my house? *Into my father's house,* I amended. I was relieved that Ithaka was peaceful and most of them had come to dinner without weapons.

When I had tucked the arms into the recesses of the bed-chamber I had shared with my grandfather, I went back to the storeroom. There I slid a dagger into my belt and slung my father's huge old bow over my shoulder. How to give it to him? No time to worry about that now; I still had to bar the door that led from the courtyard to the banquet hall.

There were no bolts on its exterior, but I managed to wedge some boards into the doorway. This would keep our neighbors from slipping out until my father granted them permission to leave. I stood back and was inspecting my work when I felt a light touch on my arm.

Even before I turned, I knew it was Poly. She had washed herself and rebraided her hair. Her tunic glowed in the sun.

"Poly," I said. "You'll never believe this. My father—he's come home."

"I'm glad for you," she said, but she didn't sound glad.

I looked at her more closely and saw tearstains on her cheeks. "*Your* father?"

"Dead." I reached for her, but she twisted away from my hand. "A fever came on the day after we left. Sotera did her best, but . . ." When she could speak again, she said, "I should have been here."

"Poly, you didn't know."

"I should have been here." She wiped new tears off her face. "Damon's gotten married."

I allowed her to change the subject. "To Kyra?"

"No, Charissa. What are you doing?" She stepped back and eyed the boards I had jammed into the door frame.

"Locking the door. I took all their weapons and my father's going to fine those leeches for the damage they've done." The look on her face stopped me. "What?" I was uneasy.

"You don't really believe that, do you?"

"I don't know what you're talking about."

"Oh, Telemachos." She sounded wearily patient. "He isn't going to *fine* them. That wouldn't be enough. He's going to kill them. All of them."

CHAPTER 34

I didn't try to convince her that she was mistaken. She was too stubborn to listen, and besides, now was not the time. My father was waiting for me.

My father is waiting for me. The thought thrilled me as I sped back to the banquet hall, feeling as though I wore the winged sandals of Hermes. *My father has trusted me with an important task, and I have completed it, and now he and I will work together and end our intolerable situation. My father is home. My father!*

The banquet hall was still in chaos. Phemios was strumming his lyre and singing something that I couldn't make out over the din of shouts and laughter. In the center of the room stood my father, surrounded by men who were inspecting him as if he were a prize bull at the market. Iros the beggar gripped my father's upper arm with both hands. "Oho!" he said. "I can barely reach around. He's a strong one!"

I started forward to knock his hands away, but my motion caught my father's attention. He looked at me, and his eyes said unmistakably, *Be still*. I controlled myself with difficulty but took hold of the dagger under a fold in my tunic.

Someone must have noticed him looking in my direction, for the hall fell silent, and all eyes turned toward me. Phemios drew his song to a premature end with a hastily muttered "And now my tale is told," and retired to a corner.

Amphinomos broke the quiet. "When did you get back?"

"Yesterday."

Antinoös, still on his bench at the table, appeared to have forgotten that he was holding a cup to his lips. "How did you make it past—" and then he fell silent.

"Past what?"

Nobody answered. Then Eurymachos turned to Antinoös and said, "I told you it was a bad plan."

"What plan?" They ignored me, just as they always had. I was going to choke with indignation. I had survived attack by Zakynthians, near-sacrifice in Pylos, abandonment in the desert, and an earthquake at sea, and they still thought I was a child unworthy of an answer.

"Did someone make a plan to try to prevent my return?" Eurymachos and Amphinomos looked embarrassed, so I knew I was right. The rest of our neighbors must have hidden somewhere, hoping to intercept me and kill me on my way home, violating every law and custom. Even Pisistratos had waited until we were out of his father's lands before robbing me and abandoning me to die. Still, mixed with my outrage was a feeling of triumph. They were afraid of me!

Antinoös put down his cup, undrained for once. "Look at him." His voice was odd. What did he mean? They were already staring at me as though I had grown a second head.

"Look at his *face*," Antinoös said.

It was Ageleos who saw it. "A beard!" he cried. "The boy finally has a beard!"

They burst into raucous laughter. "So he's not a girl after all!" someone shouted, and another voice called out, "Set up the ax handles!" A manservant ran from the room as though to obey this strange order.

My father turned to Antinoös. "What's this about ax handles, master?" His cringing tone and the "master" made me wince, but I bit my lip and watched as Antinoös took a swig of wine.

"It's a test." He wiped his mouth and raised his cup to signal that it was empty. A manservant hastened over with a pitcher and filled it to the brim. "Whoever wishes to marry Penelopeia must do what Odysseus did to win her. He strung his longest bow and lined up ten ax handles with the heads removed, and then he shot an arrow through the empty bolt-holes." He downed the wine. His words were becoming slurred; I wondered how strong the drink was. He gestured to the group of beggars. "I think we'll let the four of you try first, starting with the big one. You have the shoulders for it." Everyone burst into laughter again when my father lowered his shaggy head as though in meek acceptance of the order.

Antinoös must have grown tired of throwing things at beggars and had thought of this new way to make sport of them. What would he do to my father if he failed the test? Something humiliating, at the very least. Painful too, most likely. Why did my father not reveal himself now?

Antinoös caught sight of me. "And what an accommodating young man this is! He bears not only his new beard but also his father's long bow. He must be anxious for a stepfather."

I forced a smile. Then a thought occurred to me, turning the false smile into a real one. I no longer had to worry about how to arm my father. "Take this," I said. Our hands touched as I passed him the bow, and the look in his eyes made my smile expand to a grin. We understood each other.

"And the ax handles?"

"Patience, young prince, patience." Antinoös' voice held an unmistakable sneer. The manservant came back, both arms full of the long handles of battle-axes that my father had left behind after removing their metal heads to take them to Ilios. New handles would be easy to make from Ilian trees; bronze ax heads were not.

We all watched in silence as the man drove the handles into the hard-packed dirt floor, grunting as he lined up the holes where heavy bolts had once held the now missing blades. They stood in a line, as tall as a short man, like soldiers awaiting orders.

My father twirled the bow as though nervous, but I saw that in reality he was inspecting it for cracks and wormholes. He must have been satisfied; his teeth flashed in his beard.

The suitors for my mother's hand were paying little heed. Most of them had never been as cruel as Antinoös, and they appeared to be waiting for this latest jest of his to end before they would take their turns with the bow. I didn't see how anyone could shoot through all those holes, though. They were large, since the heavy ax heads had been held in place by large bolts. Still, how could any arrow be shot with such precision as to fly through all ten of them?

Then my father notched an arrow onto the string. He raised the bow, and everyone fell silent. I hardly contained my glee as I saw doubt pass over the faces of the more intelligent of them. The ragged cloak fell off my father's shoulders, and when he pulled the string the muscles of his back bulged.

Antinoös must have sensed that something unexpected was afoot, for he said, "Here, man . . ." in a strained voice. As though in answer, my father swung his great bow around in a wide arc and loosed the arrow.

Eurymachos leaped at my father, but it was too late—the long arrow had already pierced Antinoös' neck, front to back. A cry of horror rose from the company as the stricken man flung himself backward. His legs kicked convulsively, and thick gurgles came from him as he thrashed and the bench toppled over.

The room fell silent except for the dreadful noises made by Antinoös as his soul fled through his clenched teeth. For a moment we all stood as frozen as the statues in King Menelaos' golden hall, and then my father fitted another arrow to his great bow.

No, I thought wildly. *No no no no no . . .*

I tried to fight back my hatred of this moment. It was my father doing this—my father, whose return I had prayed for ever since I was old enough to carry a struggling dove to sacrifice at Poseidon's temple for his safe journey home, my father who was going to make everything better. Surely what he was doing was for the good; it was necessary. He was the king—the strongest, the bravest, the most generous. He was well within his rights to rid his hall of these parasites.

But to shoot unarmed men, guests at his table, invited or not, and heavy with wine—was this the act of a king?

He pivoted again, and this time his arrow was pointed at Amphinomos. I threw myself forward and knocked the bow up so that the arrow discharged harmlessly at the ceiling.

My father bellowed at me, but I couldn't make out his words. I supposed it was an order to stop, to allow him to continue in his revenge, but instead I seized the bow with both my hands and twisted it sharply. Whether he was too surprised to keep hold or whether his grip was weak because he held the weapon with only one fist to my two, I do not know, but suddenly I found that I alone grasped it. I propped its end on the floor and stepped one leg between the cord and the bow, using my hip to bend it with all my strength, and slipped off the cord. I tossed the disabled weapon to the floor and turned to face my father just as his huge hands gripped my neck.

He shook me, then lifted me nearly off my feet. He was going to crush my throat; I knew it. But I managed to slide my hands and then my arms up between his, and with all my strength I brought my upper arms down on his wrists. His grip loosened, and air rushed into my chest as I spun away, tripping over the bow but not losing my footing. I leaped over a bench and yanked the dagger from under my cloak.

I swung to face him, expecting to feel him on me, but he was several arm lengths away. Amphinomos held one of his wrists, Eurymachos the other. My father strained against them, his feet scrabbling as he tried to get a purchase on the floor, which was slippery with wine and Antinoös' blood.

"Let me go!" he shouted. "Amphinomos! Eurymachos! Don't you know me?" Doubt flickered across their faces. They looked at each other over his head, and then at me.

"It's Odysseus," I said. "It's my father. Don't you know him?" They did not loose their hold.

"I'm your king." He spat on the floor at my feet.

"You're not the king," I shouted. His small, pale eyes bored into me, but I felt nothing for him except contempt. "A true king wouldn't behave like this."

"Oh no?" His tone was mocking. "What do you know of kings?"

"I've seen some. I met Nestor and Menelaos."

"True kings both."

"No!" My voice came out louder than I had intended.

"Both men are brave," he said. "I can attest to that. When we were at Ilios—"

"And both are strong," I agreed. "And both are generous. But Menelaos' bravery led to nothing but the destruction of his kingdom. Most of the men of Sparta died in Ilios, and after all that time and death he has nothing to show for his courage but a broken wife and a child who is not his own. His daughter's life has been ruined. And Nestor may be strong and brave and generous. I have no reason to doubt that he is. But his people hate and fear him, and one day they will rise up against him and his son. This I know."

My father struggled against the hands restraining him, but they held fast. "So what quality does my wise child think a king should possess?"

The gash left under my eye by Daisy's claw sizzled. I raised a hand to its sting, and to my astonishment I felt a smooth, clean scar there, no longer the open wound of a few days ago—even an hour ago.

Then I knew. As the fourth wound healed, I realized that I knew the fourth thing that made a king. And this knowledge was the *thing that was not.*

CHAPTER 35

"Compassion," I said. It was compassion that had made me give Damon permission to stay home and tend to his family, that had stopped me from killing the sea creature, that had led me to jump from the boat in search of Poly. Compassion was something I had and that my father had never possessed. Maybe in the old days all a king had to do was to rule with a firm and heavy hand and buy his subjects' loyalty, but something had changed in our world since the cruel war at Ilios.

I nearly laughed out loud. *Return to the place that is not, on the day that is not, bearing the thing that is not. On that day the king will return.* Daisy had not said, "On that day your father will return," or "Odysseus will return." She had not cared about my father and his long absence; she knew who the king was. Even my grandfather, somewhere in his confused mind, knew. I was the one who'd had to learn it.

My stomach clenched as though I was about to vomit, and I

felt an almost physical pain as I tore from my soul the idea of my father that I had held for all these years. I realized that I no longer needed that idea. I was no longer a little boy searching for a man to admire and worship.

I grew aware of the unmoving people around me. My father seemed to remember them too, for he turned his head and said, "And what do all of *you* think of this?" Silence. A few eyes flickered as men looked at their neighbors and then back at us.

"Your time has passed," I said to my father. "You are no longer the king of Ithaka."

"Oh no?" The amusement in his voice would have infuriated me just a few minutes ago, but now I recognized it for what it was, the blindness of a man who refuses to see that the world has changed while he has remained the same.

"No."

"And who is?"

"*I* am." Maybe I was not yet as strong or brave or generous as my father, or even Menelaos or Nestor, but I could learn to be those things. What my father could not learn, because he *would not*, was how to deal mercifully and justly with his subjects.

My father guffawed, as though expecting the company to join him in his laughter. But they stood like statues. Even Antinoös had mercifully stopped thrashing and was lying still. "Behold your king!" my father jeered, and he spat in my direction. I winced, expecting the others to mock me along with him. But they didn't. Instead, I saw doubt dance across their faces.

I sensed movement behind me and glanced over my shoulder. I dared not turn around all the way to see who had come in, but the glimpse of a familiar head of shaggy dark hair was enough to lift my heart. Damon. And then another movement, and without looking I somehow knew that it was Polydora who had slipped in beside him. The *thock* of hooves on the floor and a whiff of horse scent told me that they had brought their mule with them, for what purpose I couldn't imagine. Their presence comforted me, although I knew that if all the men took my father's side we stood no chance against them.

If my father noticed Damon and Poly, he paid no attention, but went on with his address to the company. "Do you want to be ruled by this boy, who thinks that a king doesn't need strength?"

"That's not what I said," I broke in, but then I realized that no one was paying attention to him. They all continued to look in my direction as though not sure who I was.

I realized that they no longer saw me as the boy who ducked work to watch girls at the beach, the child who was terrified of the sea. I was not just the son of Odysseus, but *Telemachos,* who had traveled farther from home than any of them and had survived who knew what hardships. They must see my scars and my sunburned face—and my new beard—and I knew that my muscles had hardened with the rowing and walking I had done.

Many of them were stronger and surely braver than I, and although my generosity had kept my neighbors fed for years, it had been forced on me. No, something else had changed in me, something more important than strength and courage and generosity; it could only be that these men too recognized the *fourth thing.*

Eurymachos and Amphinomos loosed their hold on my father, and he stepped away, shaking his arms as though to get rid of the feel of their hands. Then a strange thing happened. Amphinomos came to stand by my side. He was followed by Ageleos. Eurymachos looked at me as though undecided and did not move.

"Now what do we do?" Amphinomos asked. I looked around to see who he was addressing and then it dawned on me, as the blood rushed to my face, that he was asking *me*. And not just he, but Ageleos and even Eurymachos and the beggars were looking at me as though expecting an answer. Everyone except Antinoös.

Antinoös. I had forgotten about what would happen once his family knew that my father had killed him, a guest at his own table. His family's retribution would be harsh and would tear apart my peaceful kingdom.

I licked my lips. "You have to leave," I said to my father. A snort was his only response, but I persevered. "You're not welcome here, and when Antinoös' family learns what you've done . . ." I didn't have to finish my sentence. Everyone knew that the only answer to the deliberate killing of a guest was another death.

"The boy—Telemachos is right," Amphinomos said. "You can't stay. No"—he held up his hand as my father started to speak—"no, we all know that your staying would cause a war between your family and his, and then between your allies and his, until every man on the island was at war with every other man." He gestured at Antinoös in his pool of blood, without looking at him. "We've been at peace since you left, and we've grown accustomed to it."

My father looked around, his jaw jutting out. I felt my whole body start to shake but willed myself to hold still when his gaze fell on me.

"Fine," he said. "Fine. I'll go. I never intended to stay here in this little place where *peace* is prized above honor."

I flushed. I too had seen the world. I had seen the lush fields and the treasures of Sparta, and the wide beaches and fine horses of Pylos. I knew how small and barren Ithaka was. But I didn't care; Ithaka was home, and it needed me.

"I can't live on this island that's too small even to feed a decent herd of horses, among men who are afraid of a little bloodshed. I never intended to stay. I only came here to find some men to accompany me on a glorious voyage, but I see that there are no men here, just women and little boys."

"What voyage?" It was Ageleos.

"Through the Pillars of Herakles." A stunned silence followed his words. No one had to say what we all were thinking. The gods had set those huge rocks to the west to give men a boundary beyond which they were not allowed to go. Nobody knew what lay past them—the edge of the world, with the sea pouring off it, horrible monsters that rose from the deep to consume entire boats, a region of demons—the poets had imagined all sorts of things. No matter what was beyond the Pillars, they were there to warn us to stay home.

"What? Nobody with a thirst for adventure?" He drew himself to his full height. "Why do you hesitate? Are you not curious to find the sun's resting place? Remember where you come from. You are the descendants of great heroes, yet you live on this little rock as though it were the entire world. Come! Your lot is not merely to exist like the beasts and hairy-backs that are born and live and die all on the same miserable acre. You are men! Power and knowledge await you but you must seize them. Come with me!"

Before he had even finished, some of the crowd broke into a cheer. "I'm with you," said Ageleos.

"And me," said Iros, standing upright in his beggar's garb.

"Take me," said Eurymachos. I stifled an indignant response; if he wanted to leave, I wouldn't try to stop him.

Amphinomos said nothing. "Well?" My father looked him in the eye.

Amphinomos hesitated, then shook his head. "Right here is fine for me."

"Good!" My father turned to face me. "And what says my son? Do you stay here to be the king of this backwater, this forgotten island? Or do you join me, your father and king, and my brave comrades?"

CHAPTER 36

It would probably be to my credit if I said that I hesitated, that I considered the possibility of an adventure on the open sea, the chance of finding lands that no man had ever seen before, the thrill of being by the side of Odysseus, the great hero of the Ilian War. But I didn't.

"I'm staying."

"What do you have here?"

His contempt made my toes curl. Then I thought of my mother and Eurykleia upstairs and felt the presence of Poly and Damon behind me. "Something you'll never know," I said.

"Suit yourself." He sounded as indifferent as though I had refused to accompany him on a trifling errand. He addressed the small knot of men who had accepted his offer. "Gather provisions for a long voyage."

I realized that I still clutched the dagger foolishly. I lowered my hand. I was starting to tell my father to take what he needed from the stores when a commotion arose outside, and a group of men led by Antinoös' father, Eupeithes, burst in the door. They were accompanied by old Pylenor, who stretched out a skinny arm and pointed at the body of Antinoös where it still lay in its own blood. "There, my lord." His gloating tone was repulsive; he surely expected a great reward for telling Eupeithes of his son's murder.

Eupeithes pushed his way forward. His long gray hair flopped over his eyes the way his son's black hair had, and his round face must have once been as handsome as the dead man's. Now it was red and swollen with rage. He stared at the corpse for a long time, and then he swung to my father. I shrank back at his hatred and was glad I had not dropped my dagger.

"You! You're back!" I realized that only Eupeithes and Pylenor among those in the banquet hall had been men along with my father sixteen years ago and thus were almost the only ones likely to recognize him. "You finally return, and the first thing you do is kill my son!" Eupeithes took a step forward, and his voice rose. "You owe me a life, Odysseus."

Oh no, I thought. *This is how it starts. My father killed Antinoös, and now Eupeithes kills my father, and then I have to uphold the family honor by killing Eupeithes, and then . . .*

I heard my own voice say, "Take me." A gasp came from behind me, and Eupeithes looked at me as though he didn't know who I was. I hardly knew myself. What was I doing? Then I drew a deep breath. If this was the only way to save my land from the horror of one revenge killing after another, my life would be a small price to pay. "Take me," I repeated, this time firmly. "Odysseus killed your son, so now you can kill his, and both will be even."

Eupeithes narrowed his eyes. "What are you playing at, boy?"

I ignored the "boy." "I'm offering you my life in exchange for your son's." I felt so calm, so sure of myself, that I knew that I was doing the right thing. "My life, and sixteen years' worth of food and wine at this table."

Eupeithes licked his lips. He glanced at my father and then at me. "I don't know. I was thinking more—"

"In the cove below the pig man's house," my father broke in, looking not at Antinoös' father but at me, "is a ship. In its hold is a treasure of bronze and silver. I will take you there, and together we can pick out a sufficient quantity to compensate you for your loss. Will that satisfy you?"

Eupeithes shifted from one foot to the other.

"Do you doubt me? Do you think I'm luring you to the cove only to bash your head in and leave your body there?" My father sounded as though he relished the thought. "Remember what you know of Odysseus. Am I not a man of honor?"

"You always were." Eupeithes rubbed his palms on his grease-spotted tunic as though they were sweating. "All the same, I'll take some of my men with me. To help me carry the metal," he added hastily, when my father glowered at him. Eupeithes turned to leave. My father stooped to pick up his bow and followed him.

"Father . . ." I couldn't let him go without a farewell. I cast my mind about for something to say. "Take what you need from the stores." He stopped but didn't turn. Though I waited, he remained silent, and after a moment he walked away.

I stood looking at the empty doorway. Someone was picking up the body of the fallen Antinoös, forgotten by his father. *As I've been forgotten by mine,* I thought.

Why had Odysseus offered Eupeithes his treasure? To save my life? *My* life, or the life of his heir, as he had done when he had turned the plow from my infant body? Or was he showing me that he was still generous, still a king, still someone who would give away possessions to retain the loyalty of those around him? I didn't think I would ever know for sure.

When the sound of their footsteps faded, I allowed myself to relax a little. Then from behind me I heard, "You don't think they'll take *all* the food, do you?"

I swung around. *"Brax?"* He was leaning on Damon's shoulder. The bandage around his chest, with its familiar blue stripes, was filthy and even more ragged, and he looked pale and weak, but he was still Brax, and not a mule.

"But you—but I—"

"You what?"

"I thought you were dead." Tears tickled my face and I brushed them off impatiently. "There was so much blood, Brax."

"I had more." He sounded amused. "I have blood for my man part and blood for my horse part. I didn't lose all that much. It probably looked like a lot, mixed with seawater. That boat had a leak, you know."

"Then why were you groaning so?"

"It *hurt*. There was an arrow in me. Remember?"

"I remember." I could never forget. But no matter. He hadn't died. He was still here. I reached out to pull him to me in a fierce hug, but he winced at my touch, so I merely rested one hand on his horse-back. It was warm and solid. I felt a tick, and out of years of habit I pulled it out. "How did you get home?"

He started to move his shoulders in a shrug but the gesture must have caused him pain; he stopped and merely raised his eyebrows. "I don't know. Something pulled that rotten little boat to shore."

"It must have been the sea creature," Poly broke in. "You

know, the one you wanted Telemachos to kill." She turned to me. "And then some man-bird found the boat on the beach and went to tell the rest of the forest people about it, and Saba told me—"

"And Charissa and I went and got him," Damon finished.

"And here I am," Brax agreed. "Telemachos, they're not going to take *all* the food, are they?"

I didn't care, and let my face tell him so; I was unable to speak.

"What do you want to do now?" Poly asked after a pause. I saw her wiping her face, although she tried to hide it.

"First, I'm going to tell my mother what happened. Then I'm going to clean this place up." Of course I meant I would clean the banquet hall, with its disheveled tables and overturned benches, and especially with the blood of Antinoös pooling on the floor, but I really meant Ithaka. My kingdom. My newly united kingdom. What a difference it would be to visit my ancestral home across the new bay without having to take a boat. I no longer feared the ocean, but I didn't think I'd ever look forward to setting sail on it.

I went down the corridor, planning what I was going to say to my mother. She was free now; my father was gone and nobody could force her into a marriage she didn't want, since she had a living husband. I wouldn't let them, anyway. They would listen to me now. I had returned to the place that was not, on the day that was not, bearing the thing that was not, and I knew what defined a king.

THE PYLIAN BARD HOMEROS composed a strange and lovely song about my search for my father and his return to Ithaka. I understand that it quickly made the rounds of the mainland and the islands. Old Phemios has learned some of it and sings episodes during our infrequent banquets. Even his cracked voice and faulty memory can't destroy the song's beauty. In Homeros' version of the tale, his patron's son, Pisistratos, was my good and loyal friend and helper. He said that I returned from Sparta to Ithaka all in one day, and that my father and I slaughtered twenty or thirty men instead of the one that Odysseus killed alone. But I don't mind. It's a better story the way Homeros tells it, and people like good stories.

Brax has learned this to his advantage. When a nymph touches the puckered scar on his chest and asks what gave him such a wound, he says, "A giant fish with a sword where his nose should be," leading to gasps of admiration. Or "A Spartan soldier." And then he stops, as though the memory is too painful, and the nymph lavishes him with attention.

Polydora won't allow these stories to be told in our children's hearing. She says they should grow up without learning lies. I acquiesce to this, since she rules in the home, as is correct. But when Brax and Damon and I meet, as our duties allow us (Damon's and mine, I mean; Brax finds it irritating that we can't always join him), I sometimes bring my oldest boy with me, and we tell him about his grandfather who blinded a Kyklops and heard the Sirens sing and used his wits to return to his well-loved family.

I never learned my father's fate. Bards have sung that he and his men sailed through the Pillars of Herakles and disappeared into the ocean to the west. Others have said that he changed his mind about his glorious expedition, and, being disgusted with the sea, he vowed to travel inland until he found a place where no man had even heard of it. He carried an oar, these bards say, and when a farmer, not recognizing his burden, asked what he was doing with that strange winnowing fan, he drove it into the ground as the corner post of a new house.

Either of these stories may be true, or neither. It doesn't really matter. Sometimes it's best to believe a poet's lies.

And now my tale is told.

DATE DUE

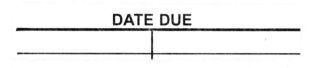